# Kate Cann

**■SCHOLASTIC**

Scholastic Children's Books,
A division of Scholastic Ltd
Euston House, 24 Eversholt Street
London NW1 1DB, UK
Registered office: Westfield Road, Southam, Warwickshire, CV47 0RA
SCHOLASTIC and associated logos are trademarks and or registered
trademarks of Scholastic Inc.

First published in the UK by Scholastic Ltd, 2001
This edition published in the UK by Scholastic Ltd, 2008

Copyright © Kate Cann, 2001
The right of Kate Cann to be identified as the author of this
work has been asserted by her.

ISBN 978 0439 95573 7

A CIP catalogue record for this book is available from the British Library

Printed by CPI Bookmarque, Croydon, CR0 4TD
Papers used by Scholastic Children's Books are made from wood grown
in sustainable forests.

3 5 7 9 10 8 6 4 2

This is a work of fiction. Names, characters, places, incidents and dialogues are
products of the author's imagination or are used fictitiously. Any resemblance to actual
people, living or dead, events or locales is entirely coincidental.

www.scholastic.co.uk/zone

This is a work of fiction and Ercos is a fictional town. I hope, however, that I've been true to the wonderful Spanish essence!

*Kate Cann*

# Chapter 1

Oh, God, he's pawing at her face again. Oh, God, stop him. If he does that *thing* he does – where he paddles his fingers down her face and grabs hold of her cheeks and squidges her mouth up . . . I'm going to kill him. I'm going to have to.

I watch helplessly as Tom squeezes in Ruth's face and makes her mouth look like a duck's bill. I stare as he kisses her, saying, *Ooo-oooh, Roofy-Roofy*. And I don't make a move to even slap him, let alone kill him.

I'm demoralized, that's what I am. Passive, helpless and demoralized. I've been on this Spanish trip one week three days, and that's approximately one week one day too long.

Tom, Ruth, Yaz and I are sitting in a fake touristy taverna at a table for four, drinking ready-made sangria and waiting for our sham paella to arrive. Yaz and I are silent, and the canned flamenco music is happily too loud for us to hear what Tom and Ruth are whispering about. Although I can guess. They're kind of gurgling and gnawing at each other across the red-checked tablecloth, and then Tom comes up for air and asks, "Well, I said I'd get us here, didn't I girls, eh?" and Ruth says, "I know, I know, you're *brilliant*, baby."

I try to make sickened eye contact with Yaz but she's staring straight ahead.

"Senor – senoritas – dinner is served!" Two waiters swoop four microwaved plates down in front of us – *crash-crash, crash-crash*. I look at the vicious yellow of the rice, the scattering of what might be seafood, and feel ill.

"Looks good!" announces Tom, as he forks a great slimy mound of it into his face.

"Yeah," agrees Ruth, lovingly. "This place is lovely."

"Although I wouldn't mind a steak, tomorrow. Or a burger or something. I'm getting a bit sick of all this Spanish crap, to be honest."

"This isn't Spanish crap," I snarl. "This is tourist crap. No Spaniard would be caught dead eating this."

"Oh, here we go again," sneers Tom. "Lors the expert on Spain."

"Don't call me *Lors*."

"Just 'cos you got your GCSE in Spanish, it doesn't make you an expert."

"I'm not saying I'm an expert. I'm just saying we should eat somewhere *real* for once, and not go in the most *touristy* place in the town!"

"You need somewhere where they've got the prices up in *English*," says Tom slowly, leaning towards me as though explaining to a backward child. "So they can't rip you off."

"Actually," I snap, "that place we walked by that *I* wanted to go in – that was cheaper. I checked the menu."

"Yeah, yeah. Understood all of it, did you?"

"Most of it. Well – some of it."

"Octopus guts and pig's colon – know the Spanish for that do you? Yum."

Ruth starts giggling as though he's hilarious, and I shoot her a look that says *traitor* and hiss, "It looked good. There were Spanish people in there."

"What's good about that? They eat all kinds of rubbish. Anyway, you should've gone in on your own if you felt that strongly about it."

"Oh, come on, Tom," says Ruth. "We've only just got here. We agreed we'd stick together tonight."

Tom splats a kiss on the side of her head, and says, "Yeah, babes, you're right, we did agree. So shut up moaning, Laura. You were outvoted, OK?"

I glare at Tom, out of words. He smirks, triumphant. Ruth looks pleadingly across the table at me and says, "Oh, come on, let's enjoy the meal, shall we?" And there's the briefest of pauses, then we all start forking up the day-glo paella and shoving it in our mouths.

It started as a joke, Tom getting the casting vote because he owns the car. It was funny about twice, then it got to be really grating. We'd pull up outside some gruesome place offering pizza at the top of the menu, and Tom would say, "Looks OK. Less than a fiver a head." And I (or sometimes Yaz) would say, "Why don't we go on a bit further, see if there's somewhere more interesting?" And Tom would answer, "OK – put it to the vote. I say eat here." And Ruth (of course) would echo, "Yes – here looks great." Yaz would usually back me up and want to go on, and Tom would say, "I'm the driver, I get the casting vote."

And he'd park the car.

I'd started to hate that bloody car.

Maybe I hated it because we were stuck in it so long each day, all through the loveliest, warmest part of the day, because Tom had this touring fixation. Maybe I hated it because it guzzled so much of my holiday money in petrol even though (as Tom gloatingly reminded us just about every single time he filled it up) petrol was cheaper here than at home. Or maybe I hated it because the car was the principal reason for us all being here together, and I'd started to *really* hate that.

*God*, what a mistake it was, agreeing to come.

# Chapter 2

The gap year. You've got to do something special. You've got to get it *right*. And so far, I've got it completely wrong. A-levels I did OK, and I'm fixed up for uni just fine. It's the fun bit I'm failing on, and failing at fun is really *failing*.

First, Yaz, Ruth and I had a celebratory summer holiday in Turkey that turned out completely naff. This was in the happy days before Ruth got swallowed up by Tom. Three great mates – three weeks in a high-rise-hotel on an overcrowded beach. Surrounded by retarded holiday reps who had ongoing bets on how many holidaymakers they could shag. Bullied into crap beach games which generally involved being picked up and carried into the sea by assorted ugly groping gits, or having something nasty tipped over you, or both at the same time. Discos in the evening with the crappest music and worse DJs; bars with sad lighting and lots of background vomiting. No interesting guys. No love, no romance.

We came home wonderfully tanned but determined to have something a bit more *real* – something beautiful, authentic, adventurous. We began to talk about going to Spain, travelling for a while, and then maybe settling somewhere for a couple of months, getting bar jobs or teaching English. Soon our talk became plans – solid plans. We got temping jobs and worked right up until Christmas and beyond, making and saving as much dosh as we could. We'd heard various scary stories about girls heading off for the heat, running out of money and having to sell their bodies just to eat, and we were determined that wasn't going to happen to us. We were going to earn a heap of cash in England, then head for Spain in the spring.

It would've been the perfect plan if Tom hadn't happened.

Ruth met him at a New Year's party. He's pretty good-looking in a thuggish sort of way, but apart from that neither Yaz nor I could see what she saw in him. What we could see, though, was she was absolutely smitten. After only a few weeks she was sleeping with him, and they were inseparable. The question of the Spanish trip came up, of course. Ruth couldn't bear the thought of leaving Tom behind, and he couldn't stand the thought of her going. She talked about staying; he talked about ditching his dead-end computer job and coming along.

It was his stupid car that decided us. Yaz and I were lulled and lured by the thought of driving down through France, of all the freedom and potential we'd have if we had a car to travel in. We worried that we'd be gooseberrying, but Tom told us he could only afford the trip if we split the petrol four ways. So Yaz and I turned our backs on all the little warning voices in our heads – and agreed.

And that's why we're all here now, silently eating our slimy day-glo paella. Tom is pointedly ignoring me, Ruth is shooting me the odd hurt look 'cos I'm "spoiling things" again. Then it's like Yaz can't bear the atmosphere any longer, and she goes into one of her happy routines – chatting away about nothing much, all jokey and bubbly. Within minutes the atmosphere has thawed and Ruth and she are laughing together and Tom's ordering up another jug of sickly sangria.

And I'm on the outside once more – the miseryguts. I can't help it. I just can't play along like Yaz. It's taking all my energy and will power not to *explode.*

We finish the meal, pay the bill from the general kitty – "No one had anything extra did they?" demands Tom – and step out into the cool Spanish night.

It's time for Round Two of the what-do-we-do-now battle. Yaz and I like to tour around a bit, look for a bit of life and action. Tom and Ruth like to book into a motel or a *pension* for the night straight away, 'cos Tom and Ruth like to have an awful lot of sex.

We could split up – just like we could eat in different places. But Yaz and I got lost in France early on, and Ruth was frantic with worry and Tom was livid, and now there's this agreement we stick together on the first night anywhere. Trouble is, the places we pull up in aren't the sort of places you'd want two nights in. So it's always a first night.

"God, I'm tired," announces Tom, predictably. He slings his arm heavily round Ruth's neck and sort of jokily collapses against her. She giggles, wraps her arms round him, supporting him. "I'm really *tired*," he repeats. Jesus, the originality of the guy, enough to make you speechless. Why doesn't he just come out and say he's horny?

Ruth laughs again, all coy and smug and loved-up and anticipatory. I can hardly bear to look at her, and I know if she knew she'd just say I was jealous.

I am not jealous. Not of *him* anyway.

Jealous in the abstract – yes, maybe. Yes, definitely.

Because the other aim for my gap year – other than travel, I mean – is to break the bleak pattern of the last three years and fall in love and get loved insanely and passionately back. That's not such a tall order, is it?

"Shall we go for a wander?" asks Yaz, looking hopefully down the street. All we can see are a couple of dead-looking bars and a café which is closed.

"We ought to find somewhere to stay," says Ruth. "Did you see anywhere as we drove in?"

"Yeah – I did," smooches Tom, into her neck. "We parked in its car park."

"That place?" I say. "That looked really grim."

There's a silence, like there usually is when I've made one of my critical comments, then Yaz pleads, "Why don't we take a wander first, take a look around?" and Tom says, "Well, let's get booked in first. Make sure of the rooms. *Then* we can go and explore." And he and Ruth start heading off back to the car, like the decision has been made by all of us. Yaz follows, and it goes through my mind to stay put, go on sit-down strike or something, but I don't, because they probably wouldn't notice if I did and then where would I be?

When we get to it the blocky-looking motel looks even more grim than it did before. It's right next to the main road; it's got a huge car park with three trucks in it, half a dozen plastic tables grouped under a plastic awning and rubbish blowing about. Tom marches up to the door and eyes the tariff notice next to it. He turns to us, beams, "S'OK! Well within budget!" and walks inside.

He rings the reception bell and books a double room and twin-bed before Yaz and I even make it to the desk. Then he and Ruth disappear giggling down the corridor, and Yaz and I are left standing.

"What happened to going to explore after we've booked in?" moans Yaz.

"Change that to after we've shagged," I snap. "Look – *we* can go out. Can't we."

"Yeah," she agrees unenthusiastically. "Don't know where to, though. Come on – let's dump our bags."

We make our way down the skinny tiled corridor. It smells of cheap pine disinfectant. The only light is from the harsh little strips overhead.

"Here's our room," says Yaz, unlocking a door.

The room is bare of everything but the most basic essentials, apart from a nasty display of pink plastic flowers on the table in the corner. I walk in, get instant claustrophobia, and want to walk straight out again.

"Shall we head back to that main street?" I ask. "While it's still light?"

"Yeah, OK," sighs Yaz.

I dump my bag in the corner, muttering, "D'you know, I'd really like to unpack that bag sometime. *When* we pitch up somewhere worth staying in." Yaz doesn't answer.

We walk out of the motel, on to the main road. "When d'you think we're going to stop somewhere *good*?" I moan, as a truck thunders past.

Yaz shrugs. "Oh, come on, Laura. You can't expect every place we stop at to be brilliant."

"Yaz, so far *nowhere* we've stayed has been brilliant."

"That little *pensión* the night before last was OK. It had a balcony."

"Balcony? More like a window box."

"*Look*, Laura – we agreed we weren't going to pre-book, didn't we. We agreed we were just going to take it as it comes."

"Yeah, but—"

"I mean – if you wanted to *know* what you were getting you should've booked something out of a catalogue, like we did for Turkey."

"*Yeah*, but—"

"And you know what Turkey was like. Phoney and fake. Just there for the tourists. At least this is *real*."

Another large truck thunders past. "Yeah, it's that all right," I agree, morosely.

We walk on in silence. I decide to shut up because I know I'm pissing Yaz off. Ever since we were kids, I've hated to piss Yaz off. It gets too lonely.

We have one drink at a bar where everyone else but us is male and over forty. We sit in the corner and they all stare fixedly at us and talk very loudly to each other as they stare. I catch, I think, the Spanish for "prostitutes" and "orphans". We leave pretty smartly, and trudge back to the motel. It's only just getting dark.

We decide to go to bed 'cos there's literally nothing

else on offer. Yaz seems OK about this. She says it's been a long day, and we'll be better in the morning for the extra sleep. While she's in the bathroom next door I slump down on the edge of the nearest narrow bed and let all the miserable, pissed-off feelings that have been lapping at my edges all evening come right in and *flood* me.

*I hate this trip, I hate it. I wish I'd never come. I'd sooner be back home at that dead-end temp job. I was happier then. God, fancy preferring a temp job to being in Spain. God, that is pathetic. That is sad. I hate myself.*

From the bathroom, I can hear water splashing, Yaz singing bits from a tune that was big just before we left England.

*Why can't I be more positive, like Yaz? She's so bloody good at being happy and cheerful – turning it on whenever it's needed, like she did in the taverna. It's 'cos she's so generous. Or maybe a bit fake? Whichever, I'm hopeless at it. I just can't act like things are fine when they're not. And I know because of this Tom likes Yaz a lot more than he likes me, and I know Ruth is beginning to get seriously fed up with me, and I'm pretty sure Yaz is getting sick of me moaning too.*

*It's down to me, isn't it? I've got to "make the best of it", like my mum always tells me to.* You're ruining it for everyone *– that's what she'd say on dire family out-ings when I complained. If Yaz can be OK about his trip, then so can I. I've got to be.*

Yaz comes back from the bathroom, and I go in after her, wash quickly, come back and climb into bed. And then the noises start, right on cue, right next door. Creak-creak-creak of the bed, and that high-pitched ecstatic yelping Ruth does. "Oh, *bloody* hell," I mutter. "Wouldn't you think they'd've got enough earlier?"

But Yaz doesn't answer me. She's jammed her pillow over her head.

# Chapter 3

We get "on the road" (as Tom insists on calling it) at ten-thirty the next day. The motel cook refuses to serve us breakfast because we're up an hour and a half later than the last of the truckers. "Should hit the coast by midday," Tom announces smugly to Ruth. "Can't wait to see you in that turquoise bikini you bought, babes."

We stop at a little supermarket and buy cartons of sugary orange juice and limp cellophane-wrapped sandwiches. We stand at the edge of the road and eat them, 'cos Tom doesn't want crumbs on his upholstery, then he chivvies us back in the car and we're off again. My mood's like a block of stone, far too heavy to be lifted, but at least that means I'm not picking fights with anyone.

At twelve-thirty almost on the dot, we catch our

first glimpse of the sea. Through a sheet of driving rain. "Easter weather," says Yaz, ruefully. "We knew it might be like this."

"Yeah, but – it's the *seaside*!" splutters Tom, as though rain at the seaside is breaking some great cosmic law.

"It might clear up," says Ruth, peering out of the streaming window at the gunmetal sky.

"And it might not," I put in.

"Jesus, Laura, why d'you have to be so *negative* all the time?" explodes Ruth.

"Sorry," I say, to everyone's surprise. "Look – let's just park and hope it will clear up, shall we?" The truth is, I've got to get out of the car. I don't care how soaked I get, I've got to *move*.

Tom parks and we pile out and edge our way along the seafront, scurrying from shop-front awning to shop-front awning. The palm trees along the road are so flattened by the weather they look like they're on a newsreel for a typhoon in Florida. Tom cheers up a bit when he finds a tacky little restaurant actually open, with a menu board offering "Full Inglish all-day brekfast" and "Ham, Egs, Chips". He disappears inside and gets his order in for a Full Inglish before the rest of us can blink the rain out of our eyes. "What you having, babes?" he calls back to Ruth. "Chips?"

By the time we've finished our food we can see through the smeary restaurant windows that the rain is easing off a bit. "Let's take a walk," says Tom.

On the beach there's more concrete than sand; great blocks of it, with holes in for the beach umbrellas. Little palm-thatched huts are dotted about, all boarded up and waiting for the season to start when they'll turn into beach bars and ice cream stalls and cafés. I walk down towards the sea. There's a spooky grey mist hovering over it, and it's surging up against the concrete blocks like it wants to wash them all away.

Yaz draws up alongside me. "Dismal, eh?" she says.

"Yeah," I agree. I'm grateful she's joined me.

"Look behind you. Look at all those tower-block hotels."

"God, yes. I bet this is the pits, high season. I'd sooner be here now."

"You mean that? You want to stay?"

"Oh – I dunno. I wouldn't mind. For the night, anyway. I'd sooner be right next to the sea than yet another motorway. Hearing the waves instead of the traffic."

Yaz laughs, says, "I bet we'd get rooms really cheap, anyway."

We wander back up the beach to join Tom and Ruth, who are wound round each other so tight you can't see where one starts and the other finishes. "This is shit," says Tom. "Let's go."

"We were just talking about staying the night," I say.

"Here?" demands Tom, scathingly. "You have *got* to be kidding."

"No. It's no worse than most of the places we've stayed."

"Oh – do me a favour. Look – the reason we came to the beach was to get some sun. As there isn't any, I say we go on."

"Yeah – but where?"

"We're heading south-west, Laura. Or hadn't you realized. It'll be hot there."

"Why don't we go inland more?" Yaz breaks in. "Go to the mountains? Everyone says the mountains are fabulous in the spring."

"Do you know what the driving's like in the mountains?" Tom demands.

"No – but—"

"Bloody awful. Narrow roads full of goats. That's why we're sticking to the main roads, OK?"

"Oh, come on – some of the mountain roads are fine, and the views are—"

"OK then. You drive."

This is Tom's trump card and this is about the fifth time he's played it. It silences Yaz. None of us has passed her test yet; Yaz has failed twice.

"Look – the weather isn't going to change overnight," pleads Ruth. "We may as well go on."

Within five minutes, we're all back in the car. Tom manoeuvres it out of the parking place using only one hand, all macho. I stare at the back of his head, hating him.

\* \* \*

The weather's really cleared up by the time we're driving through our fifth town-centre. There's been no reason to stop apart from a service station, to fill up with petrol, get a drink and go to the bog. Then, at about seven o'clock in the evening, Tom announces he's knackered ("Can't stay this gorgeous unless I get my beauty sleep, girls") and we pull up in a town that looks very similar to all the other towns we've stopped in. And we have a very similar meal; and check into another scruffy Spanish motel.

Yaz and I walk into our room. It's possibly the most basic we've been in yet, and that's saying something. There's a tiny window in the far wall, high up like the window in an old-fashioned jail. I pull a chair over, stand on it, and peer out. At three huge over-flowing dustbins and some crates of empty bottles. "Groovy," I mutter.

"I'm taking a shower," says Yaz, and heads for the dodgy-looking cubicle leading off the room. I know she's disappointed in this trip, I know it – just as disappointed as me. But she won't admit it. Maybe she thinks if she doesn't admit it somehow it won't be true.

I gaze over at the cell-window. The dipping sun's just catching it, turning it gold and tantalizing, like it's saying – *You're missing it. You're missing the real Spain.* And I get this *stab*, this real physical stab in my guts, of pure anger and frustration at the way things are going, and I just want to roll back on the bed and howl.

God, *stop it*. Stop it. Make the best of it.

"*SHIT!!!*"

"Yaz?" I'm on my feet, heading for the bathroom.

"Oh – SHIT – *SHIT!!*"

Yaz bursts out through the rickety sliding door, naked, dripping wet, hair all foamy. "*Cockroach!!*"

"Oh, yeuch – you sure?

"*Sure* I'm sure! You go in there and look!"

I fetch my heaviest shoe from my bag and crane my neck round the bathroom door. The water's still streaming into the shower tray, but there's no sign of scuttling. I take a step inside and revolve slowly, neck prickling, eyes scanning the walls. Nothing. "I can't see it!" I call.

"I am *not* going back in there!"

"But you're all soapy – your skin'll dry up and flake off—"

"*I don't care!*"

I peer behind the cheap basin. The hole in the floor for the pipe to go through hasn't been sealed – it could let in a whole swarm of cockroaches. "I think I know where it's gone," I say.

Yaz's face peers nervously round the door, and I point to the hole in the floor. "Oh, brilliant," she says. "Route 66 for roaches."

"It's gone, though. I promise."

"Yeah, but it can come back again, can't it. With a load of its friends. *Christ!* It probably runs *tours*."

"Look, Yaz – get back in the shower. I'll stand over the hole. With this shoe."

"No way."

"Don't you trust me? Look at you – you're all scuzzy. You haven't rinsed the shampoo out of your hair. It'll *ruin* it."

Yaz loves her gorgeous, long, chestnutty hair. She looks at me desperately and squeaks, "Promise you won't let it get by you?"

"If it so much as sticks an antennae out – I'll smash it. Now go on – while there's still some hot water left for *me*."

She ducks back under the shower again, going, *Oh God oh God oh God* in a very loud voice, and I crouch by the basin feeling like a prat, waving the shoe menacingly. In about two seconds flat she's plunging past me, dripping wet, out into the bedroom, leaving the water running still.

I turn it off and follow her through, laughing. "Oh come on, Yaz, it was only a bug!"

She stops frantically towelling her hair and spits, "Cockroaches are not just *bugs*. They're *evil*. Did you know they can survive *nuclear war*?"

"Can they? Wow."

There's a silence while her mouth works. Then she suddenly howls, "*God*, this is a *shit-hole*! God! Look at this towel – it's like a rag. I bet it's not even clean. This room is the pits. Look at these *beds*! It's like a bloody prison cell in here. It's awful. *GOD!* I'm getting through all this money and I haven't had any *fun* yet! This is meant to be a *holiday*!"

I gaze at her, delighted. She's doing it for me! She's throwing the tantrum I've been wanting to throw all *week*! "I thought you thought it was OK?" I squeak.

"Whatever gave you that idea?"

"Well – you didn't say anything when we booked in—"

"What's the point of saying anything when Tom and Ruth are just going to railroad over us? *He's* got the car. We'd be stranded without him and he knows it."

"But – I thought you reckoned it was good, the way Tom organized everything and saved us money on rooms and—"

"Tom is an *idiot*. I can't *stand* him!"

"Oh, *bloody hell*, Yaz! Why didn't you say all this before?"

"Because I was trying to pretend it wasn't true."

"*What?*"

"I didn't want to face the fact we'd made a total cock-up of our big trip, did I?"

"But – I thought you liked it. I thought the three of you were OK and it was *me* who was spoiling things—"

"*What is there to spoil?* This is a totally shit holiday. I've had it to here with trying to put a brave face on it. *It's shit!*"

I'm so full of relief that she feels the same as me that I think, *Thank you, cockroach*, then I collapse down on the nasty lumpy bed and *dissolve*. "I don't know what the hell you're laughing at," she snarls.

"I'm just *glad*," I say. "Glad you agree with me."

"Do you have to have a shower?"

"No – why?"

"'Cos we're going out. *Now*."

# Chapter 4

Five minutes later we're strolling down the main street, and Yaz is *venting*. It's like all the stuff she's been politely sitting on for the last week, in the hope that things will suddenly, miraculously, get better, is spewing out of her like hot ash from a volcano.

"This has to be one of the most crap, boring places in the whole entire *world*! There's no one here worth looking at, let alone pulling! There's a reason it's got no clubs or decent bars or restaurants or *anything*. No one wants to *come* here." She pulls up alongside a scruffy bar with three old men sitting outside on a bench, each with a beer in his hand. "Wow, check out the local talent," she snaps.

"Yaz! They might understand you."

"No, they won't. Anyway, they're too busy ogling

your legs. Let's go. *God*. Don't bars let women in or something?"

We pull up alongside a second bar that looks more promising, because it has a group of youngish-looking locals in the corner. "Come on!" she raps out, and she's inside and standing at the bar pointing at an advert for beer, holding up two fingers and saying, "*Dos por favor*," before I can argue.

We find a seat in the corner under a peeling bull-fight poster and both take a long pull of beer. Yaz is still simmering wonderfully. "Tom is such an arse-hole. The way he makes Ruth map-read for him, pulling her up all the time, it makes me want to puke. He just wants to see all the main roads in Spain from the inside of a windscreen."

I laugh. "Yup. All the way down to the Costa del Sol."

"But that'll be just like Turkey! We didn't agree that!"

"Nope. But the problem is we never really agreed anything, did we? We headed out here all 'let's take it as it comes, let's see what happens' – and let *Tom* happen! We might not've had a plan but he sure as hell does."

"We should be braver, that's the problem. We should strike out on our own more."

"Yeah, but that's hard when you're always pitching up somewhere new. You end up feeling like a bit of luggage."

"And acting like it." Yaz rakes all her hair back off her face and wails, "Oh, God, Laura – it's shit, isn't it? We've got to decide what we're going to do."

"As in—"

"As in have it out. Have a *row*. Tell them we can't go on like this. *Right?*"

"Right!" I echo faintly. Then I add, "When – tonight?"

"D'you fancy going round to their room and prising them apart? No, tomorrow. Maybe over lunch, when we're all sitting down together. Just say – 'let's talk about where this holiday is going'."

"What if it turns into a real row?" I ask. "I mean – what if we end up going our separate ways?"

"Are you prepared for that?"

"Um – I think so."

"Good," Yaz snaps. "Me too."

On the long, exhaust-fume-filled walk back to the motel, Yaz says, "I hope they've worn themselves out by the time we get in. I don't think I can *stand* listening to them doing it one more time."

"No," I agree. "It really gets to you after a while."

"He must be good," says Yaz gloomily.

"Yeah, he must be. I mean – he's got nothing else going for him, has he."

"Not visibly. No – he must have hidden talents. Have you noticed how he's got more and more *pigsmug* over the holiday, and she's got—"

"Shut up, Yaz. Don't wanna think about it."

"– she's got a moony, satisfied-looking smile on her face most of the time, and whenever he asks her to do something for him—"

"– which he does *more and more*—"

"– she jumps to it as though running around after him is one of the main reasons she's here on this planet."

"The other night I heard her say, 'I *like* spoiling you, baby!'"

"Oh, *throw up*."

"And then he went into one about how '*he'd spoilt her*' that morning, and they both went into all this smutty giggling. . ."

"Laura, spare me. I'm gonna be sick, I mean it."

There's a pause, and I say, "We're getting bitter, aren't we."

"Yup. We're sex-starved and bitter."

"We're gonna start getting those mean lines round our mouths if we don't get laid soon."

We're both laughing as we make our way into the Cockroach Motel. I feel happier than I have done practically since the start of this trip. Tomorrow, we're really going to sort it out.

"Those sausages we had this morning – they were ace," Tom's saying, sparklingly, as we chug along yet another minor motorway at about eleven-thirty the next morning.

"They were, weren't they?" agrees Ruth.

"Ruth – you *loathe* sausages," snaps Yaz.

"No, I don't."

"You *do*. You used to say just the look of them made you feel ill."

"Did I?"

"Well, she likes 'em now, don't you, babes?" demands Tom. "Especially those ones we had this morning."

"They were OK," mutters Ruth.

"They were lovely and fat," Tom says. "And not exploded. I can't stand sausies when they've exploded."

I feel like my head's going to explode if I hear much more about Tom's sausages. I'm a bit nervous, if you want the truth. I know we're going to be stopping soon, for a late lunch, and then we're going to hit them with our Holiday Demands. I have no idea how that will go, but any challenge to Tom's authority is bound to be unpleasant. I slide a look sideways to Yaz, hoping for some emotional contact, but she's staring out of her window.

We drive on for a bit in silence, and then something wonderful happens.

We get lost.

"It *can't've* been that turning, Roofy," Tom snarls. "Look – we're heading off into nowhere here."

Ruth has her head stuck so far into the map you'd think her eyesight had suddenly failed. "It's OK!"

she squeaks. "We did go wrong – but take the next left, we'll be back on the main road."

We do take the next left, but instead of leading us back to the main road, it gets rougher. Fields stretch ahead on either side, full of spring flowers and blissed-out-looking cattle. "Are you sure this is right?" growls Tom.

"Yeah!" says Ruth. "Just keep going – it'll be fine."

We do keep going, on and on, but there's still no sign of the main road. I wind my window down; there's no sound of it either. It's beautifully peaceful. A flock of tiny, twittering birds wheels away from the car, settles in a thorny-looking tree by the roadside.

Tom slows, swears. "I don't see no turning, babes."

"I'm sure this is right," insists Ruth, stubbornly. She shoves the map at Tom. "Look!"

"*Not while I'm driving!*" he snaps.

"Well – *stop* for a minute then," Ruth snaps back.

"I can't stop here – you can see how narrow it is! There's barely room for a car to pass us!"

And then the road starts to climb, curving gently upwards. It widens slightly, swings round a bend, and suddenly we're driving through a perfect little old town, white-painted houses on either side of us. Tom swears again. Within minutes we hit what must be the town square at the centre. Here the houses are grander, with swishy black balconies and tubs of early flowers. Benches made of the same iron lace as the balconies flank the square, with trees all out in blossom shading them, and right in the middle there's a little fountain splashing away.

Yaz, Ruth and I all let out an "oooh" of pleasure. Tom swears again. "Where is this?" he grunts. "Can you see a name up anywhere? *God* – bloody typical – no road signs anywhere. . ."

"This place is gorgeous," Yaz says. "And it's way past lunch time. I say we park."

"When we don't even know where we are?" splutters Tom.

"We'll *ask* someone," I put in. "We'll show them the map, and ask them."

Tom's face acts like I've just asked him to wear drag. "We don't need to *ask* anyone. I'll have a look at the bloody map – I'll sort it out."

"How will you," asks Yaz sweetly, "when you don't know where we are?"

"*I'll work out where we bloody are.*"

"You know, Tom," Yaz says, even more sweetly, "I think you'll find that asking for directions doesn't *necessarily* mean your dick'll drop off." Then she suddenly lurches forward in her seat, stabs a finger past his face, and shrieks, "There! Parking place!"

Tom automatically jams on the brakes, and Ruth goes, "Go on, angel. *Park*."

And, seething visibly, Tom parks.

As soon as the engine's off, Ruth, Yaz and I yank open our doors and clamber out of the car, and we're hit by the glorious scent of orange blossom. "Oh, this is lovely," I breathe. I head hungrily across the road, on to the square, followed by Ruth and Yaz. We gaze all about us, sniffing the heavenly air.

"Wow," breathes Ruth. "This place is *humming*."

I know what she means. The square has a real atmosphere – a presence, almost. It's quiet now and nearly empty, but at sundown everyone will gather here, like they do in squares all over the country, to talk and argue and party and fall in love . . . and then this extraordinary shiver runs through me, and I think, *This is it. This is the Spain I've been looking for*.

"God," Ruth goes on dreamily, "I bet this place has a history. Duels and stuff. Can't you imagine a girl on one of those balconies, looking down at her two lovers, slashing it out for her?"

I can imagine me up there, I think. This is where I could fall insanely in love and get loved insanely back.

Across on the other side of the square, two boys on a bench – one on the seat, one perched on the back – swivel round to stare at us. They have jet-black hair and tanned skin and they look very relaxed. "Spanish boys have got fabulous eyes, have you noticed?" whispers Yaz. "Kind of deep, and sexy." The two boys continue to stare at us. It's not annoying, somehow, like in England. They're staring because we're the best thing around to look at, and that feels good.

"What they goggling at?" demands Tom, stomping up beside us.

"Ruth," Yaz and I say in unison – and then we laugh.

"Yeah, ha ha," snaps Tom. "Come on – d'you wanna find somewhere to eat or what?"

I get a flash-vision of Tom trawling the side-streets for a Pizza Hut, and without really being sure what I'm doing I start to cross the square, towards the two boys. I tell myself I haven't made up my mind to talk to them, not yet – I can always turn back. But as I draw near, one of them smiles in welcome and calls out a greeting.

"We're tourists," I explain, in my wooden Spanish, opening out my hands all supplicatory. "Can you tell us somewhere to eat?"

They both grin at me then, exchange a few words together, laughing – then the better-looking of the two gazes meltingly at me, says they know an excellent place, and asks if I want him to show us. I nod eagerly – and then Tom pitches up beside me once more.

"What the hell d'you think you're doing, Laura?" he snarls. Everything about him says I'm a forward tart and he massively disapproves of me.

"Just asking directions, Tom," I say. "Since you seem to have a problem with doing that."

The boys laugh, like they understand what's going on even if they don't understand the words I'm using, and stand up. Then the best-looking one jerks his head encouragingly over to one of the tiny roads leading off the square, and the two of them start to meander over towards it. I turn back to the others and call out, "Come on! They're going to show us a restaurant!"

"*God*, Lors!" explodes Tom. "Why do we have to get involved in your pathetic attempts to pick up men?"

"Oh, don't be so dumb," says Yaz, and we both set off after the boys. I don't look back to see if Ruth and Tom are following, and I know Yaz won't either.

# Chapter 5

"How d'you know they're not gonna lead us down some back-alley to mug us?" hisses Tom from behind.

"Well, we're leading the way," says Yaz, "so if you see us getting mugged, you can make a run for it."

"Don't be so *flip*, Yaz," snaps Ruth. "Tom's only being sensible."

"I agree," smirks Yaz. "That is all he's being."

The two Spanish boys turn round, and the really good-looking one starts to speak. I try to follow what he's saying, get sidetracked by watching his mouth move, feel my own mouth dropping open, and hastily snap it shut again. "What's he saying?" hisses Yaz.

"He's saying we're late, but it should be OK. Spanish people eat lunch for *hours*. I think he says it's well into *siesta* time."

"*Cama*," says the good-looking one, "*bed*." And they both laugh knowingly and I feel kind of assaulted in the most gracious possible way, and my knees go all weak with my next few steps.

"The one on the left is *gorgeous*," murmurs Yaz.

"You keep off, I saw him first," I say, all joke-angry, but inside I feel this weight coming down. I'm no competition for Yaz – never have been. She has this great figure that's slim and curvy at the same time, and long, wavy, chestnut hair, and a really pretty face. I'm OK – Yaz is always saying how she envies my long legs – but I'm just not so desirable, somehow. I've got a boyish figure and short mouse-blonde hair. Soulful eyes, I've been told (at least twice) but my nose and mouth are too big for my face. I've just about got used to pretty much every guy we meet making a beeline for Yaz, but it still hurts me, knowing the majority of guys I go for are going to fancy her more.

It's the minority I've got to find, isn't it? A minority of one. He must be out there, somewhere.

Ahead of us, the two boys have started climbing up half-a-dozen broad stone steps to an old wooden door. It looks kind of secret. Flowering vines and wisteria trail all down the walls, across the steps beside our feet.

"Diego!" calls one of the boys, banging on the door. An older man opens it and the boy speaks Spanish to him at top speed, far too fast for me to follow, with lots of gestures backwards at us.

"Probably negotiating what his cut's gonna be," says Tom, sourly. "For bringing us here. If this is way over our budget, Laura, you can bloody well pay the extra."

"*Fine*, Tom," I snap. "Whatever."

In front of us Diego has broken into a welcoming smile, then he beckons us through the door. We walk through semi-darkness past a bar with three sleepy-looking men sitting at it. Then we go down some steps into a fabulous room, full of light, like a white-painted crypt, each corner curving down into a squat pillar. About twelve tables are spaced across the stone floor, all festively cluttered, two still with people eating at them.

Diego's calling out orders as he walks; someone appears from a side room and whisks off the white linen cloth from a table in the middle, then someone else appears, shakes out a fresh one, and rapidly lays it with glasses and cutlery. "This is going to cost a *fortune*," announces Tom, with relish. I feel a bit apprehensive myself, but I don't let it spoil my pleasure in it all.

We take our places at the table. Behind us a huge log smoulders in the massive fireplace; in front of us glass doors are open on to a terrace filled with plants. "Oh, I *love* that," breathes Yaz, flapping open her napkin. "Fire going, doors open. It's kind of decadent, isn't it? My dad would *die* at the heat loss."

I glance up longingly at the door we came in by,

looking for our guides. They're both standing there, watching us and smiling. They wave, then disappear into the darkness of the bar.

God, I wish they'd stayed. I wish that gorgeous one was sitting here now opposite me instead of Tom. "We never thanked those guys!" I wail.

"They'll get their thanks," snorts Tom. "Depend on it. Where's the menu?"

A waiter arrives, takes our order for water and beer. Then Diego appears in front of us, smiling proudly, and explains it's a set menu, fixed price. His cook is excellent, he says, everyone is always happy to eat what he prepares. Then he names a price per head, wishes us a pleasant meal, bows and disappears, just as the waiter brings our drinks.

Hastily, I convert the euros into sterling, double check it 'cos it seems so low, then, full of relief, translate as best I can for the others. I take a swig of beer, and turn on Tom. "This *whole meal* is gonna cost roughly what that revolting microwaved pasta gunk did last night."

Tom looks defiant. "Yeah, but we won't know what we're getting, will we?"

"*So?* That's part of the fun, isn't it?"

"Not if he dishes up complete shit, no."

"Oh, for *Christ's* sake, Tom! Take a risk, can't you?"

"I took a risk going away with you," he growls, "and look where that got me."

"What d'you mean?" I demand.

"I mean you never shut up complaining. Moan, moan, moan the whole bloody time. I've had it up to *here*."

The dislike in his voice – it's like violence. Ruth murmurs, "Oh, *To-om*," and looks over at me, eyebrows raised, little smile, all "sorry-aren't-blokes awful?" I can't smile back at her. I feel really hurt, even though I can't stand the guy, even though I don't care what he thinks of me.

Yaz has gone all stiff in her seat, like a terrier before a fight, and I remember with a jolt that we'd decided to discuss *where the holiday was going* over lunch. Yaz hasn't forgotten though. "OK," she says. "Let's have this out."

"Have what out?" quavers Ruth.

"If Tom's gonna start laying into Laura, I think we should talk."

Tom glares. "Talk away."

"You say Laura complains. Well, maybe she complains 'cos this trip isn't exactly turning out the way she hoped it would."

"Well, tough," snarls Tom. "It's not my ideal trip, either. Not with you two always hanging around."

"Tom, that is *so unfair*," Yaz erupts. "We *discussed* the whole thing of you two being a couple, and wanting time on your own and everything. And we're on the road so much Laura and I never get a *chance* to take off on our own!"

"We want to spend less time in the bloody *car* each

day," I burst out. "Just travelling about without really *seeing* anywhere!"

Tom looks at me like he wants me to die, then sits back and folds his arms. "OK. You take over. You plan the bloody trip."

"*See?*" I explode. "That's always your attitude. You won't discuss anything. And if we suggest anything different you tell us it's *your car*."

"Well, it is."

"Yeah, but that shouldn't mean you decide where we go *all* the time, should it?"

"Look, Laura – I'm not your fucking chauffeur. I'm not here to take directions from you."

"We're paying for half the petrol! And half the insurance!"

"Well, big deal. It's still my car."

"Oh, I don't *believe* this—" I spit out, and Yaz interrupts, "Look, Tom. We're upset 'cos we don't feel we've got any sort of *say* in this holiday. Where we're heading – or what we're *doing*. We just want a bit more discussion, you know?"

"Oh, *fantastic*," barks Tom. "So you want a sodding *committee-meeting* every night, do you? Well, you two might have nothing better to do, but believe me, *we have*. Right, babes?"

There's an electric silence. Ruth – whose head has been flicking from us to Tom and back again like she's at a manic tennis match – says nothing. Then she puts her hand on Tom's arm. He lets it rest there a second or so, then shakes it off. And then the waiter appears, and a large tureen of fish soup is placed in the centre of the table, all steaming and fragrant, with four lovely blue bowls.

"What's that *shit*?" snarls Tom.

Yaz purposefully picks up the ladle and starts doling it out. The smell from the soup is divine and I suddenly realize I'm ravenous. I look up, and see that Ruth is near to tears. But it doesn't stop me picking up my soup spoon, and dipping it into the bowl that Yaz hands me. "God, this is good," I murmur. "This is *real*."

Tom's refusing to touch his soup. He picks up a hunk of bread and starts cramming it in his mouth, spraying the table with crumbs. Ruth blinks very fast and takes a mouthful of soup all reluctantly, as though she's betraying Tom. Then she clears her throat and says, "Let's sort this out. Please don't fall out. *Please*."

"I'm not falling out with anyone, babes. It's them."

"Yeah, but—"

"Yeah but *what*?" Tom snaps, turning on Ruth so aggressively she shrinks back in her chair.

"God, don't jump down her *throat*," I blurt out.

"*Don't you tell me what to do with her*," he storms at me. "Don't you try and interfere between us, all *right*?"

There's a long pause, during which we realize everyone in the restaurant's looking at us. No one speaks, or eats. The occupants of the table nearest to us stand up and walk out.

Then Yaz mutters, "Ruth is right. Let's sort this out."

"Go ahead, duchess. *Sort* it out."

"Look – we knew it'd be difficult, all on top of each other—"

"In your dreams," sneers Tom.

"– we know you want time alone, the two of you," Yaz goes on, doggedly. "That's one of the reasons we *want* to find somewhere good to be for a while. You know – where Laura and I can take off on our own a bit—"

"Nothing to stop you taking off," says Tom. "God – I'm certainly not trying to stop you."

"That's just the point!" I squeak. "I hate the places we stay over in. It's all road . . . and grotty motels . . . and road again! And all we're doing is heading south and we haven't *agreed* that!"

Tom leans menacingly across the table towards us. "Has it occurred to you two that I might want to get to the south just so we *can* stay put for a bit? And get some space between us? And not spend the whole fucking time with you two breathing down our necks? *Jesus!*" Then he throws himself back in his chair, hard. Ruth is looking at him, horrified.

"Look, let's all calm down," Yaz murmurs. "It's just – I thought we'd *explore* more. *Relax* more. Let things happen."

Tom picks up his bottle of beer, takes a pull and glares at us. "*Let things happen*. Look girls, it's not my fault you haven't pulled yet. Is it?"

"Oh, *come on*, Tom," erupts Ruth, to my delight. "They're not talking about pulling blokes. They're—"

"Keep out of this, Ruth," snaps Tom.

"*What?*" demands Ruth. "*What* did you say?"

"*I said, keep out of it.* This is between me and them."

I fix my eyes on Ruth, and I know Yaz does too.

And she doesn't let us down. She turns right round in her seat, faces Tom square and explodes, "Just who the *hell* do you think you are?"

# Chapter 6

For the next couple of seconds I have the deeply pleasurable experience of watching Tom's face go into a triple take of sheer disbelief. *Babes* has turned on him and there's no mechanism in his head that can deal with that. It's *fab*.

"These are my *best friends*," Ruth is ranting. "Don't you dare tell me to keep out of it! God! I'm right in the middle here! How d'you think it feels – watching you and them fighting like this? And you've got the *nerve* to tell me to keep out of it!"

"I just didn't want you caught up in a stupid row, babes," wheedles Tom, "that's all." He puts his hand on her arm and she jerks it off again. *Fab*.

"It didn't have to be a row, though, did it? They just wanted to discuss the holiday, Tom! You didn't have to be so bloody *nasty*!"

"I *wasn't*!"

"Yes, you were," I put in.

"*Shut it, Laura*," storms Tom, and Ruth says, "Laura, you're not making it any better! I can't *force* you to get on with Tom, but you could be a bit less prickly sometimes!"

"Oh, that's nice," I snap. "So now it's all my fault, is it?"

Ruth takes a deep breath and says, "No. No, it's not all your fault. That's what I'm trying to say. I think you've got a point, and I think we should discuss it."

"We were discussing it!" insists Tom.

"No, you weren't. You were *fighting* about it. And you weren't giving an inch, and I agree with a lot of what Yaz and Laura said!"

Tom turns in his seat and looks at Ruth, utterly devastated and betrayed, like he's just discovered her in bed with someone else. "What d'you *mean* you agree with them?" he demands.

"Well, you have just kind of railroaded over everyone, Tom!"

"Look – if we had to *discuss* every bloody road we took—"

"I'm not saying that. It's just – more *generally*, we should've talked—"

"*Talked*. About what, for Christ's sake?"

"There's nothing wrong with *talking*, Tom! Maybe you should try it sometime!"

"Don't you pull that with me, Ruth! We do talk!"

"Look, there's no need to lose your temper!"

"Oh yeah? When you're sitting there telling me the whole holiday's been shit?"

"*I am not!* I'm just saying we should've discussed what we all wanted from the holiday. I mean, it has all been a bit—"

"A bit *what*?"

"A bit *samey*!"

"*Samey*," hisses Tom. "Course it's *samey*. It's fucking Spain, isn't it. You can't expect it to turn into fucking Italy halfway through."

"*Tom, would you not swear at me please?*" shrieks Ruth, and Tom smashes his glass down and growls, "*I'm not fucking swearing at you!*" and Ruth wails, "All I'm asking you to do is *discuss* things more!"

There's an explosive pause. Then Tom turns on us, face rigid, and grits out, "OK, *girls*. Where is it you want to go? *Exactly?*"

"Seville," says Yaz, brightly.

This is where Yaz is brilliant, I swear it. This is where I really rate her peacemaking skills. Without pausing for breath she starts describing how fabulous Seville is, and how she's sure it's not that far from here, and somehow the whole atmosphere shifts around. The nasty energy coming off Tom fades a bit, and Ruth calms down and wipes her eyes, and soon Yaz, Ruth and I are talking like we've agreed we're going to Seville, and Tom may be sulking, but at least he isn't arguing with us.

"It's nearly Easter," Yaz is going, "they have all these amazing parades, church parades, with candles and big floats and stuff. . ."

"Groovy," growls Tom, but only half-heartedly.

"And it's just a fabulous, beautiful place. My aunt told me. She says it has all these winding alleys and tall houses and big squares – she says it's best at night, it's dead romantic."

The second course arrives. It's visibly chicken, so Tom deigns to eat some, even though he pushes all the lovely fat olives and strips of red pepper to the side of his plate. Yaz turns excitedly to me and gets me to promise to ask Diego for directions of how to get to Seville. "We could set off there straight away," she says. "Couldn't we, Tom?"

When the meal's over, I go up to Diego and pay the bill, and ask him about Seville. He produces a little map for me that he says I can keep, and I understand him better than I ever thought possible, and he seems to understand me. He even jots down the address of somewhere we'll find beds for the night, in a little hotel run by one of his cousins. "Seville will be busy," he explains, "because of the *fiestas*, but you tell Juanita I sent you – show her this card – she'll find you beds."

I report back proudly to the other three, and we head straight back to the car. Tom has gone into irritating-passive mode. He refuses to look at the map

Diego's given us, just says, "You tell me where to go then, babes." Then he follows directions like an automaton. A couple of times, Ruth gets really confused, and when she can't tell him which turning to take he just stops the car and waits until she's worked it out. She's upset anyway, because of the row, and now Tom's attitude is making it worse, so Yaz ends up hanging over the back seat and helping her find the way. This works really well, which must piss Tom off enormously. Which is *fab*.

# Chapter 7

We get to the outskirts of Seville about six that night, while the light's still good. "There, that sign," I say, pointing. "*Centro*. Diego said to head for the *centro*."

Tom bad-temperedly swings his car into the left lane, hurtles round a corner. And suddenly we're on a huge roundabout with cars coming from all directions. "*Jesus*," snarls Tom. "Haven't they heard of bloody lane discipline over here? Where's the fucking *sign*?" He careens round the roundabout, and we all peer around for the sign in a state of chronic anxiety. But there's nothing saying *centro*, and we end up where we started from. "Oh, *brilliant*," Tom snarls. "Right – I'm going straight over." He floors the accelerator. Someone blares a horn at him and he blares back, swearing.

We hurtle on to the next junction. "There!" shrieks Yaz. "*Centro!*" Tom swerves to the right, following the sign. Ruth, Yaz and I all have our mouths open, halfway to screaming *slow down*. The road forks – no new sign. "*Which one do I take?*" storms Tom. "Typical – they direct you here, then they abandon you!"

"Take the left!" squawks Ruth.

Tom takes the right. The road narrows. A car is double-parked ahead of him, hazard lights flashing. "*Brilliant* parking, mate!" he bellows as he shoots round it. A car heading towards us blares its horn. "*I had time!*" yells Tom, blaring back.

Ruth slams her hands over her eyes. "*Centro!*" shrieks Yaz, pointing. "Straight on – *centro!*"

"*I can see it!*" snarls Tom, and hurtles on. It's like the car doesn't need petrol any more – it's powered by the force of his fury. I'm digging my nails so hard into the palms of my hands I'm about to draw blood.

One more enormous scary roundabout, clearly signposted this time, one more near-miss ("*learn to fucking drive!*") and we're into the centre. We just have time to heave a collective sigh of relief, and begin to take in the beauty of the place, before the roads start getting really narrow. Cars parked all along; sometimes no pavements. Tom manoeuvres slowly, neck muscles rigid. Stand-off with Ford Sierra coming the other way; Ford Sierra reverses. Tom grins briefly.

We pass a narrow road to the right closed off with chains; another blocked by rubbish dumpsters. We all know we're just circling, retracing our route, but no one dares mention this. "*Great*," Tom hisses, as he narrowly avoids scraping the car on a wall round a really tight bend. "Look – this is bloody stupid. I'm not damaging my car just so you lot can see *poxy Seville*."

One more hideous, gut-churning tight corner, and a parking space appears. Tom pulls over into it, half-on, half-off the pavement like all the other parked cars.

"It's a hell of a walk to the hotel Diego told us about from here," Yaz ventures, examining the map.

"Well, that is *tough shit*," snarls Tom. "There's no way I'm taking my car along these stupid alleyways any further."

"It's not *that* far," says Ruth.

"It's far enough!" explodes Tom, and Ruth wails, "No, no – I meant for us to *walk*!"

We get the bags out of the car boot in silence. Normally Tom would take Ruth's for her, but he very pointedly just picks up his. Ruth is looking all tearful again. I'm longing to take her aside, tell her to stick to her guns, stand up to Tom, no, better still, *ditch* the tantrum-throwing power-freak *bastard* – but I don't.

"Car's bound to get broken into, leaving it here," Tom announces, with grim satisfaction. "We'd better take everything."

"So why *leave* it here?" I spit, and stomp off out of earshot before he can do his "all right – *you* drive" bit. One day I'm going to say, "OK then," and get behind the wheel. As I've only ever had two lessons in my life, that should shut him up.

We start walking. Tom has switched off into a silent rage, and Ruth keeps shooting him anguished glances, so Yaz takes over the map. She makes quite a good job of keeping us moving. We get further into the centre of Seville, passing bars and shops, and the streets get more crowded with every step. But after about fifteen minutes, just as my arms are really beginning to ache from carrying my bag, Yaz stops, studies the map frantically for a few minutes, then admits we've taken a wrong turning.

"Oh, *great*," says Tom, in hideous triumph. "So exactly how lost are we, Yaz, eh?"

"We're not *lost*," snaps Yaz. "Just – we need to go back over that road we just crossed, and go back to that little parade of shops, and—"

"Retrace our whole fucking journey, yeah? *Brilliant*. Well, I'm having a beer first, OK?" And without looking back to see if we're following him, he stomps into a little bar just ahead of us.

"Right, he's gone – let's make a run for it," I gurgle, than I look across at Ruth and wish I'd kept my mouth shut. She has two fat tears running down her cheeks, and her chin's wobbling like crazy. "Oh, Ruth," I say. "I didn't mean it."

"It's not that," she sobs. "It's just – we've had our first *fight*!"

Yaz and I work hard not to exchange a look. "Is that so bad?" Yaz asks, gently.

"*Yes!* Yes, it is! We usually get on so well – we never argue about anything. Oh, God – he *hates* me now!"

"No, he doesn't," soothes Yaz. "You should've seen how upset he looked back at the restaurant, when you stood up to him. . ."

"I know. He couldn't *believe* I'd turn on him like that—"

"Oh, for God's sake, Ruth," I rap out. "You did *not* turn on him. You stood up for your two mates, right? He's pissed off now 'cos, like most men, he likes getting his own way, particularly when it involves cars and roads. But he'll calm down soon, and then everything'll be better for us all having had this out! It will, honestly!"

"Yeah, Ruth," says Yaz. "We needed to thrash this out, didn't we. Tom'll come round."

Ruth is looking tragically over at the door to the bar, like her whole reason for living has just disappeared through it. "I've got to go in after him," she breathes. Then she turns all defensively to me and says, "I know what you're thinking, Laura. But you wait till you meet someone you just – *fall* for! I *really, really* love him. I can't bear it being like this!" And she picks up her bag and scoots into the bar.

Yaz turns me, raising her eyebrows so high they disappear into her hair. "Jesus *Christ*," I say acidly, "if falling in love means you turn into a brain-dead doormat, I'm gonna stay well out of it."

"Oh, come on Laura. She's not as bad as that."

"*Almost!* God, if she doesn't watch it, she'll be right under his thumb. All he's got to do is throw a moody, and she's grovelling at his feet, all apologetic. . ."

"She stood up to him back in the restaurant."

"Yeah, but then he gives her the silent treatment for a couple of hours, and she's racing after him like this!"

"God, I hope she doesn't apologize."

"She will. *Urgh!* I'd like to hear what she's saying to him right now. No, come to think of it – I wouldn't. I'd probably slap her one."

"Or puke," agrees Yaz.

We're standing on the pavement, bags at our feet, reluctant to follow Ruth into the bar. I feel all churned up, all boiled up inside. "She's *wasting* herself on that arsehole!" I erupt. "She must be *poleaxed* by lust."

"Well, he is pretty fit. I like his chin."

"His *chin*? "

"Yeah. It's got this sort of dimple in it – haven't you noticed?"

"No. I try not to look at him."

"He's got a good body."

"Yeah, but he's so proud of it it really turns you off. Ripping his shirt off whenever there's a bit of sun."

"He wants to get his tan started early," Yaz sighs. "Oh, come on, Laura. We'd better go in. I'll buy you a beer."

As we walk across the pavement I say, "I bet he's not even that good in bed. I don't see how he can be, he's such a jerk."

"Laura – whatever he's doing, it's good for Ruth. You've *heard* them!"

"Don't remind me," I snarl, and stomp through the bar door.

Once we've bought our beers we make our way over to the only seats we can see – a little bench under one of the windows. We can't join Ruth and Tom because they're at a tiny, marble-topped table only just big enough for two. Not that we'd think of joining them – they're fully occupied. At first glance I think they're arm-wrestling, but then I see it's some kind of urgent lovey-dovey handclasp. Tom's talking very intently about a centimetre away from Ruth's face, and she's gone all bent-headed and swoony and *grateful*. I get this urge to stand behind Tom's head with a placard saying, "Stand up to the bastard!" I don't have a placard though, obviously, so I just glare, *hard*, but as Ruth wouldn't notice if a bomb dropped through the roof she doesn't exactly spot this.

"D'you really think it's done any good, having that fight?" I ask Yaz, as we squeeze on the bench side by side.

"Yeah," she says. "I mean – we got our way, didn't we? We're here – in Seville!" She takes a pleasurable sip of beer. "And this place is *great*."

I haven't taken in how good the bar is yet, because – like always when I go somewhere new – I've been concentrating on not looking like a prat, fitting in and following the rules. Which takes on a whole extra dimension in a foreign country. Waiter code, for example. Do you sit straight down, go to the bar, or hover hopefully? But now we're seated and drinking and no one's pointing at us laughing, so I've got time to look around me.

The first thing I notice is, it's mostly Spanish people in here. All ages, all talking loudly and laughing – the buzz is great. I notice three guys in their twenties who've just noticed us, but they're not that special, so I pass on to the amazing legs of ham complete with hooves hung over the bar, and the swirly blue and ochre tiles, and the black-framed flamenco photos going way back to when photos were first invented, and the glass-fronted case full of plates of olives, ham, chunks of cheese, little seafood tarts. . .

"Are you hungry?" murmurs Yaz.

We stare as a wonderful plate of *tapas* is carried over to a nearby table with two middle-aged couples at it. "Yes," I say. "Now I am."

"Next round," says Yaz. "Shall we? We could just point at that plate, say *otra más por favor*?"?

"You're learning. Yes, let's."

I stare over enviously at the plate of *tapas*, still lying untouched in the centre of the table. It's still untouched because an unholy row has broken out over the top of it, loud enough to make even Tom and Ruth look up.

"*Eeenglish*," one of the women spits. She's stylish, clearly Spanish, with a sharp fierce face like a hawk and short black hair. "*Eeenglish* men! You have *no* understanding!"

And the clearly English bloke beside her goes "*Shhhh*."

"*Shhh!* You see? *Shhh!* Our whole relationship has been *Shhh*! I should never have come to you! It was stupid, it was great mistake!"

Across the table from them, the other couple sit frozen, silently drinking their white wine. Both are fairly chubby – the woman looks positively luscious, with lots of rings on her hands and wild, streaked blonde hair. She catches me looking across at them, and winks.

It gives me quite a shock. Why would she wink, with that row building up just across the table from her?

"All the time – you want to calm things *down*!" the Spanish woman's ranting. "You want to calm *me* down so much I may as well be dead! I feel like I'm being buried – buried *alive*!"

The man next to her forms his mouth into a *Shhhh* shape again, but nothing comes out. "You don't know what living is – you never have!" she storms. "*Ach* – I've had enough of it!" Then she gets dramatically to her feet, knocking her chair over as she does, and sweeps outside. The man gives a little squirm of pain and rushes out after her. The fattish couple exchange a look, like they're used to this kind of thing happening, and the man gets up, picks up the chair, fishes his wallet from his back pocket, and heads to the bar. Then the woman looks over at me again – and this time she beckons.

I look down quickly, embarrassed. Then I look up again, and she beckons again, more energetically this time, and smiles so warmly that I stand up right away and go over to her. "Want to finish this plate off?" she asks, in this matter-of-fact, slightly upper-class voice. I hesitate, and she says "Look – I just can't bear to waste it. It's only just arrived – you saw. Couldn't help noticing you drooling. Here – have some *jamón*." And she picks up a bit of bread with two plump, perfectly-manicured fingers, drops some serrano ham on it, and hands it to me.

"Mmm, thanks," I say, sticking it in my mouth without thinking twice. It tastes *fab*. "But aren't you – I mean – mightn't they come back?"

"No. Part of the ritual. He has to trail after *her* – we have to trail after *him* in case she tells him to get lost and we need to mop him up." She looks at me, all comic-despairing. She's got the most fabulous sea-blue eyes. "I'm getting sick of it, frankly. But there you go."

Her husband comes back from the bar, says, "OK, Bella – shall we follow the happy couple?" and she picks up an olive, pops it in her mouth and beams at me. "Bye," she says. "Enjoy our *tapas*!"

And they're gone.

# Chapter 8

In two seconds, Yaz is over beside me. "What was all that about?"

"Dunno," I say, attacking the tapas in earnest. "Free food?" I'm explaining in between chews when the two vacant chairs at the table are yanked out, and Tom and Ruth sit down.

"*All right*," says Tom, dispatching two little tarts at top speed. "This is all right!"

"*Oi*, Tom, go easy on those," I snarl. "Have some olives!"

"Can't stand olives," he says, ramming the two largest bits of cheese in his face while Ruth looks at him adoringly. "God – that woman though! Shouting the place down like that! That bloke should've smacked her one."

"He's joking," says Ruth at me, not meeting my eye.

"I am not," says Tom. "You yell at me like she did, babes, and I'll lay you out."

Then Ruth mock-hits him, and he grabs her hand and mock-bites it, and says, "Come on, babes, you *like* getting *laid out*," and then they touch foreheads and go all giggly together, and Tom says, "You know what that woman's problem was, don't you? You only had to look at her bloke. She wasn't getting enough!" I feel like I'm about to vomit, probably over Tom, so I stand up sharply and go over to the bar and get another beer each for Yaz and me. I'm damned if I'm getting them for those two as well.

When I get back to the table, most of the cheese and all the bread has gone, and Tom's talking about finding the hotel before it gets too dark. All his good humour has come back, which actually makes him more of a pain in the arse than when he was sulking. He demands the map from Yaz, studies it for a bit, then announces he'll get us there fast, no problem.

So we drink up, clear the last of the *tapas*, and leave.

Outside, Tom lives up to his promise. He takes Ruth's bag off her and marches on ahead, slowing every now and then to consult the map that Ruth dutifully holds out for him at eye level.

"God, look at that," I sneer. "She's acting like some kind of *slave*."

"Except she's getting her bag carried," points out Yaz, which shuts me up.

I like the little hotel from the minute we've walked through its front door. It's got a tiny black marble reception desk and a black marble floor, and low, moody lighting. I elbow Tom out of the way and explain as lucidly as I can to the girl behind the desk that we've been sent by someone called Diego, then I show her the restaurant card he jotted the hotel address on. She breaks into an enormous grin and calls "Juanita! *Juanita!*"

A stately woman appears from a door across the hallway, smiles at us, and takes the card the girl's waving. Then she too breaks into an enormous grin, and starts cross-questioning me about her *primo terrible* which I think means terrible cousin. I tell her how well he looked, and how good his food was, how much we enjoyed the meal, and she glows like I'm praising her personally.

She's got a bit of English, and between us we're getting on fine. She's worried about finding us rooms for the night though. "You could maybe all share?" she asks. "I have big family room with—"

"Absolutely *no way*," breaks in Tom, with a snort of incredulous laughter. "*Christ.* This is my *girlfriend*, and we need privacy, we need—"

"Yes, *OK* Tom, I think she's got the *message*!" I hiss.

"I know!" she suddenly announces, pointing a finger heavenwards. "Of course – those Belgium men leave after dinner. Yes – perfect rooms. Two rooms."

"*Great*," says Tom. "How much?"

Juanita ignores him, which makes me like her even more, beams at me and says, "The one I give to you two girls – it's one of my favourites! You'll *love* it!" Then she quotes a price per head that's only a bit more than all the motorway cells we've been staying in up to now.

"Fantastic," says Tom. "Come on – let's go." And he grabs Ruth round the waist, all leery.

"The rooms are not ready yet," says Juanita, sternly. "Leave your bags. Go to the *fiesta*. It starts soon. Come back in two hours." She pauses, glares at Tom. "No – *three* hours."

As we make our way out of the little hotel, Tom's looking like thunder and Yaz and I are trying hard not to erupt with sadistic laughter. Ruth worms her way under Tom's arm and they both walk off fast together like partners in a three-legged race.

"That was *hilarious*," mutters Yaz, as we hurry after them. "There was Tom – practically getting his kit off in the foyer—"

"– all ready for a passionate reconciliation scene with Ruth—"

"– and Juanita kicks us out to wander the streets for three hours! Oh, *look* – I can't keep this pace up. Can't we all agree to meet back at the hotel?"

We shout after them, suggest we'll pitch up at the hotel separately. Ruth turns round and wails, "But we agreed we'd stick together on the first night somewhere new!"

"This is different," says Yaz, authoritatively, as we draw up beside them. "We know where we're staying for the night, we've dumped our bags there and we don't need to use the car again."

"Oh," says Ruth. "OK then."

"See you tomorrow, yeah?" I say. "At breakfast, maybe."

"Don't count on it," leers Tom. "I plan on staying in bed late. *Right*, babes?"

# Chapter 9

It's a fine evening – not hot, but a lot warmer than England at Easter-time. We head down a likely-looking side street and it leads us to a tree-lined square, full of people milling around. A couple of stands have been set up, selling drinks and tasty-smelling roasted nuts and popcorn. One of the far streets has been roped off; little red velvet and gilt chairs are lined up all along the edge of it. Self-important elderly people in posh clothes are weaving in and out, claiming their seats.

"Things are hotting up," says Yaz. "The procession can't be long now."

"*Por favor!*" squeaks someone behind us at waist height. We turn round and come face to face with a miniature member of the Ku Klux Klan.

"*Je-sus!*" I breathe.

"Don't *blaspheme*," snaps Yaz, moving out of the way to let the tiny Whites Rights member past. "This is a religious festival, for God's sake!"

"Well, he gave me a shock! What's he doing here?"

"He's a *penitente*," hisses Yaz. "My aunt told me about them. *Penitentes* wear those hoods to look stupid, so they can humble themselves in the eyes of God."

"Did the Ku Klux Klan understand that when they pinched the outfit idea?"

"Doubt it."

"God, that's so *weird*. He's only about eight. What's he got to repent? Not eating his vegetables?"

"It's just a *symbol*, Laura. Of human guilt. The Catholics are really hot on guilt."

"Yeah, but making a little *kid*—"

"Oh, I think the kids *like* getting all dressed up. Parading around, getting lots of attention. It's like Halloween, isn't it."

"Ha! I bet the priests wouldn't like you saying that!"

"Oh, you know what I mean. I don't suppose the kids really understand all the heavy repentance stuff. Look – there's two more over there stuffing their faces with popcorn."

Somewhere in the distance, a single drum has started beating. It sounds unbelievably ominous, like someone's about to be executed. A hush falls over the crowd of people in the square, and everyone starts craning their necks towards the roped-off road. A gang of kids about our age push in alongside us, sliding their eyes sideways, eyeing us up, and I eye them back for as long as I can hold out.

Then the music starts. Some kind of brass band, playing music with a measured, tragic beat. And then the procession appears, round the bend in the road. First, loads of spooky monk-figures in hoods, barefoot and carrying crosses. Then the band, everyone walking in step, slow and solemn. Following them, about twenty pint-sized *penitentes*, most with an overdressed mum walking proudly alongside. Then the drummer, keeping to his deadly beat. Then some grown-up *penitentes*. Then a float, moving slowly and ponderously, swaying from side to side. On top of the float is a grotesque statue of Christ, carrying his cross, with three soldiers behind him laying into him with whips. Blood streams down Christ's plaster back. "Oh my God," hisses Yaz. "That is *gruesome*!"

As the float passes, the kids next to us cross themselves, managing to look quite cool while they're doing it. One of the girls keeps licking her lips, like she's a vampire turned on by the blood. Under the canopy covering the float you can see the feet of maybe twenty men, all inching forwards under its weight.

"Enjoying the show?" asks a cultured voice. We turn round, and there's Bella, the lush blonde from the bar who gave us her *tapas*, with her husband.

"Hi!" I say. "Yes. Well – it's kind of weird."

"Death, blood, drums, guilt, sin – all *enormously* erotic," Bella beams. "Mind you – I'm an old convent girl."

We're not sure what to say to this so I squeak, "That *tapas* was delicious! Thank you for . . . um . . . letting us have it." Then I think I might've been tactless, because of *why* she let us have it, so I add, quickly, "Did you find your friends?"

Bella rolls her sea-blue eyes skywards. "*Did* we. *Enormous* punch-up. Practically had to separate them in the street. She's gone off now, booked into a separate hotel – he's gone to bed with a bottle of whisky and a box of paper hankies. Sorry, I sound callous. It's just one gets a little fed up with it. They've been married eight years, you know. One would think they'd've calmed down a bit by now, but actually they seem to be determined to go the other way. Ah – *look*. The torches! I love torches. Pagan fire in a Christian festival. And here's another *pasos* – *stupendous* – oh *look* at it!"

A bit stunned by her onslaught of words, we turn our eyes back obediently to the procession. This time it's Christ on the cross, sprouting from a huge, voluptuous bed of white lilies. "Isn't it *heavenly*?" breathes Bella, inhaling their scent greedily. "God, I *love* Spain." And she throws her head back on her plump neck, shaking her mane of hair back from her face. Her husband puts both hands on her shoulders, and she rubs her face against first one hand, then the other, sensuous as all hell.

*Why them*, I think, enviously. *Why those two middle-aged people, and not me.*

# Chapter 10

The tail end of the procession winds down the street, tagged by a determined-looking matron towing a miniature *penitente* who clearly had to derail for a bit to have a pee. Some of the crowd of onlookers start to follow the procession; the rest turn towards the bars round the square, pushing their way through the doors and grabbing the outdoor tables. There's a real party feel to it, like everyone's really elated – it's infectious. Three sexy-eyed, olive-skinned boys wander very slowly past us, up far closer than they need to be, staring unblinkingly, and I stare back.

"Let's go, Bobby!" exclaims Bella, spinning round to face her husband. "I want a lovely glass of *manzanilla*. And food!" She seizes his hand and turns to us. "Do you know Seville?"

"We just got here tonight."

"Oh my goodness! Have you got somewhere to stay?"

"Yep," I say proudly, every inch the accomplished tourist. "We've booked into this gorgeous little hotel on *Calle Sierpes* for the night."

"And after that? Are you planning to stay here long?"

"Well. . ." I say, and without really meaning to I'm giving her a run down of our gap-year outline, complete with Tom's hideousness, and the need to stay put for a bit so we can make some money to fund the months ahead. While I'm talking, Bella stares at me intently, then she says, "I *do* sympathize with you. Couples can be an absolute nightmare, can't they – ignoring the needs of others."

"Yes," says Bobby, in his contented, fruity voice. "And so *frantic*! If they're not tearing each others' clothes off, they're tearing each others' eyes out."

Bella laughs, pats my shoulder, says "Well – we must find a restaurant. They'll all be heaving!" and trots off, hand in hand with Bobby.

We watch them go. "Wonder how long they've been together?" Yaz muses.

"Ages, I bet. They make you think marriage might work, don't they? Except I wouldn't want to get that fat."

Yaz laughs. "Come on – let's go for a tour around." And we start walking, weaving our way through all the people milling about, soaking up the festive atmosphere. We feast our eyes on the gorgeous ochre and orange colours of Seville, and the smell and sound of the horses drawing carriages, and the palm trees like huge green ostrich fans on the tops of long poles, and the fountains – everywhere you look there's a fountain, streaming and splashing. It's all so romantic it kind of chokes me up, and, much as I like Yaz, I wish I was here with someone I was in love with, and I know she's wishing that too. We ogle the olive-skinned Spanish boys, but they seem as exotic and out of reach as Seville itself.

Neither of us admits it, but we're nervous about going into the packed, heaving bars we keep passing. They're glamorous and alien – totally different to the half-dead roadside ones we've experienced up to now, totally different to the just-for-tourists ones on the Turkish coast. These are Spanish, first and foremost, and you feel you need to know what you're doing before you can step inside.

Then we cross a beautiful open square and pass a large, open-fronted bar with a group of Americans standing outside. They've all got drinks, and they're all looking benign and out-of-place, far more out of place than us. Yaz says, "Shall we?" and I nod, and we plunge inside the bar.

I know it's going to be me who orders the drinks because my Spanish is better. I squirm my way through to the packed counter, and stand there, hoping the white-shirted, black-waistcoated men serving have clocked me, and my place in the queue. They have, of course. Spanish barmen – like the waiters – are mega-efficient. They take their jobs very seriously and they do them very well, and you'd just better not hold them up by dithering. I get my money out ready.

"*Dos cervezas por favor!*" I squawk as the barman spins round on me. I've got two uncapped beers and two glasses in front of me before I can blink, and I'm not sure whether to leave a tip or not so I leave a big one and elbow my way triumphantly back to Yaz.

She's standing up against the wall, craning to see something that's happening at the very back of the bar. "They were *dancing*," she hisses. "There's a guy with a guitar, and these two girls. . ." The men in front of us blocking most of our view suddenly shift and walk away, and we move into the space they've left, closer to the back of the bar. I stand on tiptoe and I can just see a little wooden stage there, set back into an alcove. A boy with a guitar is sitting on the edge of it, concentrating on trying out a chord. He tries it twice, three times, then he starts to play. And then a boy standing nearby starts this finger-drumming in the palm of his hand, and a girl joins in, and another boy starts drumming really loudly on the table. Then there's some laughing and teasing and two girls – one in jeans, one in a short dress – jump up on the stage and start dancing, all poised and confident and powerful, feet moving fast, hands held high, fingers working this complicated routine.

I'm totally impressed. "Is that flamenco?" I breathe.

"Not sure. Thought you had to wear big spotty frocks with flounces at the bottom."

"It *is* flamenco. I'm sure it is."

"It's bloody sexy, whatever it is. Look at the way they're so aware of their bodies."

"Yeah. And so aware of showing them off, all stretched out like that."

The beat's infectious. Several more people nearby us have joined in the drumming. And the girls are laughing, moving round each other, and people on the floor are calling out to them, encouraging them.

We move closer to the stage. Two of the boys notice us, nudge each other, turn to stare at us with big grins on their faces. And almost straight away the girls on the stage dance forward, all hostile and challenging. As if they'd like to pick up imaginary flouncy skirts and shoosh us out of the place, like we were hens in the kitchen. It's sort of a joke, but not quite, and Yaz and I feel uneasy and immediately act like we're engrossed in conversation and not watching them at all.

"D'you want another drink?" I mutter. We've both finished our beers.

"No," says Yaz, to my relief. "Let's go."

Outside, we're filled with this ridiculous sense of achievement, 'cos we've survived a real Spanish bar on *fiesta* night, and we link arms and walk straight across the beautiful square. "This must be heaven in the heat," murmurs Yaz.

"Well, we'll find out, won't we," I say. "We're gonna come back, right?"

"If we can make Tom agree. Oh, God, Laura – d'you think that row we had in the restaurant will've done any good? D'you think he's going to start listening to us now?"

"We'll make him."

"Yeah. And we'll *talk* about where we're going next – we'll agree on it, we won't just let him—" Yaz stops dead, jerks her head towards a doorway we're about to pass.

"Ah," I say, as I take in what she's looking at. "They definitely got over that row they had, then."

Tom and Ruth are in the doorway. And he's got her backed right against the wall and she's got one arm wrapped tight round his head and one slung round his neck. She's half disappeared beneath him and his whole back's moving with the energy he's putting into snogging her. "*Jesus*," gasps Yaz. "That is *so not clever*." We watch as Ruth winds her right leg round

Tom's left one. "At a religious *fiesta*, for Chrissake. And that is someone's *door*. They'll get *arrested*."

"By the Spanish Inquisition, with any luck," I say drily. "And I hope Tom gets tortured."

"You really don't like him, do you?"

"I hope they chop off his balls and serve them up as *tapas*."

"*Laura!* That's a *disgusting* thing to say!"

"Yeah, OK. But it would give us a bit of peace tonight, wouldn't it?"

# Chapter 11

As it turns out, we have perfect peace. We're in a room far away from Tom and Ruth, a beautiful room with two beds like princess beds in a fairy tale, all frilly covers and fat cushions. There's a round marble basin in the corner, an old oak wardrobe, and a huge, beautiful mirror on the wall reflecting the glow from the pretty lamps and reflecting us as we move about, smiling, getting ready to go to bed.

The best thing about the room, though, is the set of skinny glass doors that opens on to a beautiful little balcony. There's just room to stand on it, side by side. We're overlooking a courtyard, with windows and balconies just like ours on all sides of us, screened by trees and flowering creepers. In the courtyard, little tables are spaced out among the huge plant pots, and lamps are shining, making shadows in among the leaves.

We lean our elbows dreamily on the rail, breathing in the jasmine scent. "Oh, this is heavenly," sighs Yaz. "It's so *romantic*."

"*Romeo!*" I call, experimentally, but no one answers. A small bat swoops into the courtyard, then swerves off again.

"I bet we'll have breakfast down there tomorrow," Yaz says, "if it's warm enough."

"Let's stay another night," I murmur. "Then I can hang some of my gear up in that wardrobe. I can leave my toothbrush out on the sink."

Yaz laughs. "Sad, Laura, sad. But – yeah. It would be nice to stay on."

"You know what? I'd really like to find work here. So we can stay in the city. Imagine having that bar we went to as our local."

"Don't push it, Laura. One night at a time." We wander in and get into our fat princess beds, and they're so heavenly and comfortable that we're asleep within seconds.

Despite Tom's boast that he's going to stay in bed making love all morning, it's him who wakes us up the next day, banging on our door. "*Come on!* Are you two getting up or what? My car's probably getting broken into while you lounge around in there!"

Yaz swears, I pull my pillow over my head. Tom hammers on the door again. Yaz swears again, louder, then she pulls on her silky kimono and yanks the door open. "Morning, Tom," she says icily.

"Yeah, yeah. Come on – I need to check the car, so we might as well get off now."

"We want to stay another night!" I squawk from the depths of my pillow.

"*What?*" snarls Tom.

"We want to stay another night," repeats Yaz sweetly. "See some more of Seville. I spoke to Juanita last night, and I'm pretty sure she'll give us cheap rates for another night."

And *I'm* pretty sure Yaz is lying, or she'd've mentioned it to me, but I wait expectantly to see if Tom takes one of his favourite baits – saving money.

"Oh, *what?*" he huffs. "Don't you want to get on?"

"No. That's the whole point – we agreed, didn't we, yesterday. We were going to take our time more, stay on in places we like. . ."

"I don't remember agreeing anything like that," grunts Tom. "Oh, look. Just get up, will you, you lazy cows – we'll have breakfast, talk about it then." And he turns on his heel without waiting for an answer.

Yaz stands and watches him as he stomps along the corridor. "Hate him, *hate* him," she spits.

Yaz was right – we do have breakfast in the courtyard. The sun's out, beaming down on the tables on the far side. Bread rolls and jam, cereal, fruit and creamy yogurt are all laid out on a trestle table, so we pile up our plates and sit ourselves down at a table in the sun. A girl of about our age trots out smiling and serves us lovely milky coffee, and orange juice that tastes as though it's been squeezed about two minutes ago. "Ah, this is the life," sighs Yaz, taking a sip of juice. "This is *fab*."

And then Tom lopes into the courtyard, instantaneously making it less fab. He heads for the trestle table, grumbles loudly about there not being any Coco Pops, picks up four rolls and no fruit, and plonks down next to us. "Where's Ruth?" I demand.

"Still in the shower," he says, all smug and suggestive, as though he went straight back to their room and made high-octane love to her again.

"Have you asked her? About staying on?"

"She's not keen," he says, spraying crumbs across the table. "Our room was crap, for one thing."

"Really?" I ask, all fake concern. "Ours is *fantastic*."

"Yeah, well, lucky you. Our bed was about three hundred years old. We had to put the mattress on the floor. And the room was right next to some kind of massive *cupboard* and some idiot was pulling out buckets and brooms at three in the morning."

"*Poor you!*" I gush. Tom narrows his eyes at me all suspicious and hostile, and then Ruth walks into the courtyard. Tom gets up and goes over to her, partly to give her a smarmy kiss, partly so he can grab extra butter and jam from the trestle table.

"They look really pale, don't they," hisses Yaz. "D'you know that rhyme?

*"Uncle George and Aunty Mabel*
*Fainted at the breakfast table*
*So all lovers please take warning –*
*Never do it in the morning!"*

"What're you two smirking about?" demands Tom, thumping down at the table again, with Ruth next to him.

"Nothing!" we both carol.

"Yeah, well. We'd better discuss what we're doing, hadn't we, now Roofy's here. Since you two want to look round Seville *again,* what we thought is we can check on the car, have a walk around, and then get going."

"Tom," says Yaz sweetly, "have you ever looked up 'discussion' in the dictionary? Only I think you'll find it's a kind of *two-way* event."

"I'm just saying what we want to do!" says Tom. "You're free to put your side!"

"Well, you know what our side is," I put in. "We want to stay another night. Don't you like Seville, Ruth?"

Ruth shrugs. "It's OK."

"Oh, *Ruth*! It's *beautiful*!"

She shrugs again. "Yeah, but—"

"And that parade! Didn't you like that? I thought it was *awesome* – I mean, *stunning,* but completely weird too."

"Yeah, well . . . it *was* different."

"It was amazing! It was like we saw the *real Spain* last night!"

"*Real Spain!*" scoffs Tom. "Lors, you are such a sad case, you know that? Spain is just like anywhere else, only it's hotter and they're mean to bulls."

"*God,* Tom, you're so *ignorant!*"

"You're the one who's ignorant. You've got some stupid girly romantic view of this place—"

"*Uuurgh* – you do my head in! Look – I just think Spain's *fascinating.* The culture – it's totally alien to ours. This flamenco thing – we saw *kids* dancing it last night, people our age. It's like it's in their blood."

"Well, they're just as sad as you are then, aren't they, Laura. They've got no decent clubs to go to, that's their problem."

"*Jesus!* I really, *really* don't understand you. I don't understand how you can be so shut off from everything different."

"Yeah? Well, if I'm *shut off* it's 'cos I like the way I live. Maybe you don't. Maybe that's the whole problem. Maybe if you'd managed to pull someone in the last five years you'd—"

"*Tom!*" snaps Ruth warningly, and Yaz goes, "This isn't helping us decide anything."

There's a pause, and the smiling girl comes out and refills our coffee cups. I sit on the routine hurt I feel about Tom's jibes about men, and decide to ignore him. Ruth stirs her coffee, round and round, and says, "We really haven't got a very nice room here. If you two don't mind – I would like to push on."

"Yeah – but where?" I blurt out.

"South. Don't look like that, Laura – we've got to get *jobs*! I dunno about you but practically half my money's gone already. And if we get to a holiday resort—"

"– we'll be sure of work," finishes Tom.

"But – what's the point? It won't be *Spain*!"

"Yes, it bloody will! You look at an atlas! And it'll be hot and great and on a beach—"

"– and full of *idiots* like Turkey—"

"– you just don't know how to have a good time, that's your problem Laura—"

"– and you're so stupid all you want is cheap beer and a sun tan—"

"*Oh, for Christ's sake, stop it!*" Ruth jumps to her feet, rushes out of the courtyard. Tom jumps to *his* feet, glares at me like it's all my fault, and follows her.

And Yaz sighs and says, "Oh, well. We tried. I s'pose we'd better go and get our bags then, eh?"

We all meet in the foyer. Tom and Ruth seem to have had another row in their room before they came down. Ruth is all wobbly-mouthed and Tom's frowning. You can tell that, in one corner of his unreconstructed brain, he's started to blame her for having such bitches for friends.

We pay the bill; Tom asks if we can stow our bags behind the reception desk for a couple of hours, and

Juanita agrees. Then he outlines his plan, which he clearly thinks is very generous to me and Yaz, and which is: to check on the car, have another walk round Seville, get lunch if it's cheap enough, come back, pick up our bags, and get off.

And head south.

Yaz and I are not happy, not happy at all, but we don't see a way out. I'm still nurturing a secret hope that I'll stumble on a perfect two-jobs offer on a card in a shop window somewhere, with good pay and full accommodation, which means that Yaz and I will be able to stay here, but even in my desperate state I know that's not going to happen.

"Why don't we split up again?" Yaz asks hopefully as we walk out of the hotel. "Like last night."

"No point," grunts Tom. "We don't particularly wanna see Seville. We'll tag along after you two. That way you won't get lost again, like you did in France."

"That happened *once*!" I erupt, and Tom holds up his hands and goes, "Hey, hey, calm down, Lors – girls just have a crap sense of direction, that's all!"

"Are you going to let him get away with that, Ruth?"

"Oh, for *heaven's* sake, Laura – it was a *joke*!" wails Ruth.

"No, it wasn't," says Tom, infuriatingly. "It's a well-known scientifically-proven fact. Girls can't park, either. It's all to do with spatial awareness."

As one, Yaz and I start walking, fast, but not fast enough to avoid hearing, "It's like their driving – that's crap too," as we turn a corner.

First we check the car, and find it in exactly the same state we'd left it in. This seems to disappoint Tom, who spends a good ten minutes examining it for scratches, attempted break-ins, hidden incendiary devices and so forth. Then we take off for our daylight tour of Seville. True to his word, Tom tags along, with Ruth, who seems to have gone into some kind of state of non-existence, in tow. Having them constantly three steps behind us completely ruins the experience. Like trying to watch a favourite film sitting next to someone who just doesn't get it, and keeps making stupid, inane comments.

We stop in front of a beautiful fountain and they stop too, and Tom spends the whole time grumbling that he's got dog-shit on his shoe, and trying to clean it off on the ground. We walk through a beautiful little cracked-tiled, overgrown square, and all we can hear is Tom saying, "They should tidy this up." We stop to admire the flowers strewn on the ground from the procession the night before and Tom says, "Crap road-sweeping service, innit?"

"What are we going to do, Yaz?" I mutter. "Are we going to take off on our own?"

She sighs. "I'm scared to. Not without a job sorted out."

I sigh. "Me too."

After that Yaz and I give up trying to soak up Seville, and we give up any idea of having lunch here, mainly 'cos we can't face the thought of sitting opposite Tom as he moans on about wishing he was in a McDonald's. We resign ourselves to getting back in the car, driving for an hour, then filling our faces at some roadside café.

We walk miserably back to the hotel, this time with Tom and Ruth in front. And as we get there we see two people filling (literally) the doorway.

"*There* they are!" cries a voice I know. "I told you we'd find the right hotel, Bobby! See – I am getting psychic! This is *fate*!"

# Chapter 12

"Hello, you young people!" calls Bella, beaming all over her face. "Are you hungry?"

"Who the fuck are they?" hisses Tom.

"You know – from the bar!" I hiss back. "They gave us their plate of *tapas*!"

We draw up in front of them. "Have you still got your car?" demands Bella, still beaming.

"Yes," says Tom, in a belligerent, who-wants-to-know? way.

"Oh, *good*! In that case, Bobby and I would like to treat you to lunch! We've got a proposition for you, haven't we, darling?"

Bobby nods happily, and they set off down the street, and, a bit dazed, we all follow. It's good Bella has offered us a free lunch, 'cos otherwise Tom would refuse to come. As it is, he lags behind, grumbling about how I always go round picking up weirdos and how it had better not make us late getting back on the road.

Soon we're inside this fantastic old bar, seated round a big scrubbed wooden table with heaped plates of meatballs, *pimientos, tortilla* and cheese in front of us, clutching cold, wet bottles of beer.

"Now, I'm sure you want to know why we've *kidnapped* you," Bella begins. "The story is this. That couple you saw us with – they've finally split up. Well, I say *finally,* they're always splitting up, but this time I think they mean it, because poor Derek's set to go off to *Australia,* can you believe, to stay with his brother, and Paloma's thrown her wedding ring into the fire. Literally. She's so melodramatic. Well, the Spanish are, you know. That's why we love them, isn't it, Bobby?"

At my side, I can feel Tom about to say something appalling like, *Get on with it you fat cow!* But luckily, Bella continues: "The four of us bought a house together, three years ago. We take it in turns to go there. *Pino Alto*, it's called. That means tall pine – it's got the most beautiful old pine tree by the gates. It's near Ercos, halfway between the mountains and the coast. Beautiful. Perfect. Isolated. *Eden*. I'd spend most of my time there painting – *heaven*. But that's come to an end now, hasn't it, Bobby?" She turns to her husband, eyes welling, and he pats her hand and says, "No Bella, no darling – I'll sort it out. You'll see. We'll buy them out. We won't have to sell it. We'll—"

"What exactly has all this got to do with us?" interrupts Tom rudely.

"I'm coming to that," says Bella, firmly. "We're off for a long tour of America the week after next – it's been planned for ages, we can't cancel now. Paloma and Derek were going to keep a check on *Pino Alto*, stay there this summer – now they can't. Paloma says she doesn't want anything more to do with it ever, *refuses* to find someone to rent it, she's being *impossible. . . Anyway*. It's up to us to sort it out at the eleventh hour – we absolutely can't leave it empty, not for that long. It's been broken into before when it's been left empty for a long stretch."

"You want us to move in?" demands Tom.

"Exactly!" beams Bella.

"How much?"

"How much what?"

"How much would you charge us?"

"Oh – *nothing*! That's the whole point. You'd be caretaking. You'd be doing us a favour."

"That is an *amazing* offer," I say quickly, before Tom can start demanding caretaker's wages. "You really mean we could stay there for nothing?"

"Indeed."

"How come you're trusting us like this?" Tom blurts out. "You don't know anything about us."

"Oh, Laura told me quite a bit," says Bella meaningfully. "And I'm intuitive about people. And I'm rarely wrong. Am I, Bobby?"

"No, angel, you aren't," Bobby replies, lovingly.

"I took to Laura and Yaz right away. And your girlfriend seems awfully sweet, too." Oddly enough, she makes no comment on Tom himself. "And I trust fate. Bobby and I agreed – if we found the right hotel, it was *fated* that you'd look after the house for us." And so saying, she picks up her huge baggy handbag from the floor, delves into it, and comes out with a packet of photos.

And fans them out on the table before us, in among the plates and bottles.

"That's *Pino Alto* from the front. That's the pine itself – and the palm tree. Isn't she *proud*? All little *fincas* have their own palm. That's the courtyard. Beautiful in the evening. That's the olive grove – it's got its own little olive grove. That's the kitchen . . . basic, but fine . . . that's the main room . . . those sofas were such a bargain . . . master bedroom . . . other bedrooms . . . bathroom . . . isn't it heavenly? Bobby, *we can't get rid of it!*"

Bobby puts both his arms round her and hugs her, and the four of us sit and stare in awe at the absolute beauty of the white house. I can't take my eyes off the first photo, with the black iron gates and the curly bars at the windows, and the great swathes of jasmine and flowering creeper falling on to the clay terrace tiles . . . it's like my dream of Spain. It's perfect. The sort of place where anything and everything could happen, the sort of place to fall insanely in love. . .

"It's *wonderful*," breathes Yaz. "Gorgeous," murmurs Ruth. And even Tom mutters, "Yeah."

Ruth drops the photo of the olive grove back on to the table. "The thing is," she ventures, "we have to get jobs pretty soon. That's why we were heading south. You know – to a holiday resort."

"Oh, *God*," says Bella, lip curling in distaste, like we were setting up as lapdancers or something. "You don't want to do that. They've completely ruined that south coast. And there's work in Ercos! Seriously – it's getting more commercial all the time. We hate it, don't we, Bobby? Although it hasn't lost its *essence*. Bars, restaurants, clubs . . . or you could do teaching English as a foreign language. Big demand for it. Oh, you'd get work really easily."

There's a pause so electric it's like the air's crackling. I look towards the far end of the bar, where the high sun's glinting through the window on to the racks of wine. I look down at the wonderful photos. I think about travelling south with Tom in the cramped Astra towards the high rise hotels on the overcrowded beach. "Let's do it!" I burst out, fervently.

"Yes," says Yaz. "*Let's.*"

"*Wonderful*," breathes Bella. "You see, Bobby? I knew it would be OK. They'll be fine, I know it. They'll take good care of *Pino Alto*. I *know* it."

Bobby leans over, kisses her hair. You get the feeling he wouldn't care what happened to the house or anything in his life, as long as he still got to be with her.

"Now, just hang on a minute," says Tom. "We ought to at least discuss it."

"*Fine*," says Yaz. "Sorry, Tom – forgot how keen you were on *discussing* everything fully. One – we'll save a huge amount of money by not having to pay rent. Two – we get to stay in one place for a bit. Three – Bella says we'll find work easily. Four – the place looks absolutely mind-bogglingly beautiful."

"Oh, it is," agrees Bella. "You'll love it."

"Why is it so important to have a car?" demands Tom.

"Because it's isolated. You need a car to get to it."

"Although there is a bus," puts in Bobby. "Down into Ercos. Once you're there."

"I don't like the sound of it being isolated," grumbles Tom. "Suppose something goes wrong? Like all the lights go out or something?"

"Then you contact Miguel. He's our sort of odd-job-man, and he looks after the olive trees. He lives nearby and he's an absolute marvel."

"Suppose it doesn't work out once we're there? Suppose we want to move on?"

"Then you give us a week's notice," says Bella. "So we can sort something else out. Now, if there're no more questions, Bobby and I will retire to the bar, and leave you four to talk frankly. And when we come back – you can tell us what you've decided."

And she and Bobby stand up, and sail majestically away from the table.

"That is the *most amazing* offer I have ever been made, and I'll never speak to you again if you bitch this up, Tom Harrison!" I spurt out.

"As if that would worry me," sneers Tom. "Yeah, OK, it's pretty cool. I just don't trust it."

"What's *amazing* is that they trust *you*! With their house! Oh, come on – we're gonna say yes, aren't we?"

"Yes," says Yaz. "*Yes!* It looks fantastic. Oh, I can't believe this."

"Ercos sounds a bit of a shit place though," grouses Tom. "If it's only just got around to opening up a few bars and clubs. I'd sooner go where there's a bit of action."

"Oh, Tom – there *will* be action. Just not fake holiday-rep-organized action. And think of the money we'll save! And if we don't like it – we can move on, can't we?"

I've got to get him to agree, to at least get us there, get *me* there, I've got to. I turn on Ruth. "Ruth, have you ever *seen* a more romantic place? Come on – you've got the casting vote. What d'you say?"

And miraculously Ruth turns to Tom and says, "Oh, Tom – let's go, baby! At least give it a try – it looks *fabulous*!"

# Chapter 13

And a mere hour-and-a-half later, we're on the road to Ercos, with the keys to *Pino Alto* in the glove department, and a new map spread out on Ruth's lap and all the instructions and phone numbers Bella gave me safely stowed in my bag. I'm so excited I keep bouncing up and down in my seat, like a little kid ten minutes away from the seaside.

"We can have a bedroom each," Yaz says. "Not that I want to get away from you, Laura, but—"

"I want that tiny one," I say. "The one with the twisty bars on the window with the vine coming in—"

"Well, we're having the big one," puts in Tom, predictably.

"Yeah, yeah," says Yaz. "God – the bathroom looked fabulous, didn't it? All marble and stuff. . ."

"Bloody cold at this time of the year," grumbles Tom. "Did she say anything about heaters?"

"Only that there's a big open fire," I gloat. "And they burn laurel wood, and it smells heavenly. . ."

Tom snorts, and reminds us all for about the five-hundredth time that it's just an experiment and if we don't (meaning he doesn't) like it after a week or so we move on – south. Then, just as he's explaining for the six-hundredth time he wants to get to the south for the summer anyway, Yaz drowns him out by singing "*We're all off to sunny Spain! Oh, viva España!*" and I'm thinking: with any luck, things'll really come together in Ercos, and Yaz and I and – who knows? – maybe even Ruth won't be in the car with him when he goes.

We make good time, only stopping once at about seven o'clock (at Tom's insistence) for Coke, chips and hamburgers. The trouble starts, of course, when the map directs us off the main road. This happens at about the same time that the sun starts to go down. Bella had told us to be sure to get to the house before nightfall so that we can find our way in and turn on the electricity and everything, and now there's a kind of anxious nervousness in the car, everyone keeping an eye on the sinking sun. It's like we're racing to the castle to stake Dracula before he wakes up.

Tom slows by each turning off the narrow road we're on, but Ruth rejects every one. Then out of the blue she squeaks, "It must be that one! Look – she's marked the bus stop. And the rubbish dumpsters on the other side."

Tom eyes the bumpy-looking lane Ruth's pointing at with acute disgust. "That is going to *seriously* screw up my suspension," he snarls.

"Well, go really slowly, baby," soothes Ruth. "It can't be far now. She said there was only a bit of rough track."

Tom lurches sourly on to the lane, and we all hold our breath as we bump forward. Fields are on each side of us, punctuated by the odd house surrounded by wire fencing. "This is *ridiculous*," he announces. "This road is crap. Imagine coming along it at night – you'd end up in a ditch."

"Bobby said there was a bus, though, didn't he," Yaz wheedles. "Into Ercos."

"Yeah, but I bet that was the only bus-stop back there," replies Tom, grimly. "I can just see you three staggering along this track, in your club gear."

We jolt along in silence for a bit, then the track forks. "Which way, babes?" demands Tom, stopping the car. Ruth, face pressed to the map, can't decide. Tom snatches the map from her, swears, turns the map upside down, swears again, and announces half the roads aren't marked down and we've probably gone hopelessly wrong and he's got *no fucking idea* where we are.

On the horizon just beyond us, the sun sinks completely out of sight. "Just drive on a bit, baby," urges Ruth, tensely. "Maybe it'll be round the next bend."

Tom snorts, and starts the car up again. The track gets narrower, more bumpy. An oncoming tractor forces us off the road into a field, and Tom has to rev like crazy to get out again. It's really gloomy now, and hard to see. We drive round a bend and we're suddenly faced by a sprawling, run-down farm house, with no way round it. A huge black dog with electric eyes in our headlights and teeth like a bulldozer runs out from nowhere and barks at us ferociously. Tom turns the car in the drive, dirt spurting from his wheels, and accelerates away. "*Jesus*," he snarls. "The Hound of the fucking Baskervilles or what? Look – I'm gonna try and get back on the main road."

"What?" I wail. "Why?"

"'Cos we're lost, Laura, that's why!" he snaps.

"Well, once we're back on the main road, we'll have another go at following the map, won't we –?"

"No! It's far too dark. We'll find a motel for the night."

My heart plummets. I know if we give up now we won't come back. Tom'll find some way of proving it's a bad idea and heading off to the south coast once more. I feel so desperate and frantic I don't realize I'm wringing my hands like a loony, until Yaz nudges me sharply. And then I spot this tall tree, across the other side of a field, and something about it makes me crane my neck round, peering at it, and then suddenly the penny drops and I shriek, "*Look!* That pine tree there!"

"So?" growls Tom.

"Don't you remember seeing that in one of Bella's photos?"

"No!" wails Yaz.

"Well, I do! I promise you – it's by the gate. It's what the house is named for! *Pino* . . . um . . . *Pino Alto*! Why don't we just head for that?"

"D'you see a road leading to it?" snarls Tom.

"No, but – if you keep going – and take the first track to the right – and we can keep the tree in sight—"

Tom slams the headlights full on, slams the gears into first. The car growls forward. I'm twisted right round in my seat, eyes glued to the pine tree like it might evaporate if I lose sight of it for an instant. And then, like a miracle, a track opens up on the right. Tom swerves into it, cursing. Dirt sprays up all around the car.

The pine tree gets nearer, and nearer. And then the track starts veering away.

I feel an absolute flood of despair. "We were almost there!" I wail. "Look how close the tree is! Why don't you just drive straight across to it?"

"Because that will mean driving straight across a *fucking field*!" explodes Tom.

"Yeah, but – it looks OK! Firm. There's grass there!"

I hold my breath. There's a tense, ballistic pause. And then Tom does possibly the first thing this trip that I actually like him for. He yanks the wheel round, and ploughs into the field. We lurch and bump across it, but we don't stop. And then we see the pine tree close up, and even better than that, we see some gates, and they're exactly the same big, black, beautiful wrought-iron gates as the ones in Bella's photo.

# Chapter 14

I'm out of the car before Tom can even put the brakes on, shrieking, "I'll unbolt it! I'll unbolt it!" I lurch at the gates, slide back the heavy bolt, wrench each gate across to the side walls gleaming white in the dusk. I feel rather than see the palm tree waving above me. I know the house is behind me, but I don't turn to look at it yet.

Tom switches off the ignition. Ruth and Yaz clamber out of the car, and he follows them. The moon's come up, it's the only light there is, and by it we can make out the L-shaped, single-storey house and the wide, clay-tiled terrace. There's a big wooden table standing on the terrace, and over it a rough trellis on poles supports a great mass of vines. You can't see much beyond the terrace – just the outlines of trees and bushes, and total blackness.

"Oh, great," snarls Tom. "We are in the middle of *fucking nowhere* here!" He thrusts his hand out towards me. "Gimme the keys, Lors."

Dumbly, I fish them out of my bag and hand them over. I think about snapping *I can do it*, but I'm lousy with strange keys, and I bet Tom isn't. As he stomps over to the door I try and read the expression on Yaz's face, but I can't see well enough. *Oh God, let it be all right*, I mutter to myself.

"*Wuuuurgh!!*" Tom leaps back from the door like a scalded cat. "There's a bloody great *lizard. . .* Jesus!"

I take a couple of steps towards the door. Then I laugh, pick up the lizard's tail, and hammer on the door with it. "It's a door-knocker, you prat," I say. "Chuck me the keys."

Tom glowers at me, then he shies the bunch of keys, hard, but I manage to catch them without wincing. I slide the big one into the big lock, praying, and I feel it turn. Then I go for the Yale lock. The first key I try is hopeless, but the second fits, and soon it's turning and the door's swinging wide, wide open.

"Oh, *well done*, Laura!" squeals Yaz, and Ruth says, "We're in!"

Trying not to look too triumphant, I grope my way round the left of the door, like Bella said to. I find a little cupboard on the wall, open it, and find the torch where she said it would be.

Then I switch it on and shine it straight in Tom's pugnacious face. "If I read out the instructions, d'you think you can turn the electricity on?" I ask, sweetly.

Five minutes later, and we're not only all lit up but we've got the water heater on, and the kettle on, too, because Ruth found some teabags and longlife milk in a cupboard. We girls are dancing about with excitement and even Tom is allowing a smirk of pleasure to distort his macho features.

The room we're in is massively long and open and *fabulous*. The door we came in by leads straight into the kitchen space, which is partitioned off from the rest of the room by marble-topped units. Beyond that, there's a long table, with two curly gothic candlesticks and eight wooden chairs. And beyond that, three fat sofas are grouped round a huge open fireplace. There are sets of shutters all along both walls, which means there must be windows behind them, which means the light in here in the day must be out of this world.

"Great place for parties!" says Yaz. Then she races straight down to the end, throws herself on one of the sofas. "I want a *fire*!" she cries. "Tom – I bet you were a boy scout. Get lighting."

"Get stuffed!" he replies, genially.

"Tea's up!" says Ruth. "And look – there's some coconut biccies here. Only just past their sell-by." She tears open the packet and stuffs one in her mouth, and soon the rest of us are beside her, grabbing mugs of tea and biscuits. The sense of relief we all feel at getting safely inside is so real you can practically reach out and stroke it.

"Come on," says Yaz. "Let's explore! The bedrooms must be through there." She points at the door to the right of the fireplace.

We jostle each other through into a tiled corridor, with four doors leading off it on the left. The first leads into a large room with white walls, plain furniture and a big double bed with brass knobs. Tom scoops up Ruth, staggers across the room with her and crashes down on to it, while she shrieks with mock-rage.

"Oh, God," groans Yaz, scathingly. "Let's go."

Tom and Ruth don't follow us into the second room. It has no bed; instead it's crammed to the rafters with paintings and easels and artist's stuff. "Bella's art room," I say.

The third room is the bathroom, all white and gleaming. It feels cold now but it must be great in the heat. The fourth room has two twin beds too close together, and a skinny wardrobe with two drawers underneath.

"Where's the room you were going to have?" says Yaz, all puzzled.

I shrug. "Maybe it was an old photo of the one Bella took over as an art room."

Yaz frowns. "It doesn't look like it. The shape was different."

We both try not to look disappointed that we have to share again. Yaz says, "It's a bit of a squeeze but it'll be OK. And it's wonderfully far away from the lovers." Then a huge yawn splits her face and she croaks, "It's been a helluva day, Laura. More like two days without a night in between. I feel absolutely shattered. Didn't Bella say all the duvets and stuff were in a wooden chest in the main bedroom?"

We head back to the corridor. To find the main bedroom door firmly shut and a pile of bedding on the floor outside it. "Oh, bloody hell," I mutter. "They're not wasting any time, are they?"

Still, we've got what we want. The sheets feel very slightly damp, but they smell of lavender. We head back to our room, make up the beds at top speed, do as little teeth cleaning and so on as hygienically possible, and get into bed.

Yaz goes off to sleep almost straight away; I can hear her breathing slow and steady. I lie there in the pitchy black, seeing the same whether my eyes are opened or closed. The silence is immense. You can hear absolutely nothing.

I decide I'm quite glad Yaz is sleeping in there with me.

# Chapter 15

I snap awake the next day with a feeling of heart-thudding panic, and blink about me. I realize where I am, and get this rush of excitement. Then I remember the nightmare journey we had to get here, and how far out in the wilds we are, and panic takes over again.

After all these jangling emotions, I need a cup of tea. I glance over at Yaz; she's still snoring softly, one hand bunched up under her chin. She even manages to look gorgeous when she's asleep, the cow. I decide to head into the kitchen and make her a cuppa, then get her to come and explore the place with me.

I hobble across the tiled floor into the bathroom next door. A shaft of bright sun through the window is spotlighting the chilly white bath and glowing on the marble floor; suddenly I can't wait for Yaz to explore the place, I want to see it now. I pee quickly, speed past the sex machines' room and straight through the living room. Then I draw back the two big bolts on the front door and step outside.

And my mouth drops open and for a good few seconds I forget to breathe, and I realize I now understand that corny old phrase "it took my breath away". There's a great bowl of blue sky, and under that, mountains. The whole of the horizon is mountains, nothing man-made breaking the outline. Then there's a vast stretch of green – trees, grassland – and as my eye travels in with it I see ranks of olive trees, and I remember Bella saying the house had its own little olive grove, and I wonder if all those trees belong to the house, but I reckon they can't, there's far too many of them. They come right up to the terrace and as they get closer they're mixed with bushes covered with glorious flowers, some red, some white; and all these lovely wild spring flowers are sprouting everywhere, daisies and poppies and beautiful graceful ones like lilies that I don't know the name for. . .

The vines over the big wooden table on the terrace are lifting and falling in the light wind, shining in the sunlight, and I think: I'll make breakfast, and I'll make Yaz get up and come out here to eat it and *look*.

Back inside, I plug in the electric kettle and wonder what I can find for breakfast. I remember Bella flapping her arm vaguely, saying, "There's some provisions in the fridge and the kitchen cupboard. Help yourselves to whatever you find." The stench of overripe cheese hits me before I've even opened the fridge door properly. Maybe when you're sophisticated, you eat it that way, but I'm not sophisticated so I hook a fork through its greasy wrapper and convey it outside where I lob it in a great tangle of leggy looking cacti next to the terrace. The only other stuff in the fridge is a bottle of champagne, a herbal pick-me-up and a tub of margarine. Anxiously, I pull open the kitchen cupboard, where Ruth discovered the teabags and biscuits last night. There's one more carton of longlife milk, but apart from that just a packet of spaghetti, some manky-looking honey, and rows and rows of jars of dried herbs. And inside the tea caddy there are only two teabags left.

Panic hits me again. I see Tom getting up ravenous after his calorie-burning night of passion, wanting eggs and fried bread and bacon, and getting foul-tempered when he finds out the cupboard is bare. I see Ruth and Yaz coming to blows over the last teabag. I see everyone demanding to get in the car, and leave.

I make one teabag do for two mugs, and hurry back to our bedroom. "Yaz! Here. Tea. Come on – we've got to get into town."

"*Mmrrrgghhhh.*"

"We need to get some *food*. Come on, Yaz, wake up."

I put her tea down on the narrow table between the two beds, and take mine into the bathroom. I strip off and stand in the bath, and turn on the spray thing attached to the taps. After a few seconds of icy water shooshing round my feet, it turns wonderfully hot, and I can shower. I towel myself dry and shoot back to the bedroom. "Come on, Yaz! You haven't even touched your tea!"

"Wassa point?" she mutters groggily. "We need Tom to drive us. . ."

"Maybe we don't! Maybe we can find out about that bus Bobby told us about. . ." It's hopeless. She's slipping back into her dreams. I feel better after my shower, though. I take my time dressing in clean jeans and a favourite ivory-coloured shirt; I spike my fingers through my hair. Then I jab on some mascara and lippy, and wander outside again. Maybe we can have spaghetti for breakfast, I think. Spaghetti with a bit of that stale marge. . .

It's absolutely silent. I find myself just lifting up my arms, looking towards the sun climbing the big blue sky, like I'm a druid or something. Then, somewhere in the distance, a dog starts barking, answered by another one. And then I hear a motorbike hum, a long way away. And the rumble of a big vehicle getting closer, rattling along on the rough road, a truck or a –

"BUS! Yaz, it's the BUS! Come on, get *up*!"

It could be the bus into town, it could be. I can

hear it right behind the house now, getting closer. I race into the bedroom – Yaz is still flat out. I grab my purse and screech, "Yaz, I'm getting the bus into Ercos, OK!?" The last thing I see as I turn to run is her gawping, half-awake face. I bet she didn't get what I said, but too bad. I hare over the terrace and out of the wrought-iron gates.

The road I'm standing on is narrow, unmade and full of ruts. I can see the tyre tracks we made last night on the field alongside it, and I can just about see the road we came off behind that, because a tractor's moving along it now. *Shit.* I bet that's what made the noise. I'm just kicking myself for getting all worked up over a tractor when a wonderful little squat yellow bus trundles into view. And I stand there, shifting from foot to foot, crippled by not wanting to make a total prat of myself by rushing over the field towards it. Then I make this pact with myself: if I'm brave enough to do this, I'll get to stay in the house. And then I'm loping over the bumpy earth to the road.

I reach it just ahead of the bus. No bus stop in sight. *Sod it, sod it!* I scream (silently) and I step out into the road and wave frantically. The bus (wonderfully) clatters to a stop beside me. I grip the bus rail, mount the first step, and peer up hopefully at the driver. He's grinning at me and coming out with a great stream of Spanish. I recognize the word Bella, and when he takes both hands off the wheel and sketches Bella's voluptuous shape, I nod furiously. "Yes – I'm staying at Bella's house!" I say, enunciating the Spanish as clearly as I can. "I want to go to Ercos!"

He waves me enthusiastically on board, asks me for one euro. The bus is only half full; there's a gang of men in rough work clothes at the back, and apart from that it's women with little kids and grannies in black with huge wickerwork baskets. I find a seat, and the bus starts up. A few metres on, we pass a little turning that I realize must be the turning off to our house. I stare at it, marking it, fixing the three spiky-looking plants beside it in my mind. The bus trundles on and our house disappears from sight.

And I realize with a kind of liquidizing of my innards that I have no real idea where I'm going, and if it all goes horribly wrong I've got no way of contacting Yaz and the others back at the house.

# Chapter 16

It'll be OK, I tell myself. It'll be OK.

The bus bumps along the track, turns into the main road, and I'm gripping the rail in front of me so hard my knuckles are white. Five minutes later we stop next to a garage; three more women and a man get on, but no one gets off. I reckon I'll wait until most people disembark, then I'll get off too, and check with the driver where the bus stop for the return journey is.

Ten minutes go by, fifteen. Inside me, fear mounts that we're not heading into Ercos at all, we're just going to keep trundling on and on until we hit Portugal or somewhere and I'll be lost for ever and I won't ever see my home again, when suddenly the trees by the roadside disappear; and the houses multiply. And then I want to shriek with joy because I see a sign that says *Ercos*. We're turning right and swinging into a road alongside a great square, a wonderful Spanish square, shaded by palm trees and flanked by benches. The driver yanks on the handbrake, everyone starts surging off, then he turns and beams at me. "RETURN!" he booms. "Bus – RETURN – there be!" And he jabs his forefinger at the other side of the square. He has very, very rudimentary English, even more rudimentary than my Spanish, but he clearly wants to practise it. He holds up his arm, shows me his wristwatch. "Each bus RETURN – ten minute to all hour!"

Just to check, I repeat what he's said to me in Spanish. We smile and nod delightedly at each other. Then I resist an impulse to fling my arms round his neck, and jump off the bus.

It's twenty to ten. I reckon if I get the ten to eleven bus back I'll have enough time to do a recce and pick up some food, but at the same time not cause too much panic over my absence from the house. If anyone's actually awake enough to notice I've gone, that is.

I cross the square, my skin prickling with how fantastic it must be in the heat, in the dark, and set off along the road beside it. I pass a bar, two little supermarkets, a bike shop, a tool shop and a clothes shop with flouncy flamenco dresses and enormous chairback hair combs in the window. Could be useful. I cross another square, smaller and more modern, with tables and chairs set out all across it in groups, servicing the restaurants all around it. There's a fountain in the middle and people having morning coffee; everything looks very fresh and new. Bella was right, I think, the place is being developed. I bet we could find work easily.

I wander further on, up a steep, cobbled street into what must be the old part of Ercos. Here, the road narrows down so much no car could get through, and you could lean out of a bedroom window on one side of the street and practically shake hands with someone opposite. In the square at the top there's a huge, ancient church, and several hotels and restaurants in grand old conquistador buildings. I cross over to the edge, grip the flimsy rail in front of me, and gaze down. Even though Bella had told us Ercos was built on a clifftop for defence, I'm awestruck by the great sandy drop of cliff beneath me, the stunning impact of the view. From here, you could see invaders coming from miles away. It's like I'm standing in the sky. Two falcons fly past beneath me, and I stare down at the backs of their wings.

After a while I pull myself away, and head down a narrow, secret-looking street leading off the old square. I pass cafés, shops, some great-looking bars, even a couple of Latino-looking clubs. I think how great the buzz would be up here on a hot night. Then I remember to check my watch. *Damn* – I've only got forty minutes till the bus goes back. *Shame* – I was just feeling brave enough to go into one of those cafés and order a cappuccino and a croissant from the tempting trays in the window. Still, I'd better play it safe – I need to shop for food. I head straight back to the square and down the steep street again.

One of those little supermarkets right by the bus stop will do, I think. I reach the nearest shop a bit breathless, push my way timidly inside and pick up a battered wire basket. Then I hover for a bit, watching a woman moving along the shelves just in front of me, but it seems to be done just like it's done in England. So I pick up two loaves of crusty bread, one white and one brown, then I get some eggs, cheese and bacon and a big box of tea bags. Still thinking about breakfast (I'm ravenous) I get straw-berry jam, butter, apples and bananas. After that I'm a bit stumped, but I remember the spaghetti and put a couple of tins of tomatoes and some onions into my basket. I'm by the tiny deli counter now. The stuff displayed there looks delicious; the girl serving it looks sulky. Still, she's only my age. I ask for olives, ham, yogurt.

On to the wine shelves. I can hardly believe how cheap it is compared to home. I get two bottles of the third cheapest red (to go with the spaghetti), then I cram a cucumber and a large lettuce with real earth on its roots on top, and head for the check-out.

There's only one woman ahead of me, and she's got her purse out, paying. I scan my watch again: a good ten minutes before the bus goes. I'm just feeling all triumphant and pleased with myself when a little old lady in a black dress edges in front of me, showing me the packet of butter in her hand, smiling and gabbling something. I don't need to try and understand her because it's clear what she wants. I smile back 'cos I don't feel I've got much choice, and she totters up to the check-out. Then another old lady – this time a big fat one with a huge overflowing wire basket – draws up alongside her and directs a stream of Spanish at her, and it's clear they're best friends and it's also clear she's going to go next in the queue.

*Shit.* If this was England I'm pretty sure I'd be brave enough to tell her not to push in, but here – no way. It's probably the law over here that you've got to let old ladies go in front of you. I stand there limply, checking my watch every thirty seconds or so and peering round anxiously in case any more grannies rush over to queue-jump.

Only five minutes till the bus leaves. But it's my turn now, and the girl is very efficient, zipping everything through and packing it into two carrier bags, and in no time I've paid and I'm out on the pavement. And there's the wonderful little squat yellow bus sat waiting, and better than that, the same driver from before, who waves to me like he's known me for years.

Sitting at the back of the bus, bumping along with a bulging carrier bag balanced against each leg, I feel dead smug. I pick bits off the crusty bread to eat and even remember to look out for the three spiky plants that mark the lane up to our house, so I can have the sweet pleasure of giving Tom directions later on in the car. The bus rocks by *Pino Alto*, I get to my feet, and the bus driver obligingly halts the bus where he picked me up before. He explains in his wonderful butchered English that the bus stop is just a bit further on, and I repeat that back to him in my wooden Spanish, and we smile at each other in delight.

Then I jump off and walk across the field towards the wrought iron gates.

To be met by Tom shouting, "Where the *bloody hell've* you been? Yaz has just phoned the police!"

# Chapter 17

"**S**he hasn't!" I howl. Yaz and Ruth run out of the house. "Yaz – you haven't phoned the police!"

"No," says Yaz, looking all kind of relieved and angry to see me. "I wouldn't know how to. But we were all going to go out and look for you if you weren't back pretty bloody soon!"

"Before we'd had breakfast!" adds Tom, indignantly.

"But Yaz – I told you where I was going!"

"See, I thought I'd dreamt that. I also dreamt about a little girl in a barrel . . . and that this masked robber had hit you over the head. *And* that we'd all drowned."

"Great omens," mutters Ruth.

"Oh, shit, I'm sorry," I say. "I got the bus into Ercos – the food situation was dire. Look – breakfast." And I hold out the two bulging carrier bags.

Tom's on to them like a dog on to its Pedigree Chum. "Fantastic! Go on, Roofy – do us a fry-up."

Yaz grabs one of them. "Oh, *brilliant*, Laura. We'd just used the last teabag. God, you've eaten half the bread. It looks fabulous though. Come on."

We all hustle into the kitchen. Someone's opened the shutters inside, and light's streaming across the main room, crossing in the middle. While we fry eggs and slice bread, and Tom complains that I didn't get any chocolate, I yabber on about how great Ercos is, how I know we can find work there. I exaggerate about how fantastic the nightlife looks and enthuse about the bus service; tell them the bus stop's right behind the house.

Ruth smirks at me. "You wait till you see what else is behind the house."

"What?"

"A swimming pool!"

My hand with its spoonful of strawberry jam stops halfway to my mouth. "But that's *brilliant*! When it's hot we can—"

"Don't get excited," says Tom, dampeningly. "We won't be doing any swimming in it. It's a wreck."

"Eat first, see it later," says Yaz. "The bacon and eggs are ready."

And we carry our plates outside, plus the teapot and mugs and milk, and as we sit down at the table the sun sails like a spaceship from behind a cloud and radiates down on us. Even Tom's looking seduced over his rapidly moving knife and fork. "Isn't it *great* here?" I gush. "Isn't that view amazing? Isn't it the most amazing bit of luck, being offered it?"

Tom's fork pauses. "Yeah, yeah, Lors – OK, it's lovely. Roofy and I've been talking."

Talking? Makes a change, I think.

"And we reckon we ought to have at least a few days here before we decide anything. Go into town, check it out – check out how easy it is to get to the beach. That kind of stuff. Before we even think about trying to get work here."

"But it's so *wonderful*—"

"You say Ercos is a hot place – fine. We'll check it out."

"OK," I mutter.

"And then we'll take a *group decision*, OK?"

"Yeah? With your car having the casting vote as usual?"

"Oh, grow up, Lors. You're the one who's so keen on having committee meetings on everything. We'll talk about it, and then decide."

"OK."

"And then we'll act on the decision. Right?"

"I said OK, all right?"

"Just so's we're clear."

To avoid decking Tom with my plate, I get up sharply, and say, "Going to show me the pool, Yaz?" She grins, and stands up.

"Oi," says Tom, "what about clearing up?"

"I did the shopping," I snap, and stomp away.

"Don't look so mad," says Yaz, as we make our way round the side of the house. "If Ercos is as good as you say it is. . ."

"It's not Tom's kind of good," I mumble. "Oh, God, Yaz – I want to stay here! Don't you?"

"For a bit, definitely."

"Only for a bit?"

"Well – it is kind of out of the way, isn't it? I want to see a bit of action this year."

"There *will* be action," I start to say – then I stop, 'cos the pool's in sight. And not just any old hole-in-the-ground dipping pool, either. This pool was designed by someone with a fetish for Olympia and a wish to swim among the immortal. It's enormous, and at the far end, there's a crumbling concrete shelter like a little temple, roof balanced on the heads of four toga-clad concrete goddesses. Shattered columns designed to look like ruins flank the edges, with fancy stone benches in between, and grand crescent-shaped steps lead into the pool. Which unfortunately is full of wide cracks and brackish-looking sludge instead of water.

"Wow," I say. "Bella never showed us a photo of this, did she?"

"No. I should think she was bloody embarrassed by it. It's way out of keeping – must have been put in by some crank owner in the 1950s. Hey – you haven't seen the other bit. There's a whole extra bit of house."

"Yeah?" I follow her round the back of the house, where there's a little square building tagged on.

"I got it open with the house keys. It's that room you wanted – the one in the photo?"

We walk inside. The room is dusty and destitute, old wooden sunbeds stacked up in the corner, but it fits round me perfectly. I recognize the twisty bars on the window and the vine coming through from Bella's photo.

"I reckon they used this as the changing room, you know, for the pool?" Yaz nods towards the wall. "Loads of hooks for clothes and towels."

We stand there, and I think of coming in here from the cold water and the hot sun. A large green gecko skedaddles out from behind a gilt-edged mirror on the wall and streaks across the ceiling. "Going to move in?" laughs Yaz.

"Not yet," I say.

We eventually drive down into Ercos at about six o'clock that evening. The time in between has been kind of wasted; taken up by getting used to the place. We've wandered round the olive grove picking up firewood; unpacked our clothes; put the food away in the kitchen. I think everyone feels a bit spaced out by the fact that we're going to be here for a while. It's nice, but it's uneasy. We're not sure it's going to work out and I feel like no one's quite meeting my eye.

It's a relief in some ways to get back in the car,

which is pretty ironic when you think about it. I manage to direct Tom into Ercos without a hitch, and he has no trouble parking by the large square. The sun's low and marvellous, making the palm trees glow. I'm casting sideways glances at everyone, anxiously watching for signs that they're impressed. Tom perks up when we round the corner to the second square and spot what could be a pizzeria. "Come on, babes," he says. "Let's go and check out the prices. I'm starving." And they head over to look at the menu pasted up in the window.

Yaz puts her hand on my arm, slows me down. "Laura," she hisses, "for Christ's sake, calm down a bit!"

"Calm down? I'm hardly saying anything!"

"You don't need to! All this desperate energy's coming off you, like you want to force us to love the place – you're acting like an estate agent! Just relax, can't you?"

"Sure," I say, stung.

I can't, of course. I feel I want to sell them on each and every good point. We have a bog-standard pizza, inside 'cos it's too cold to sit out, then I tow everyone up the steep cobbled street to see old Ercos at the top. We look at the breathtaking view; then we stick our heads round the door of one of the clubs, and even though we decide not to pay the entrance fee, even Tom agrees it's got potential. Then we have a drink at one of the little bars. Tom mellows with a pint of lager inside him. "Yeah, OK, Lors," he says, patronizingly. "It's OK, so far. I tell you what we'll do. We'll drive out to the beach tomorrow, yeah? Roofy and I really want to see what the beach is like. And if it's OK and it's not too hard to get to . . . well . . . we'll think about staying for a bit, yeah?"

I want to grab the smug git round the neck and kiss him, just for saying that. Instead I offer to buy him another lager, and driving home I'm dead tactful and feminine giving him instructions – even when he takes a wrong turning. Then I make everyone tea before we turn in. They're having it so good they're going to want to stay here for ever.

# Chapter 18

When I wake up the next day, I can't work out what the strange noise is. It's a loud humming and thrumming, with this scary splashing sound underneath it all. I haul myself out of bed with some half-awake idea that someone's let the bath tub overflow, and totter next door. It's only as I stand looking at the empty bath that I realize the window in the corridor looked different. I turn back to it. Rain is sheeting down so heavily outside it's like standing under a waterfall.

I walk through to the living room, open up the shutters one by one. Waterfalls on each side, filling the room with a grey-white light. It's weird, surreal. Kind of scary, kind of romantic—

"Bloody *brilliant*, eh?" snaps Tom, erupting like a

boil through the far door. "You can't even see through the windows!"

"No gutters," I mutter. "Bella said Spanish houses don't always have gutters."

"Typical. Well – so much for going to the beach. You got the kettle on? I'm taking some tea back to bed."

All that day, the rain doesn't ease for a second. We eat the rest of the food I got from Ercos; in the evening I make very dull pasta sauce with the tins of tomatoes and onions, and we open the cheap red wine. Tom begrudgingly lights a little log fire but the chimney won't draw properly and smoke fills the room. Yaz tries to improve things with a sheet of newspaper but Tom shouts at her and we end up just letting it die in front of us.

Everyone goes to bed early. No one says anything to me. They don't need to. I know what they're thinking.

Next morning, the rain's still there, but a little less heavy. Tom announces with the voice of a dying martyr that he and Ruth will drive into Ercos, get some provisions. They find a couple of hideous yellow rain capes on the back of the front door, put them on, and trudge out to the car. But then the trouble starts. The engine goes but the car won't move; its wheels are stuck fast in thick, red viscous mud – mud that's been created in just twenty-four hours from the packed earth beside the terrace. Tom revs and revs the car but the wheels just spin and dig in deeper, while great globs of mud fly everywhere. He swears horribly, cursing Spain, cursing the rain, most of all cursing me. Ruth and Yaz fly off to try and find a plank of wood or something to jam under the wheels, but I can't move. I stand under the inadequate shelter of the palm tree filled with heavy despair.

This is it, I say to myself. The end. Tomorrow, I'll arrange a flight home. This trip is a failure. I've failed. There's relief in admitting you've failed.

"Do you want some help?" says a voice I don't know. Deep, Spanish and something else – American maybe?

I look up.

"Do you want some help?" the voice says again. It's coming out from a hood on a tall, broad-shouldered shape that's just come in through the gates.

The shape moves closer. Under the hood there are two dark, sexy eyes, a strong straight nose, black hair plastered down by rain. I find my voice. "We're stuck," I croak, idiotically.

He shrugs. "The rain. Everywhere is mud." Then he turns and heads out of the gates without another word.

"Who the fuck was that?" snarls Tom through the car window, over the sound of the anguished engine.

"Dunno. He asked if we wanted some help, and then—"

"Pissed off. *Typical*."

Just then, Yaz and Ruth appear, with a thinnish-looking length of wood. "Oh, *what*?!" explodes Tom. "That won't be any bloody good!"

"Well, it's all we could find, Tom!" snaps Ruth. "You get out the car and get soaking wet finding something better!"

"Look, babes, don't get angry with *me*. It's not *me* who's dragged you out to this God-forsaken hole."

"I'm just saying there isn't any other wood!"

"Oh, give it a go then. Shove it under the wheels."

"*Me* shove it? Can't you get out and help?" Ruth sounds near to tears, and this, as usual, is enough to shift Tom from his seat. In fact I'm beginning to suspect her of turning her tears on at will. He takes the wood from her, and starts jabbing it into the red mud in front of the front wheels.

And then the stranger reappears through the gates, with a thick plank balanced across his shoulders. He pauses by Tom. "No good," he says. "Too small." Then he drops his plank down on top of it, gives it a couple of hard kicks into place, and says, "Now try."

You can tell there's a battle going on in Tom's Neanderthal brain between the side that wants to tell this superior-acting newcomer to eff off and the other, slightly more intelligent, side that recognizes he might get some help here. He grunts ungratefully, gets back in the car, and switches on the engine. As it revs into life, the stranger moves swiftly behind the car and heaves on it. I join him, and we push side by side.

He has fabulous hands. Brown and strong and slender. The car revs harder, then surges up and out of the mud and skids towards the gate. It's almost a disappointment.

Tom jams his head out of the window and shouts, "Come on, babes, get in!" Then he adds gruffly, "Thanks mate."

"Where are you going?" demands the stranger.

"Ercos," says Tom, in a who–wants–to–know voice.

The stranger shakes his head. "No. Not yet. Flooding on the lower road. Even the bus has stopped." His English is excellent, but a little stiff maybe, like a coat that hasn't been worn for a long time.

"Oh, that's bloody brilliant," Tom growls. "So we just sit here and starve do we? Look – who are you? You *live* here, do you?" The last question is delivered in this scathing voice, like anyone who lives here must be sick or mad or both.

"I'm Juan," the stranger replies. "The son of Miguel. The—"

"Oh, the odd–job–man, right?" says Tom, all relieved, like now he's pigeon–holed Juan as a member of the lower orders he can relax.

"He's an olive farmer," says Juan coolly. "And he helps Bella look after this house. He sent me to check you were OK. In all this rain."

"Yeah, well we're not, mate, OK? We're fucking fed up. And starving. That's why we've got to get into Ercos."

Juan shakes his head. "Tomorrow. The roads will be better then – the rain's stopping. I'll fetch you some food for today. My aunt always has lots of food. You go in and get warm, and dry, and wait. . ."

"No chance of us getting either, mate. Couldn't get the fire to light."

"Let me see," says Juan, and strides across the terrace and through the front door. Yaz and I are practically barging each other out of the way as we hurry after him.

I step inside the kitchen. Juan's pulled his hood back, he's shaking back his black hair. The eyes, the nose, the jaw, the *mouth* – everything shifts into perfect balance. He's possibly the most gorgeous, most romantic-looking guy I have ever seen in my whole life.

And beside me I can positively feel Yaz thinking, *OK, Laura – which one of us'll have him?*

# Chapter 19

"Can I take my coat off?" asks Juan. Yaz and I nod like a pair of car-window dogs on a speed track, and he slides his wet bulky coat off his shoulders and drops it in a corner by the door. I'm glad to see it wasn't just his coat making him look broad-shouldered. He's strong. Either he spends a fair bit of time at the gym, I think, or he helps his dad a lot.

The others push their way into the kitchen and come face to face with him, and I can't help noticing even love-sick Roofy looks pretty impressed. Tom, of course, looks deeply threatened, which isn't exactly a surprise, since Juan is clearly superior to him on just about every level there is. "You won't get that fire going," Tom says, aggressively. "The chimney's crap."

"The chimney's fine," Juan replies. "I helped

point the bricks; I made sure there were no cracks."
He heads over to the fireplace, adding, "It must have
been your fire."

*Uh-oh* – now he's gone too far, criticizing Tom's
fire-lighting technique. Tom's face bunches up like a
fist but luckily Juan drops down on his hunkers in
front of the grate and is spared the sight of it. He
pulls a knife from his pocket and starts slicing wood
shavings off a charred log, then he arranges the half-
burned wood from last night on top of them.
Pretending I'm deeply interested in how to build a
fire, I gaze at his beautiful profile, ogle his hands as
they move. He strikes a match, ignites the shavings,
and sits back on his haunches watching as the little
flames lick up. "I'll get some logs," he says. "There's
a store at the back of the house. That wood you col-
lected is a bit damp. For the chimney to draw it must
be hot."

And he leaves the kitchen.

I resist a very strong impulse to grab Yaz by the
arms and jump up and down shrieking about how
gorgeous he is, because I don't want Tom to have that
kind of ammunition. Instead I say, "God, that was
lucky – him turning up!"

Tom snorts. "Yeah, well, if I'd known about the
store of logs. . ."

"*Tom* – his fire's already better than anything you
managed," says Yaz, cruelly. "Yours was crap, face it."

"*Yeah*, well – let's see how good *his* turns out. I still

say that chimney's blocked. Anyway, he's a bit of a pushy bastard, isn't he? Barging in with his plank of wood without even. . ."

"Oh, come on, Tom," I snigger. "Just 'cos his plank was bigger than yours." Yaz and I go off into a great insulting peal of laughter, and Ruth glares at us and wraps her arms round Tom, saying, "Don't be bad-tempered, baby! He's gonna bring us some food, isn't he?"

Juan comes back in, all wet and macho, arms full of logs, and dumps them by the side of the fireplace. Then he puts two on the fire, and says, "That will be burning soon. I'll go and get you some food." And he's gone, and Yaz and I only come out of our daze to shout, "Thank you!" once the door's closing.

He puts his beautiful head back round the door. "Don't let the fire go out," he says.

No chance of that, I think. Not the one inside me, anyway.

And then we wait for him to come back again. "I'm *starving*," moans Tom. He sits down on the sofa and glares at the fire, as though willing it to start belching smoke into the room and prove his point about the chimney. It doesn't, though. The logs catch and flare up, and Yaz adds another, and soon even at the kitchen end of the room I can feel some warmth. The laurel-wood smoke smells heavenly.

For some reason I'm rearranging the knives and

forks in the cutlery drawer, then drying glasses that are already dry. Yaz won't look round, she won't meet my eye. I know she thinks Juan's fabulous, just like I do. If she likes him, that's it, I think. I can't compete with her. I pick up another shiny glass, and polish it furiously.

There's a kick at the door. I open it, and Juan's standing there, both arms supporting this huge canvas bag full of stuff. "My aunt – she's very generous," he explains, apologetically. "And she likes Bella – she says she can't let Bella's friends go hungry."

Tom advances greedily from the fireside. "What we got?"

"Pork, fresh pork," says Juan, dumping the bag down on the counter. "My uncle killed a pig last week."

There's a tiny shocked pause as we let this sink in, then Juan starts unpacking his bag, saying, "She sent a big jar of pickle to go with it. And bread . . . and a cake. Potatoes, and onions. Tomatoes. And eggs. You want me to make omelette – Spanish omelette?"

"Yes *please*," I say fervently, at the same time as Tom's saying, "No – you get off, mate," but if Juan hears him, he doesn't register it.

"Oh, this is so wonderful of your aunt, to send all this!" gushes Yaz. "Let's have a real *feast*! We can fry some of this pork, and if you make an omelette too. . . Have you had lunch?"

"No."

"So can you stay?"

"Sure – if that's all right."

"Course it's all right!" coos Yaz. "Fan-*tas*-tic!" Juan smiles and produces two bottles of wine from the bottom of his bag. "Fantastic!" squeals Yaz again, dancing across the kitchen to get the glasses I've been needlessly polishing. "God, Juan – I'm so glad you came by! Or we'd've starved to death! Or *frozen*."

He shrugs. "My father sent me. Bella phoned, told us you should have arrived, asked us to check on you."

"God, Juan – how come your English is so good? It's brilliant!"

At this, Juan breaks into a grin, revealing a beautiful set of even white teeth. "My grandad's American."

"Yeah, I thought I could hear an American twang—" I start to say, when Yaz interrupts with, "*Wow!* Does he live here?"

I'm going to slap her in a minute, I think.

"Yes – he moved to Spain. He taught me English. We speak it together, sometimes. And last year, he took us all on holiday over there. Pasadena – where his people live. It was *amazing*. So full of energy and . . . and excitement. I want to live there."

"In America?" scoffs Tom. "It's crap – you don't wanna move there."

"When did you last go?" demands Juan.

"Well, I – I wouldn't *wanna* go, mate. I meet enough Yanks to know I couldn't stand being surrounded by 'em on a daily basis."

Tom laughs at his own witticism, while Juan frowns at Yaz and says, "Yanks?"

"Unbelievably old-fashioned term for Americans, Juan. Ignore him."

Then Ruth breaks in protectively with "You know, my jeans are *still* damp. I'm going to get changed. Are you coming, baby?"

This question from Ruth would normally have Tom going off into a leery routine about wanting to be there when she peeled her jeans off, but right now Tom's more interested in keeping his end up with the Spanish-American intruder. "I'm not too bad, babes," he says. "Don't be long, yeah?"

Ruth peevishly struts out of the kitchen, and Tom says, "No, seriously mate, if you want to see life, come to England." (Tom pronounces this *En-ger-land*, like a football chant.) "Not America."

"I'd love to," says Juan. "I've never been. I love the . . . the *culture* there."

"Yeah, it's brilliant," says Tom, who wouldn't recognize culture if it jumped up and bit him on the nose. "It's brilliant in England. Best country in the world."

He glares at Juan, challenging him to contradict, and Juan shrugs and says, "Shall we start cooking?" He stoops down to a cupboard and pulls out a huge skillet that fits over two gas rings. "I know where things are," he says, a bit apologetically. "I've cooked for Bella and Bobby."

"*Really?*" sneers Tom, as if this alone makes him, Tom, the winner in the Real Man contest they're having, when suddenly a short, unearthly shriek splits the air, followed by another, and *another* –

"That doesn't sound like *my* car alarm. . ." muses Tom.

"*It's Ruth!*" I shout, racing out of the kitchen and through the door at the end, and into their bedroom.

Ruth's standing there, in front of the mirror. Her mouth is open and the screams are still coming, rhythmic and terrified. Her face is ashen and her eyes are fixed on the reflection of an enormous, coal-black spider that's slowly stalking across her neck.

I take a pace forward; my eyes shoot from the mirror to the spider itself. It looks like a horror-film hand closing in on her face. "Oh *shit*," I moan, helplessly. Tom, behind me, squawks, "Babes! Don't move! It's a fucking *tarantula*!" At this, her screams get louder – they join together. "Get it *off* her, Tom!" I wail.

Tom moves towards her very, very slowly, one hand outstretched and trembling. And then Juan pushes through from behind, lunges out, knocks the spider to the floor, and stamps on it. Just like that. Wham, blam.

Ruth bursts into tears of relief. Tom puts his arms

round her and snarls, "Fucking *hell*, mate. It could've bitten her, you doing that."

"It would only have nipped her," says Juan. "It's not a tarantula. These kind of spiders – they're usually outside. It must have come in to get away from the rain."

"What took you so *loo-oong*?" snivels Ruth.

"I thought you were a car alarm, Roofy," explains Tom, uncomfortably.

"Wow – *Juan*," breathes Yaz, all wide-eyed with hero worship. "How could you *touch* it? How could you—"

"Did it drop down on you, babes?" interrupts Tom. "From the ceiling?"

Ruth takes in a huge glugging gasp of air. "I picked up my jumper from the *floo-ooor* . . . and pulled it on – and I saw it in the *mir-ror*! On my *ne-eeck*!"

Tom starts to smother her hair with kisses, while Juan says, "It would have crawled into your jumper for warmth."

"Spare us the wildlife lesson, mate, OK?" snaps Tom.

"Are there lots of those spiders here?" wavers Yaz.

Ruth muffles another howl and Juan shrugs. "A few."

"OK, everyone out," says Tom, masterfully, one hand on the door. "Let me calm her down."

We troop out, and Tom slams the door after us. "Three guesses how calming her down's gonna end up," mutters Yaz.

"Yeah, well," I mutter back, "Tom just lost the Real Man contest he was having with Juan. He needs to make up some ground!"

So now it's just the three of us in the kitchen. Juan heats up the skillet, peels some onions and unwraps the pork, while Yaz hovers at his elbow like an eager kitchen assistant. She doesn't do all that much, but she does make an excellent job of getting between me and him. I crack six eggs and whisk them for the omelette, then I stand watching him make it, pretending I want to learn about cooking.

"You going to lay the table, Laura?" asks Yaz loudly.

I can't think what to say to get out of it, so I grab a fistful of cutlery and troop sourly out to the long table. I lay five places, then decide it's so gloomy outside with the rain still streaming down that I'll light the stubs of candles in the curly gothic candlesticks. "Can you chuck me your matches, Juan?" I ask.

And he turns, gives me a completely heart-stopping smile, and tosses a box across the marble counter. God knows how I manage to catch them after that smile, but I do. The candles look wonderful once they're lit. They glow in two little constellations, and the fire glows beyond, and I hurt with wanting it just to be me and Juan here, alone. We'd eat, then we'd move on to the sofa right in front of the fire, and darkness would fall outside, and—

"Laura? You couldn't empty the kitchen bin, could you?"

I bare my teeth at Yaz in what might be a smile, and head back to the kitchen.

# Chapter 20

Fifteen minutes later, the omelette's made and the bread's sliced and the pork is sizzling deliciously in the skillet, almost cooked. And Yaz has moved in on Juan so successfully I feel like my stomach has turned to lead. She's kept up a constant stream of conversation, commanding all his attention. It's like they're the only two in the kitchen. And now she's helping him make tomato salad and they're up so close they're practically touching.

"I'll open the wine, yes?" he asks.

"Oh, *yes*," breathes Yaz. She holds out two glasses and when he's filled them she hands one to him and they both take a sip, looking into each others' eyes.

*Fantastic. Great, Yaz. Shut me out completely, why don't you? What's that sickening old expression? All's fair in love and war? I hate that expression. This isn't fair. It isn't fair that you're prettier than me, with all that bright personality, and he looks at you all the time and laughs with you and doesn't notice me at all.*

Juan pours a glass of wine for me and hands it to me with that heart-stopping smile he has, but I know he's just being kind. He goes over to the stove, prods the meat with a knife. "It's done," he announces, all satisfied.

"Fantastic," squeals Yaz. "I'll get the plates."

"Should we knock for the other two?" Juan asks doubtfully. At least twice while we were cooking, one of Ruth's famous yelps of passion could be heard above the clatter around the stove.

"I'll go," I say, wearily.

"Are they – are they married?" he asks, almost shyly.

Yaz bursts out laughing. "*Jesus*, no! Ruth might have lost it – we *hope* temporarily – but she's not that dense."

Juan shakes his head, like he doesn't really understand. "It would be so hard to – *be* with someone like that here. You have more freedom, in England, don't you."

Yaz giggles, not sure how to answer this, and I say, "It depends on how you define freedom." Then I feel a bit embarrassed and walk off. I march along to the sex machines' door and bang on it, sadistic and loud. "Lunch up!" I shout.

"Thanks, Lors," floats back Tom's voice, all snug

and smug and sleazy. "We'll be out soon as we've got our clothes on."

*Yeah, great Tom, rub it in like you always do*, I think savagely as I stomp back to the main room. *I'm a kind of double gooseberry now, aren't I. Double green, double sour, double prickly . . . I should give up now. Say I'm ill, give up and go to bed. It'll hurt less.*

It really is a feast being laid on the table, though. The best meal since we've come to Spain, easily. The delicious smell lifts my spirits just a bit. I'll eat before I go and shut myself away and die of misery, I think. Sort of a condemned girl's last meal.

Tom and Ruth emerge from their room and fall greedily on the wine. Yaz chivvies everyone to sit down, then she and Juan proudly dish out the food, piling up the plates. And we eat. It tastes every bit as wonderful as it smells and looks. No one's saying much – just the odd muttered compliment – there's no need. Everyone's basking in the goodness of the food and the warmth of the fire blazing away at the other end of the room. The candles glow on the faces of the two couples and the rain splashing outside just adds to the romantic cosiness and I'm forking away at top speed to stop myself snivelling on to my pork and pickle.

"I'm supposed to be working on the pool here," Juan suddenly announces.

"Really?" says Yaz, all quivery, a piece of bread

halfway to her mouth. "I didn't know Bella was restoring it."

"She wants the pool. She's not sure about the statues. Although she says they're . . . kotsch?"

"Kitsch," I correct him, and he grins at me, "Yes. The agreement was – I work on the pool when I have a space in my other work. This rain has made most building work impossible—"

"So you're a builder, are you mate?" demands Tom, smirking.

"I can build things, yes," says Juan. "Bricklaying. I work for my uncle's firm. But it's not . . . what I want to do for ever. For the rest of my life I mean."

"What *do* you want to do?" asks Yaz, leaning towards him on her elbow, all flattering and intent. "For the rest of your life?"

"God, I don't know yet." He says "God" like he's trying it out, like he's never said it casually before, like we all do. "I want to travel, that's for sure. I want to see more of the world. . ."

"Me too," murmurs Yaz.

"But not just travel like a tourist – I want to *live* in other places. . ."

"Oh yes, I know what you mean," she says.

*No, you don't!* I want to shriek. *It's me that wants to do that – you just tag along! You're quite happy being a tourist and I had to practically break your arm to get you to even come here!*

"I'm saving to get to America," he goes on. "My

grandfather's people – they could help me get work—"

"Not sure you'd get a green card, though," says Tom, dampeningly. "They're really tightening things up. Anyway, like I told you – England's better."

"And if you came to England, *we* could help you get work," says Yaz. She'll be asking him to live with her in a minute.

"So," barks Tom, in a back-to-business voice, "what were you saying about the pool, then?"

"I just wondered if you'd mind me working on it a bit, while you were here," Juan says. "If it wouldn't disturb you. . ."

"No problem at *all*," says Yaz, eyes shining. "You turn up whenever you want. That's OK with everyone, isn't it?"

We finish eating, and move from the table to the sofas. We stoke up the fire, and talk, and open the other bottle of wine; then we shut the shutters on the gloom and rain and make tea and eat Juan's aunt's fruit cake, and talk some more.

It's a lovely afternoon, and I'd really enjoy it if I weren't in the role of pathetic-loser double-gooseberry. It's sheer masochism that keeps me here, sat on the floor, while the other two happy couples sprawl on a sofa each. Yaz and Juan aren't exactly a couple, not yet. But it can only be a matter of time. There's this feeling of grief lapping at my edges, grief that this wonderful boy wants Yaz and not me; I know it's waiting to engulf me later on, when I'm on my own.

There's a pause in the sleepy conversation. Juan checks his watch, and groans, "I have to go. My father'll murder me. I was supposed to help him chop more wood before dark." He stands up, grins at Yaz, stretches his arms back behind his head, showing impressive muscles under his shirt.

"Are you going to get into *awful* trouble?" asks Yaz, with this little-girl round-eyed look.

"No. I'll set up a spotlight. I'll chop it in the dark!" He turns to go, and we all shuffle to our feet to see him out, even Tom. As he reaches the door he grins again, takes a step towards Yaz, and she kind of rushes towards him. He takes hold of her by the arms, kisses her on both cheeks, then he turns a bit awkwardly to me, and ducks and kisses me, once on each cheek, and I freeze with how close he is, with how good he smells, a tangy male smell that's woodsmoke and cotton and aftershave and him all mixed up. . . We separate and he laughs, as though he's relieved or something, then he turns to Ruth and kisses her twice, too.

At this, Tom, of course, siezes up like a pitbull on red alert. He clenches up his fists and his face and for one horrible moment I think he's going to stonk in and head-butt Juan. I pull open the door smartly, so that if Tom does lunge he'll collide with that instead, and Juan shuffles out. "Goodbye!" he says. "Thank you – it's been great!"

"So we'll expect to see you soon, shall we?" breathes Yaz. "Fixing the pool?"

"Sure," he says. "Tomorrow, maybe." And he disappears into the dusk.

"*Fuckin' smarmy little git!*" explodes Tom, as I close the door.

"He's not little," swoons Yaz. "He's about eight centimetres taller than you. *Actually*."

"Yeah, well, he's smarmy and a git, anyway. The way he grabbed Roofy like that—"

"*He only kissed her goodbye!* That's the way the Spanish do it, on both cheeks! I think it's lovely!"

"Yeah, well, it's pretty clear why *you* thought it was lovely, Yaz. You couldn't peel your eyes off him all afternoon. Your tongue was so far out of your mouth it was getting covered in rug fluff!"

"*Charming*," says Yaz, haughtily.

"He'd better not try it again," snarls Tom, darkly. "Not with you, babes."

"Oh, baby, don't be daft!" gurgles Ruth, flattered, as she curls herself under his arm. "It's *Yaz* he's interested in."

"Yeah, Yaz, made a bit of a conquest there, didn't we darlin'?" Tom jeers. "When you gonna move in on him, eh?"

Yaz huffs in pleasure, refuses to answer. She strides over to the fire, picks up the empty wine glasses, and sweeps back, chinking, to the kitchen.

\* \* \*

Pretty soon after that I say I need some air and walk out on to the dark terrace. "Don't be an *idiot*," I lecture myself. "You knew right from the start he'd go for Yaz and not you."

I round the corner of the house and stand looking at the derelict swimming pool. The moon's broken through the low cloud, lighting up the concrete goddesses and the stone steps. *I haven't met anyone as gorgeous as him for* ages, *though*, I think, savagely. *Ever, in fact.* Shit, *it's not fair.*

Then I take off, and walk. I walk right round the edge of the grounds where the fence separates the olive grove from the road, over gluey, rutted earth that could turn my ankle at any minute. I don't care, I walk on, and the olive trees look like strange little twisted people in the dark, holding up their arms to warn me of something.

Once I've been round the fence perimeter twice I feel a bit calmer, and I go back to the house, leaving my muddy shoes outside. Tom and Ruth are lying in front of the glowing hearth, coiled pulsatingly round each other, and they barely look up as I come in. Yaz has disappeared. I noisily fix myself a mug of coffee, and head straight for our bedroom.

Yaz is sprawled on her bed, idly filing her nails. "Where did you disappear to?" she asks.

"Oh – just for a walk. I heard an owl."

"Groovy. Did you make me a cup of coffee?"

"No. Share this." I hold out the mug to her and I want to talk about Juan but I can't. It's like she's the enemy.

"I think I'll have a bath," she murmurs, comfortably, taking a sip of my drink. "Not much else to do, is there? I wasn't going to hang around in there with those two. Honestly, they get worse. It was baby-talk this time. I think I prefer it when they grope each other."

"I'm sorry I hung around so long," I say, dully. "You know – when Juan was here."

"*What?*" laughs Yaz, all bright and fake. "Don't be silly – what are you talking about?"

I was right, we can't discuss it. Something like this happened before, when we were fifteen and both fancied the fabulous Aidan Jones in the year above us. We both went after him and Yaz got him, even if it was only for three and a half weeks till he moved on to someone else. But while we were both stalking him, we couldn't talk about it. It was like, because we were friends, we had to pretend we weren't doing something so unfriendly as fighting over the same bloke.

And now it's the same. Now we can't talk about this.

# Chapter 21

I wake the next morning and hear banging, metal on stone. Yaz's bed is empty. I pull on my cotton dressing-gown and wander out of doors, but I kind of know what I'm going to see, even before I turn the corner to the swimming pool.

There she is, perched on the edge, all cool and exotic in her blue kimono with her lovely foxy-brown hair all round her shoulders. And Juan is standing in the pool, sleeves rolled up, chipping away at the sagging tiles on the pool walls. As I walk round the corner they both start laughing at something. I think about turning tail, going back to the house, but Juan spots me and calls out, "Good morning, Laura! I hope it wasn't this noise that woke you up?" I shake my head, and he goes on, "I wanted to get started, before the rain sets in again."

"Juan's been telling me about this club," Yaz says. "He says it's the best in Ercos – he knows the DJ there, he plays great music."

"*Las Estrellas*," he says. "I'll take you all there tonight, if you like. Friday's the best time to go."

"Is it Friday today?" I ask feebly. "I'd lost track."

"You want to go, don't you, Laura?" demands Yaz.

"Sure," I say, "I mean, I guess so." Then I troop inside again, and leave them to it.

The prospect of being my new green prickly sour self at the club that night with two infatuated couples isn't exactly thrilling me, but it's better than what's presented to me at about seven o'clock that evening.

I'd spent most of the day mooching about and reading; Juan worked on the pool, and Yaz had kept him company. He went home about five, promising to be back at nine to take us all to the club. The rain had held off long enough for Tom and Ruth to drive into Ercos and buy a load of provisions and it seemed to put them in a domestic mood. As dusk fell over the olive grove, they lit the fire again, cooked a watery stew for the four of us, which they served up with rice, and then announced that they weren't really up for a night out.

"You two go. Juan'll look after you," says Tom. "We're gonna have a long bath together, aren't we, babes? With that champagne that's in the fridge. And then kinda relax in front of the fire."

In other words, they're planning a total sex-fest,

and everyone has to be off the premises. I try and persuade them to change their minds but they're so wrapped up in Tom jamming his tongue in Ruth's ear they don't hear me, and it's so demoralizing being completely ignored that I give up.

I get tarted up dispiritedly in the bathroom, alongside Yaz who looks more and more gorgeous with every bit of make-up she applies. "I'm not going too wild," she says, "not till I see what everyone else wears here at night. I don't want people thinking I'm a prostitute or something." Then she pulls back all her hair from her face and smiles happily at her reflection in the mirror.

I thought I'd steeled myself to go through with this, but when Juan arrives looking devastating in a white shirt and black leather jacket, and he and Yaz kind of melt together for a hello kiss, I hear myself saying, "Look – I'm feeling really weird. Seriously. I think it's Tom's cooking. I think I'd better stay behind—"

"Oh, *Laura*," moans Yaz, "you can't do that! You'll be all right – I feel fine, and I ate his stew."

"Well, maybe it's a bug then. I really don't feel up to coming."

There's a pause, then Juan says, "I think we'd better all stay here, then."

"*What?*" I squeak. "No, honestly – I couldn't stop you going – and anyway, Tom and Ruth'll go ballistic, they're running this huge bath right now and they've taken candles in with them and everything. . ."

"It will be very awkward," says Juan, all serious, "if I turn up with just one girl. Everyone will talk. Everyone will assume Yaz is my girlfriend –" Yaz smirks – "and it would be wrong to go to clubs with a girlfriend before I've introduced her to my parents. It would be the wrong way round."

"Blimey," breathes Yaz. "You're a formal lot, you Spaniards, aren't you?"

Juan shrugs, smiles apologetically. "It must seem really old-fashioned to you. But believe me, Ercos is a small place, and a lot of people I know will be at the club tonight – the gossip would be terrible. It'll be bad enough as it is – everyone will notice you two!" And he smiles.

"Oh, come on, Laura!" squawks Yaz. "Say you'll come!"

"If you feel ill at the club – I'll bring you straight back," adds Juan.

There's a pause while I try to stand firm and they both look at me like their whole future's in my hands; then I mutter, "OK." And I'm thinking in horror – my *God*, he's desperate to get her there, my *God*, I'm their *chaperone* – just like those little old ladies who sit in the corner with a fan – this *cannot get worse*!

"*Thanks*, Laura," says Juan fervently. "Let's go!"

Juan's right, *Las Estrellas* is fantastic. You know whether a club's going to be any good the minute you walk through the door, don't you? And even in my slumped state I know this is good. You can tick it all off – sounds, lighting, mood, bar, seating. It's raw, compared to some of the classy London clubs I've been to, but there's an energy here that makes up for any lack of sophistication. It's pretty crowded. A few pale tourists, but apart from that they're nearly all Spanish, and they're buzzing and full of it and dressed to kill. Next to them I feel really drab.

We check in our coats, make our way to the bar, Yaz right up close to Juan, and me trailing behind. And suddenly we're surrounded.

"*Hola*, Juan! Where you been, *hombre*?"

"We missed you!"

"It's been weeks – why didn't you call?"

"Who are these girls?"

"They both yours? Lucky *dog*!"

Five boys, three girls. I can just about follow their Spanish and it's clear from all the greetings and the body language that Juan's a bit of a leader, a bit of a star (which he would be, wouldn't he, looking the way he does), and that turning up with two strange girls is the kind of unexpected and glamorous thing he tends to do. The Spanish girls all crowd in and kiss him; one hangs possessively on his arm. They dart little hard glances at us; they're like the flamenco dancers in that bar in Seville, challenging our right to be here, wanting to shoo us away.

Juan laughs, lapping it all up. He's bolder, more jokey, more flashy speaking in Spanish and I'm not sure which I prefer. He introduces us, explains why we're here, says, "And now we'll talk in English, right?"

At least one of the girls seems to understand him – Nuria, he called her. She fixes me with her coal-black eyes and says, "You don't come to a club to *talk*. Do you?" She raises her arms, shimmies like she can't wait to start dancing.

I giggle my agreement like a complete inadequate, then turn away, take refuge in the drink-ordering chaos that's going on. Jesus, I think, they're full-on female, these Spanish girls. It's not just the sexy dark eyes and the curvy figures and the super-feminine clothes and tottering high heels. It's the whole way they move and laugh and scintillate and direct energy at you like a blowtorch. I feel like some kind of uptight schoolgirl in comparison. Even Yaz is looking undermined. She keeps pushing her hair back then tugging it forward again, and she only ever does that when she's not feeling confident.

Over the speakers, the DJ shifts his act up a gear. He wants to get the whole club out on the floor. Then something with a fast beat starts up, and everyone but me and Yaz acts like an electric current's gone through them. Our group moves off to the centre of the floor, taking us with them; two of the girls are towing Juan along. They all bully their way to a space and start up this wild, skilled, Latino-style dancing – strutting, flouncing, turning, swaying, and there's all this communication between the dancers: response, counter-response, response . . . they look fantastic, and whatever they do they keep the beat, like it's choreographed for a video. I jerk about like a nerd on the outskirts of the group, next to Yaz. There's no way I'm trying to dance like that, even if I admire it, not yet anyway – I'd make an idiot of myself. I know Yaz is thinking the same. We're out of place.

Then Juan tries to get Yaz to dance Spanish-style. I watch him take her hand with an ache of jealousy I'm almost getting used to. He's got flamenco in his blood, that's for sure. Nothing flashy or embarrassing – just the way he holds himself, the sure way he moves. It's incredibly sexy. Yaz seems overpowered by it – she won't respond, she giggles, shakes her head, waves her hands like she's pleading for mercy. I can see the Spanish girls assessing her, dismissing her . . . then another record starts, and one of them claims Juan as her partner.

It's getting pretty bleak, being nerds on the outskirts of the group, dancing to music we've never heard before. Yaz looks over at me, raises her eyebrows above wide eyes in that club code that means, "Rescue me!" I nod, and we back away, and one of the Spanish girls smiles and points to the far side of the club.

"See, I know you think Tom's an idiot," Yaz is saying, peering into the long mirror above the line of basins, liplining her already luscious mouth, "well, he *is* an idiot – but I can understand why he wants to get to a holiday resort where there'll be more English people. I mean – I feel dead out of place here, don't you?"

I shrug. "Kind of. But I like it that it's different."

"Hmmm. . ." says Yaz, unconvinced, and moves on to mascaraing her eyelashes.

We're still not talking about Juan. We're not even mentioning the whole reason why we're here in this club. We loiter about titivating in front of the mirror for a bit longer, then we head back to the floor. And just as we're reaching our group, there's a shift in the music. Something comes on that was just getting big as we left England, something we *know*. . .

"All *right*!" crows Yaz, spinning round to me, and suddenly it's our turn, our place. We start to dance, this controlled, robotic dance that goes with the music, different right down to the core to the way the Spanish girls dance. And we grin, and mouth the words – we're showing off, full of claiming this alien sound as ours. Juan's group watch us, laughing, trying to follow the way we're moving – they can't do it, though, not like we can. I feel like we've proved something. When the Latino beat comes on again, I loosen up a bit, and Juan smiles across at me. He doesn't take my hand, but he dances alongside, and I follow a few of the steps, and he shouts, "You're good! You're good!"

\* \* \*

Later the three of us take a break, and head for the bar. Juan absolutely refuses to let me pay for the next round of drinks, even though he bought the first. I don't push it 'cos I reckon to insist would cast a slight on some Spanish machismo code of his. We lean back against the bar rail, Juan in the middle, and Yaz says, "It's great here, Juan. You were so right about it."

Juan smiles. "You should come in the summer. It's on a lake, this place, with a beach – when it's hot they open up the whole of the back, and there's an outside bar, and lights in the palm trees, and people dance on the sand and go in the water to cool off. . ."

"That must be heaven," sighs Yaz. She turns towards him, puts her glass down on the bar on the other side of him, like she's tracing out a barrier against me. They start to talk about the other clubs in Ercos, and I feel start to feel really awkward. I shift about for a bit, ignored, then I say, "Won't be long," and troop off, letting them think I've gone to the bog again. I don't, though, I slip outside and walk down to the beach Juan was telling us about.

None of the lights are on, just the light from the moon hitting the water. It's a big lake, with a couple of boats moored alongside. As my eyes get used to the gloom I register this hunched, sexy shape in one of the boats – a couple. A lump comes into my throat, just as if it was Juan and Yaz out there, and then I hurry back indoors.

I can't see them anywhere inside – they've gone

from the bar. I wander self-consciously across the floor, weaving between all the gyrating people, and come up against Juan's group of friends. Nuria, the girl who speaks a bit of English, asks where he's gone. "*No sé*," I say – *I don't know* – and she smiles at my Spanish, asks, "Is your friend with him?"

I shrug, because I don't know that either, but I can take a guess.

I hang around on the edges of the group again, watching them dance and have fun, only joining in enough to avoid looking like a complete loser. I'm just starting to feel really panicky about what's happened to Yaz and Juan, wondering if I've been abandoned here to make my own way back to *Pino Alto*, when I look up and see a guy that could be Juan over on the other side of the floor. He's all wrapped up with this girl who could be Yaz, and he could be kissing her.

# Chapter 22

I turn my head away; I can't bear to see. Then I make myself look up again, and they've gone. I spend the next fifteen minutes on some kind of miserable edge, scanning the crowd for them, waiting for proof that Yaz has pulled Juan. I finally collide with them by the club's main entrance. They're close but not actually touching, and Juan asks me in his beautiful deep voice if I'm feeling OK. I want to start crying when he says that, but I mutter about being tired instead, and he says he'll take us home. We get into his car and he drives us back, right through *Pino Alto*'s gates. Then he gets out of the car and kisses us both Spanish-style, but Yaz first, and he holds Yaz for longer, I'm sure he does.

And then Yaz and I go to bed, and I still don't really know if she's got off with Juan, and I can't ask her, because we're still not talking about this battle that she's winning.

Next morning we wake at about the same time and bicker drowsily about who should get up and make tea. Then we hear the crunch of feet on the gravel behind the house, followed by chipping and scraping from the swimming pool. Yaz smiles, all secret and intense, slips out of bed, grabs jeans and a T-shirt, and goes into the bathroom. She spends a long time in there, making sure she looks really good. I hear her come out, go into the kitchen. She'll be making coffee, maybe fresh orange juice too, to take out to him.

Suddenly I can't stand it. It was them I saw last night snogging, I know it was. And I know I've got to face them soon, wrapped up in each other, so hot they'll make Tom and Ruth look tired. But not yet. Not yet.

I get dressed, grab my bag, and bolt.


And now I'm sitting alone on the bus into Ercos, trying to think out a plausible excuse to tell Yaz why I sneaked off without even letting her know I was going. Which is hard when I'm not even sure what I'm doing. All I am sure is I've got to get away.

The bus bumps along, spraying dirt up from the muddy track, and all the passengers are chatting cheerfully because at last the sun's making a serious effort to come out. The Spanish sun isn't watery and half-hearted, like it is in England. When it finally breaks free from the grey cloud it's rich and warm and the water in the ditches sparkles. It doesn't cheer me up, though. Not a bit.

It'd be a lot easier if our society didn't have all these unspoken conventions about not expressing ugly feelings, wouldn't it. If I could just go up to Yaz and say, "Hi. I'm off because I'm sick with jealousy over you and Juan – in fact I shall probably vomit if I see him touch you. OK?" But I can't, can I? I've got no *right* to feel that strongly. I've never actually had anything with him, and it would be pitiful and grotesque to try and stake any kind of claim on him. Even the claim of being upset.

Put up, shut up, grow up – that's the social code.

The bus stops at the square, and I get off. The sun shines on the pretty buildings, the pavement glows, and I'm flooded by a sense of how it would be in the summer, sitting out round the little wrought-iron tables under the palm trees as the night comes in. . . I walk down the street and my situation hits me like a wet towel. What am I going to *do*? I can't stay here if Juan and Yaz get together, I won't be able to stand it, all eaten up with jealousy, hanging around like a spare part . . . what's the alternative though? Flee back home like the ultimate in losers?

I feel lightheaded with misery. And *hunger* – the last food to pass my lips was Tom and Ruth's mushy stew at seven o'clock last night. I drag myself along the street a bit further, then pluck up courage to push through the door of a quiet little café on the corner. I go up to the counter, order hot chocolate and bread rolls. The Spanish words flow off my tongue almost without my brain being engaged, and that cheers me up just a bit. The waiter beams, waves me to a table in the window – I feel he wants me on show to the street, and that cheers me up a bit more.

The hot chocolate is frothy and creamy; I break off bits of roll to dunk, savouring the luxury, and as I do that, I brood.

*You can't just up stakes and go home, you can't. That would be such an admission of defeat. And you've got more right to be here than anyone – it was you who struck up a friendship with Bella, so it was you who got the house; it's you who speaks Spanish; it's you who held out for the real Spain, and didn't just drift along to some holiday camp on the South Coast.*

I've reached the last dribble of the hot chocolate, the last lump of bread. And then the solution hits me. To give my life some shape and purpose and to avoid hanging around at *Pino Alto*, suffering – I've got to get a job. Fast.

I pay, take off, walk along the street towards the steep road that leads up to old Ercos, wondering if you go about getting casual work here the same as you do in England. I pass a bar with a card in the window saying it needs bar staff, and hover reading and rereading it, my heart thumping with the mere thought of going in and applying. "You've never done bar work before," I mutter to excuse my cowardice. "Look for a restaurant. Or a café."

That could be the answer. Right through my A-level years I worked at *Greedies*, a café near us, and I got great tips. I can't see any cards in the restaurants or cafés I pass, though. And as I peer through the windows, it occurs to me that the level of service required in Spain is a bit above the level *Greedies* trained me for. And I'm not sure my Spanish is up to it, anyway. I'm beginning to feel my resolve trickling away, depression taking over again. I turn back, head along a dull, modern-looking street, turn off that, walk along another almost the same. Mostly offices, some houses. And then I see a little black painted sign saying, *School for English*.

The sign is on a thin, three-storey building, with a prospectus sheet in a gilt frame in the front window. And tucked in the frame is a hand-written note saying, *Teaching staff needed – apply within.*

Without giving myself time to consider I march up to the front door and ring the bell. A sour-faced woman in a track-suit opens it; I say I'm here about a job, and she ushers me without comment or enquiry into a room leading off the hall. Inside, there's a glamorous-looking signora behind a big desk, piles of jet-black hair looped on top of her head. I cough, but she doesn't look up. "Excuse me," I say, in as cut-glass-correct an accent as I can muster, "I saw the sign in your window asking for English teachers, and I—"

As she hears my voice the woman starts, stands up, launches herself round the desk at me, practically embraces me. "*Eeenglish*," she breathes. "You *are* English?"

"Yes, and I've got English A-level, Grade B, but I've never studied teaching, and I—"

"No matter!" she gushes, twirling a red-nailed, ring-heavy hand. "*Conversation*. You can make good conversation, yes?"

"Oh, sure . . . I mean, I do all the time. . ."

"And *idioms*. Our students – they don't want textbook English. They want *idioms*."

I haven't the faintest idea what an idiom is, but I gush, "Oh, of *course*. I'm *always* using idioms. All the time."

She beams at me, showing a scary amount of gum. "Your accent is *perfect*. Now. What we do here – we are not just a normal school. We have the teacher and classroom situation, but we have other methods too. We have businessmen come to us who need to progress fast. So we have small intimate *groups*. We have drinks; we relax; and that way we make the best conversation."

There's a pause. The horrible thought comes into my head that all this is a cover for a branch of the sex industry; that any minute now she'll be producing the suspenders and plunge bra I'm supposed to wear as I teach. "Is it only business*men*?" I ask, nervously.

She laughs, defensively. "Usually. We're a little behind you English feminists here in Spain. Give us time."

"How big are the groups?"

"Only eight or so pupils. They pay more; they get more individual attention and . . . and *comfort*. I'll show you one of the teaching rooms. Come."

Thirty minutes later I'm back on the street. And I've got a timetable in my hand – two afternoons and two mornings a week – and an agreement about the very generous pay and I'm absolutely *triumphant*. My fears about the sex industry were totally unfounded. I really do just have to sit around on a comfy sofa and drink coffee and chat. True, I have to have ideas about what to chat about, and I have to be charming and patient, so they'll like me and want to come back. But basically I think it's a peach of a job. And by the end of our time together, Concepción – for that is the signora's name – and I were positively best mates. She even promised to help me spruce up my Spanish a bit, when she had the time.

I pick up a few groceries and head back to *Pino Alto*, simmering with determined well-being. Stuff love, I think. This job – it's my sword, my protection against all the hurt that's waiting for me when Juan moves in with Yaz, and they kick me out to sleep round the back in the swimming pool changing room with the geckos. And you know what? I won't care.

I've got a job, I'll be making money, I've got freedom. . .

When I walk through the gates, Yaz is lounging at the table on the terrace. "Juan's gone," she purrs. "You've *missed* him."

# Chapter 23

"You've missed him." She means that in every sense of the word there is, I know she does. The smug, languid smile on her face suggests he spent the last two hours before he went just declaring his love for her.

I shrug, then I launch into a counter-attack of telling her excitedly about the job I've landed. She shrugs, put out that I didn't wait for her to go job-hunting, and comments snottily that the job doesn't sound like a whole load of laughs. Acidly, I offer to make her some lunch with the bread and deli stuff I bought. Offhandedly, she thanks me.

"Butter or mayo?" I ask.

"Butter," she says. "Please."

We're speaking in these clipped, flat tones, barely looking at each other, both playing the same stupid fake game, both not talking about the real issue. The real issue as in Juan. What would be honest would be for her to squawk, "Nyah – nyah – *jealous*!" and for me to walk over and whack her round the head.

As I turn to go she says, "Oh, by the way – Juan's promised to take us all out tonight to one of his favourite bars. He says they do great *tapas*."

"That'll be nice," I say, thinking, *She's still not really pulled him then*. Not if he's asked all four of us.

And I disappear into the kitchen.

The day passes and it's basically crap. When I tell them about my job, Ruth's pleased for me but Tom shakes his head wearily as though I've just confirmed his worst suspicions about the state of my brain. "You should've *waited*, Lors," he says. "We don't know we're staying yet, do we?"

"Well, *I* know," I snap. "*I'm* staying."

"Sure you are. All on your own, eh?" And he laughs, patronizingly.

The sun disappears again, clouds gather overhead and Tom and Ruth decide it's too risky to make it to the beach. "Maybe you can get your bikini out tomorrow, babes, yeah?" Tom leers. Instead, they head off in the car towards the nearest shopping centre, leaving Yaz and me behind. We spend the time avoiding each other around the terrace and the house, exchanging the odd constipated word.

But after less than two hours, Tom and Ruth are

back again. Tom's fuming and Ruth's upset. She explains tearfully that they took ages to navigate the ringroads leading to the shopping centre and when they got there it was awful. "*Total* rubbish," seethes Tom. "I was buying trainers and this arsehole assistant kept making out he couldn't understand me. Then – once I'd finally got them in a bag – this cow tried to take them off me when we were going into the supermarket!"

"She only wanted to staple the bag up," snivels Ruth. "It's to stop shoplifting. . ."

"Well, I couldn't understand what she was on about. She kept trying to get the bag off me – I bloody nearly decked her. I wish I had done—"

"Oh, *Tom*—"

I leave them to squabble, wander off round the side of the house, sit looking at the sludge-filled swimming pool as the rain starts to fall yet again. I'm full of this kind of bleak resignation that our stay at *Pino Alto* isn't working out.

Tom isn't too keen on being taken to a bar by Juan but – as he dragged Ruth out of the supermarket with the bag for his trainers unstapled but before they bought any food – it's either that or go hungry. So we all cram into Juan's car at nine-thirty that night, Yaz (of course) in the front seat beside him.

Juan drives into Ercos and right up the narrow winding streets to the old part of town, where he parks with ease in a very small space. "Wow," breathes Yaz, "you're a brilliant driver! Those streets are *scary*."

"Oh, I'm used to them," says Juan, and Tom – terrified we might think Juan's a better driver than him – chips in with, "Yeah, it's only a matter of doing it a few times, Yaz."

The bar is down a back-street, down some steps, in this wonderful cavern-like cellar. It's a good place, and it's already heaving. As we push our way through to buy drinks, I recognize several of the faces from last night, and Nuria grabs me and kisses me like I'm an old friend. "We're in luck," shouts Juan, above the noise. "They've just got the barbecue going – I'll get us some food."

We find a table and seats at the far end of the cellar, where a stone lion's head on the wall is spurting water into a great marble bowl stacked with empty wine bottles. "This is *brilliant*," squeals Ruth.

"Too packed," grumbles Tom.

"Oh – come on, baby! The *Dog and Fox* is as packed as this on a Saturday night."

"Yeah, but not with—" he breaks off, and we all know he was going to say something appalling like "bloody foreigners", but we let it go because Juan arrives with a large platter full of drool-making food. Everyone pounces on it, except Tom, of course, who prods suspiciously at a mound of what look like tiny Catherine wheels and demands, "What's that?"

"Pork," explains Juan. "They curl it up and skewer it, then put it on the grill . . . try one, it's delicious."

"No thanks, mate," sniffs Tom. "Looks a bit fatty to me."

"Oh, for *God's sake*, Tom," I erupt, "whenever I see you with a beer in one hand you've got a packet of pork scratchings in the other!"

"That's different. . ."

"You bet it's different. This is food and that's crap."

"Have some *tortilla*," laughs Juan. "Or an olive."

"I hate olives," Tom says, bunching up his face like he's being mocked, and just then a whole group of people descend on us – some from last night, some new – and start talking and pinching food and asking Juan about his new friends. I can follow more and more of their chat, even join in a bit. I like them – the way they're such fun, so energetic. I like the way that girl's whole face is behind what she's saying – the way her hands are in on it, too. I like the way that boy's got his arm slung round Juan's neck, although I know Tom's right now suspecting him of being queer.

A boy asks about *Pino Alto* and I wheel out my Spanish to tell them all about it. Juan's listening, and when I stumble over a word he supplies it, or encourages me, says, "Go on, Laura." I wish he wasn't so bloody *kind*, as well as gorgeous, 'cos it only makes everything worse and me want him more.

"So when can we have a party?" asks one of the boys. "At your house?"

"Never," says Juan, "you'd wreck it."

"Well, we could set up speakers out on the terrace. . ."

"Ah, *great idea*," says Nuria. "I've seen that terrace – superb for *dancing*!" She's shimmying in her seat at the very thought, arms half lifted . . . one of the Spanish girls laughs, another girl applauds, then one of the boys starts drumming flamenco really hard on the table. Another boy joins in, laughing, matching the rhythm, and the sound lifts. It's incredibly sexy. I feel it right down my spine, right down my legs to the ground – everyone at the table moves with it. Two women standing near us turn round and start clapping to the beat, and someone's shouting to the barman, and then the music from the speakers gets louder, and suddenly people are standing up and dancing, clearing the tables back and just *dancing*.

My heart's thumping with it, with the way it happened, the *speed* it happened.

Tom snorts, throws himself back in his chair with his arms folded, and says, "Oh, bloody hell. This is going to be embarrassing."

"*Shut up!*" I hiss.

"Any minute now they'll be passing round a tambourine for money. . ."

I glare at him, hating him, and Juan leans towards

me. "Laura?" He takes hold of my arm just above the elbow. "You going to dance?"

I don't move for a minute. I think – I wish he wouldn't do this. He really doesn't have to look after me like this. Two of the Spanish boys are pulling Yaz out on to the floor. Tom turns to Ruth, looking incredibly pained, and says, "I hope you don't expect me to start prancing about, babes."

And I think, *Stuff it – I'm going to* dance*!*

# Chapter 24

It's easier to dance in this dark cavern-type place than in the club last night. There's less room, and we're all crowded up against each other, jockeying for a bit of space, but that's good, 'cos I don't feel so exposed, so on show. I let myself slide into the rhythm of it, not as flamboyant as the Spanish girls, but there with it just the same. "Hey Laura!" Juan calls, above the noise. "You're good!"

He moves right opposite me, and we're dancing together. He's wonderful. So relaxed, so full of it, like the music's making him move, like it's flowing through him with his blood. I catch the energy from him, and suddenly we're *really* dancing, a whole body communication opening up, response on response on response, getting wilder, trying different things but keeping together, it's fantastic, it's magic, I want it so much that –

I freak.

I can't take it, I have to stop it. "Hey," I squawk, "I got myself a job today."

Juan stops too. He looks at the floor, then he looks towards me. "In Ercos?"

"Yeah. Teaching English." We move towards the outskirts of the group. My heart begins to slow a bit. I tell him all about my job, and he says he knows the school, it's new, but it's already got a classy reputation. "What's an idiom?" I say.

"*What?*"

"I told Concepción I could do idioms, and I've no idea what they are."

Juan laughs. "Isn't it like – slang and weird phrases? Like – 'raining cats and dogs'?"

"Oh – *right*. Oh, that's good. I can do those by the bucket-load. Bats in the belfry."

"*What?*"

We both laugh, and I explain what that means, and he says, "*Le falta un tornillo*," and I say, "What?" and then Yaz appears right next to us. "Hey, Juan – come on! You said you'd show me some flamenco moves!"

Juan turns away with her, and I flop down at the table next to Ruth and grab my drink. "He's off," grunts Tom, nodding towards Juan. "Moving in on Yaz. God – look at him. Fucking poof."

"Just 'cos he can dance, Tom," I mutter. My eyes

are riveted to him. He moves like . . . he moves like an *angel*. Why did I stop dancing with him? *Why?*

"I hate all that posey Spanish crap," sneers Tom. "*Look* at 'im. Anyone'd think he was in a bullring."

Juan's holding himself really taut, really upright, and Tom's right, it is a bit like a *matador*, it's got that same strong centre, the same power, but it's much more fluid, much more exciting . . . he's not dancing like he danced with me, though. Even allowing for my judgement being totally warped by need and greed and jealousy, I can see that. He just isn't lifting off, like he did with me. I sit there, watching him showing Yaz some steps, and I'm overpowered by the memory of dancing with him, what it *felt* like to be up so close to him. . .

"Oh, I'm hopeless," giggles Yaz, stumbling to a stop. "I just don't get it!"

"Shall I get you another drink?" says Juan.

"Sure. I'll come with you." And they disappear into the crowd.

On the way back in the car, Juan says, "D'you know the name for what happened tonight?"

"What?" breathes Yaz, looking sideways at him all adoring.

"When everyone started to . . . *move* . . . get up and dance. D'you know what it was called?"

"A load of people making prats of themselves?" queries Tom.

"*Duende*," says Juan, ignoring him. "It's like – the spirit of music, of *fiesta*. It's just suddenly there, it gets a hold on people. People used to say *duende* was a goblin."

"A *goblin*?" scoffs Tom.

"Yeah. Casting a spell on people. You can't force it – it has to just happen. Bit like the *craic*, in Ireland."

"Well, there's a lot of similarities, aren't there, between the Irish and the Spanish," I put in all excited, 'cos I know about this. "They reckon loads of Armada galleons on the way back to Spain got ship-wrecked near Ireland, and the Spanish sailors settled in Ireland and married Irish girls and taught them their dances and music and stuff. . ."

"Hah!" snorts Tom. "I wouldn't be pleased about your link with the Paddies if I was you, Juan. You know how we see the Irish in England, don't you?"

"No," says Juan, "how?"

"As a bit lacking in the brain department, mate, that's how." And he sits back, guffawing.

I glance sidelong at Ruth, to see if she'll pull him up, but she's gone into her non-existence mode, which she's doing more and more nowadays. Mind you, anyone saddled with Tom would want to be non-existent, wouldn't they, when you think about it. I consider pulling him up myself, but I just can't be bothered – he's not worth it. And then I hear Juan say, "Is this some kind of joke thing you do, Tom?"

"What?"

"This – old-fashioned racist stuff. You can't mean it, surely. Is it like – irony? I know you English are supposed to be very good at irony."

There's a wonderful, pregnant pause, and then both Yaz and I start laughing. "*What?*" asks Juan, spreading his hands on the steering wheel. "What have I said?" He knows exactly what he's said though. He's acting the innocent but his eyes are gleaming with triumph.

And meanwhile Tom's huffing away and probably trying to work out what "irony" means. "Oh, yeah, ha ha, girls," he growls. "I'm not a racist, mate. Just a realist."

"Really? These two things – they're similar in England, are they?"

"What you mean, similar?"

"Well – it's easy to get the two confused?"

"Look – there's no *confusion*, mate. Racist is like – hating someone just 'cos of their race. But if you're a realist you just know what's what."

"What's what. Oh – *right*. Now I understand."

Yaz and I start sniggering again, and Ruth nudges me hard and says, "I never knew that about the Armada. That they stopped off in Ireland on the way back to Spain."

"Yeah," says Tom, "after we'd kicked their arses for them. Trying to invade En-ger-land! Fucking *no* chance!"

# Chapter 25

Yaz and I wake up late the next day, and lie in bed chatting for a bit, but we're still not talking about the thing that really matters to us. I still don't know if she's really with Juan or not. I'm beginning to wish she'd get on with it – it's like I want the axe to fall, finish things. "Shall we get some tea?" she says. "See if Tom's left any bread for toast?"

We stagger together into the main room, and stop dead.

Tom and Ruth's cases and bags are standing there, right by the front door, all packed tight and bulging.

Ruth won't look up from the sink where she's washing some mugs up. "Morning," says Tom. "You lazy cows."

Yaz finds her voice first. "Ruth – what *is* this?"

"We're off," says Tom, calmly.

"What? *Why?*"

"Oh, come on Yaz – it's obvious, isn't it? It's bloody boring here! I mean, yeah, nice house and everything, but Ercos itself is hardly the most happening place in Spain, is it?"

"I thought last night was great!"

"That pokey little bar? No one in there but Spanish people!"

"That's what *was* great," I hiss. "It's really different, it's—"

"Oh, stow it, Lors. We want to go south."

"But it's rent-free here!"

"Yeah, and it's just as well it is, 'cos we're not exactly going to find jobs, are we?"

"I got a job!"

"As a poxy *teacher*! I want to get work as a bouncer or behind a bar, and I don't see that happening round here – they'd want you to speak Spanish!"

"You could *learn*."

Tom looks at me like I've just suggested he paints his toenails pink, and doesn't deign to answer. There's a silence. "Ruth?" I say. "Are you going along with this?"

She turns from the sink, but she won't meet my eye. "I'm sorry, Laura," she croaks. "I feel awful about this, but—"

"Babes – what d'you feel awful about?" erupts Tom. "We're not just sneaking off and leaving them, are we? Girls, you can come with us, or stay here.

Fair dos. You got half an hour to make your minds up." And he beams at us, overcome by his own generosity.

"But why didn't you *discuss* it?" storms Yaz. "With us? Before you just – decided to piss off?"

Tom looks genuinely bewildered. "But we *are* discussing it," he says. "I'm asking you – do you wanna come with us or not? I can't say fairer than that, can I?"

"I thought we were all going to stick together?"

"We can do. We can all go."

"But what you're saying is – what you've *decided* without consulting us at all – is we can't all stay here."

"*Obviously* not. If Roofy and me are going. Which we are. Come on Yaz, it's a fair choice."

There's absolutely no point in arguing with Tom. His whole face is shining with how straight and even-handed he's being and how he's giving us a real choice. "Look," he says. "I'll go off and have a bit of a walk around, let you girls talk it through. OK?" And he leaves the kitchen, smiling.

"Don't start on me," says Ruth, the minute the door shuts behind him. "*Please*."

I'm struck by the wavery note in her voice, and I look at her. I feel like I've been so wrapped up in myself, I haven't looked at her properly for ages, and now I get a shock, 'cos her face has changed. It's like the old Ruth has gone missing, like I don't know her any more.

"I'm not going to start on you," I say. "I just need to know . . . if you really do *want* to go! You loved it when we first got here."

"Yeah – it's nice. But – well, Tom's right. It's so *quiet*. And he – he really is set on getting to the south coast."

"Package-holiday heaven."

"Oh, Laura, you're such a *snob*."

"I'm *not*. And that's not you talking, that's Tom."

Ruth's eyes flare. "It is *not*. If you weren't such a snob, you'd come with us." She turns to Yaz. "What about you? You gonna come?"

There's a silence. Yaz is chewing one side of her mouth, looking uneasy. "Well . . . I can hardly leave Laura here on her own. . ."

"No," says Ruth. "And anyway, you want to stay and see how things develop with Juan, don't you? Can't blame you, I guess. But have you thought about how shitty that's going to be for Laura? When you two are all into each other and she's left out on her own?"

Well, *thanks*, I'm thinking. *Glad* you're so sure my fate is to be constantly blokeless.

"Why don't you both come with us," Ruth goes on, "then you can meet *loads* of guys. God – most of the reason they go to those resorts all along the coast is to meet girls."

"I don't want to meet the sort of guy who goes to a place just to meet girls," I snap.

"That is so arrogant, Laura."

"No, it's not. I don't want someone just up for a bit of stupid conversation followed by sex."

"God, Laura – you know your problem? You read too much of that *Wuthering Heights* stuff when you were a kid. You're hopelessly idealistic."

"No, I'm not!"

"You are. If you weren't, you wouldn't've got so hurt by that loser Ryan Morrisey when you were sixteen."

"Oh, for God's sake—"

"If you want to meet someone, go somewhere where there's loads of guys. Come south with us."

"*No.*"

Ruth lets out a great *paaaa* of irritation, turns back to the sink. "Never mind about cross-examining me," I say. "You still haven't answered my question."

"What question?"

"Are you sure you want to leave here?"

"I've *told* you, Tom—"

"*Tom's not you!* Come *on*, Ruth. It could be great here, and you know it. And you don't want to split the three of us up like this. I *know* you don't."

Ruth shrugs, miserably. "I'm not having a row with him, Laura. I hate it when we row."

"Oh, *Ruth* –"

"He says – he says he gets so hurt when I'm angry with him. 'Cos all he cares about is making me happy, and when I'm pissed off it makes him feel he's failed.

And then he gets angry, too, 'cos he thinks I should know that, and be more sensitive and value what we have and not get angry with him in the first place. . ."

My brain's staggering just trying to follow Tom's rules for a successful relationship. "So that means you're going to do just want he wants, does it?" I demand.

"*No*," snaps Ruth. "All it means is—"

"Have you decided, girls?" Tom's face comes grinning round the front door. I resist an almost overwhelming urge to smash a fist into it.

"Yeah, baby," says Ruth, dully. "They're staying."

# Chapter 26

After Tom's Astra has driven off along the dirt track and disappeared from sight, Yaz and I make a late breakfast and sit together uneasily on the terrace to eat it. "Have we done the right thing?" she says, nervously.

"The *only* thing," I assert, glumly. "Giving up this paradise – when it's rent free? Those two are mad."

"Well – Tom is, anyway. D'you think we've let Ruth down, making her go off on her own?"

"Yaz – no one made her! God!"

"Are you scared? Being here on our own, I mean?"

"No. There's a bus, and I've got a job. And there's . . . Juan and his friends. We won't be isolated."

Yaz smirks when I say Juan's name, and I wonder if we can talk about him now at last, about the fact that we both like him, about the fact that he's probably the main reason we're both staying on. "I'm going to have to find a job, aren't I," she says. "Like you."

"Yeah."

"Juan'll help me find one." And she stands up, picks up her plate and mug, and drifts back to the kitchen.

Over the next couple of weeks, life starts to fall into a pattern. I start work at Concepción's School of English, and it goes well. I don't have any real idiots in my class, and they're all so eager to learn they're a doddle, they're hanging off my every perfectly-pronounced word. One of them acts like he'd like to hang off my chest, too, but I always sit as far away from him as possible and when he asks me out for a meal "to make more conversation", I tell him it's against the rules of the school and that's that. On my third shift there, Concepción asks me if I'd like to fit another shift in, and I say yes. Right now I need the support of this routine, and it feels good beginning to stack up some money.

I'm known on the bus now, too, 'cos I'm travelling at regular times, and people say hello to me. I'm known in the café where I get a cappuccino, and sometimes lunch, and I'm known in the little super-market. My Spanish is growing more and more polished. It feels great, making a go of living in a different place. It helps me deal with the total crash in my emotional life.

Yaz still hasn't found work. Her Spanish just isn't good enough for anything other than table-clearing and washing up, and she won't lower herself to that. I suggest to her that I ask Concepción if she could work at teaching English, but she's pretty snooty about that too, so I don't push it.

I'd sooner be there on my own, anyway. I strike up a friendship with Luisa, a fellow teacher. She's Spanish but her English is good enough for her to teach it. She's crazy about all things British, and she's delighted to have me as a new friend. She's a bit old-fashioned; she says she doesn't go out much in the evening. But she does take me home for a huge traditional Spanish lunch, and she promises to show me the mountains. All in all, I'm pleased with the way I'm coping, pleased with the life I'm beginning to map out for myself, a life that's separate from *Pino Alto*.

Separate from Juan and Yaz.

The weather's still wet and uncertain, and Juan says he can't get on with his building work. He's up at the house nearly every day, working on the pool. I don't know what goes on, the times I'm in Ercos teaching, or off with Luisa. I don't want to know, not any more.

The day Tom and Ruth left Yaz announced she was moving into their room, and made a big fuss about washing the sheets and sweeping the floor. . . I didn't bother to argue. I was happy to have the old room to myself. But it means we're further apart than ever. Juan and Yaz don't act like boyfriend and girl-friend, not in front of me, but that doesn't prove anything. Maybe they're just being tactful.

Juan says he's got to look after Bella's friends, especially now Tom and his car have abandoned us. He took us out clubbing again, and we met up with a gang of people, so my gooseberry status wasn't too painfully obvious. And the other day he turned up here in the evening with Nuria and some other friends; they bought drink and food and we made a fire and sat round talking until dawn broke. . . Yaz and I fit well into his group, although I can feel that a couple of the girls are beginning to get a bit possessive about him, a bit pissed off with these interloping English girls. Even so, we've planned a party this Saturday out on the terrace, and we talk about making a trip to the beach soon as the weather gets better.

If it wasn't for the ache I feel all the time, watching him across the room, with his black hair and eyes and the way he moves, watching him laugh, knowing I can't have him, it would all be wonderful.

Saturday, the day of the party, I don't have to work. I sleep late, and when Yaz tries to wake me to take me on a shopping trip with Nuria and a couple of the other Spanish girls, I bat her away. I feel exhausted somehow; worn out right down to the bones. I go back to the escape of sleep.

I finally wake up at about midday. I can hear the familiar sounds of Juan chipping and scraping in the swimming pool. I lie back, arms behind my head, listening for a while, then I get washed and dressed and make my way to the kitchen. I cut open the big net of oranges I bought yesterday, and pull out four – then six. They're so cheap compared to England, you feel you ought to use a load of them. I slice them in half and press the halves one by one on to the little electric juicer. Soon I've got a half a jugful of fabulous fresh juice. *I'll take him some*, I think. *It's only being friendly.*

It isn't, of course. It's being masochistic, like pressing on a bruise. Outside on the terrace, it's really warm, but the air is grey and heavy, with big bloated clouds hanging overhead. I walk round to the swimming pool, stand there watching him work for a few moments, then he catches sight of me and I call out, "Want some juice?"

"Laura!" He grins at me, welcoming. "Wonderful. Thank you."

I sit down on the edge of the pool, letting my legs dangle, and hand him his glass. He doesn't sit beside me; he stands a metre or so away, and I watch his throat as he tips his head back to swallow. "I'm trying to finish that side today," he says. "Before the rain sets in again."

"I can't believe how wet it's been," I say.

"Ah, it makes up for later. When it won't rain at all. The olive trees need it now, for their roots."

I think of the tree roots, parched and gratefully soaking up the rain, and for some reason that makes me feel all choked up and I think I'd better get back inside. But before I can stand up, the first fat raindrops start to fall. "Uh-oh," he says. "Here it comes. . ." And then suddenly the sky's sheeting down, a great, soaking, tropical-style rainstorm. I scramble to my feet, and he slams down his glass and jumps from the pool, and we're both racing for the little changing-room. He shoves the door open, ushers me in in front of him, then stands there, laughing, shaking the rain out of his hair like a dog. His eyelashes are spiky with the wet.

"Oh my GOD," I squawk. "I've *never* seen the sky open like that before!"

"My orange juice," he says mournfully, "I didn't finish it."

"Well, it'll be nice, mixed with fresh rain."

He smiles, wanders to the back of the room. "D'you want to sit down, Laura? There's some old sunbeds here." And he starts dragging a solid wooden sunbed across the floor towards me.

"Check it," I say, nervously. "Check it for spiders. You know – like that one that jumped on Ruth. You said they crawl inside to get out of the rain."

Juan laughs. "They'll have to *swim* inside in this." He starts pummelling the cushions. A sleepy little moth spirals up from one, but no spiders.

He's left the door open. We sit side by side on the

sunbed, looking out at the deluge. It's like sitting behind a waterfall. The rain's crashing on to the clay tiles, streaming away in sheets, and the air smells alive. "Where's Yaz gone?" he asks.

I sigh. He wishes he was here with her instead of me, of course he does. "Shopping," I say.

"Ah. She didn't come round to the pool to see me, this morning. She must've known I was there, though."

I shrug, sourly, and he goes on, "I think – I think I've really annoyed her."

"Yeah?" I murmur, unenthusiastically, thinking, *Great. I'm about to be asked my advice on how to heal a lovers' tiff.*

"Yeah. You see – Oh, God, there's no way of saying this without sounding like some arrogant idiot. But the problem is – she. . ." he trails off, then he takes a deep breath and blurts out, "She likes me a lot more than I like her."

# Chapter 27

The rain drums on the roof, hisses on the tiles outside. The air's so thick with water vapour it's like a mist wreathing round us. And I can't help it, my heart's soaring, *soaring,* with what Juan's just said.

"I'm sorry," he mumbles. "She's your friend, you're going to take her side. But—"

"What's been happening?" I croak.

"Well – nothing. But she wants it to. I was at fault for . . . it's just – Oh, God, it's a mess! It's my fault. Well – not all my fault. I'm not used to English girls. Maybe you work differently?"

"Juan – you're not making any *sense*!"

"Aren't I? No, I don't s'pose I am. Thing is – she came after me quite strong. When I first met you all, I mean. She thought I liked her, well, I *did* like her, but she thought I—"

"Fancied her?"

"Yes. She put her arms round my neck at *Las Estrellas*, that first time I took you all there – d'you remember?"

I nod. Of course I remember. I remember seeing them up close together. It felt a stone had been swapped for my stomach.

"I couldn't push her off, could I? So I ended up kissing her. I felt I'd insult her if I didn't kiss her. That was a mistake, wasn't it?"

"Well . . . not a major one." My stomach isn't a stone now. It's cartwheeling.

"I think it was. It told her I wanted her. When I didn't. And then – she acted like we had something special between us. And she didn't seem to mind that I didn't play along. And then . . . it happened again. That bar we went to, just before Tom and Ruth left? I . . . I sort of kissed her again."

"*Again?*"

"She came on to me – she started kissing me! Don't look at me like that, Laura! I couldn't just push her away, could I? It would've been. . ."

"Insulting?"

"You're laughing at me."

"No, I'm not. It's just I've never heard of anyone snogging someone out of politeness before."

"You don't believe me, do you? You think I'm a bastard. *Hijo de puta!* OK, maybe I am. A bit. It's just – Spanish girls are different. They make you do all the running. They make you crawl, if they can. I'm not used to girls doing the running, being this direct."

"And Yaz isn't used to boys turning her down. Not that you *did*, exactly, did you?"

"No. No, I should have done, I should've been straight. Now she thinks I really like her, and the only reason I'm not coming on to her is 'cos I'm shy or . . . or too afraid of the Catholic church or something. She comes and sits by the pool while I work – she talks to me, flirts with me, like she's trying to convince me, wear down my resistance . . . and then she gets cross and marches off. . . I don't know how to put things right. *Joder*. I'm up to it in my neck, aren't I."

"Up to my neck in it," I correct him. "You know, it's simple really. You've just got to *tell* her."

He looks at me, horrified. "What – that I don't find her attractive? How *can* I?"

"Look, Yaz is pretty sure of herself. Usually she gets any guy she wants. And if you've flirted with her and kissed her – *twice* – well, you can't blame her for thinking you like her, can you? So you owe it to her to explain that you were being polite. Or a *hijo de puta*. Or an idiot. Or all three."

He looks up at me all hurt and surprised, then he laughs, really laughs, showing all his teeth. I leave a little pause, then I say, casually, "Did anything happen at the club we went to the other night?"

"Nothing. I made sure we stayed in a group. You remember."

I do, of course. We'd danced in a group all night and I'd longed for Juan to move opposite me, but he hadn't.

"I suppose I did encourage her, to start with," he goes on. "A bit. If I'm honest – a lot of me liked the way she went after me. It was an ego trap."

"Trip."

"Trip. I was down. I was fed up. I was full of – what the hell does anything matter. It was no excuse though."

There's a silence, then I ask, "Why were you down and fed up?"

The rain has eased, and it makes the silence stronger. "Why?" I ask again.

"*You* know," he says.

"I don't," I say. "If I did, I wouldn't be asking you, would I."

"*I* took a hint from you!" he kind of erupts. "Why couldn't she? She ignored all the hints I made, that I want her as a friend but no more, she came after me. . ."

"What hint?" I ask. Little spooky fingerings of hope start running up and down my spine. "What hint did you take from me?"

"You made it clear you weren't interested in me," he says, sulkily. "That's what. Look, it's OK."

"Why did you think that, Juan?"

"You didn't want to come out with us. That first night."

"That was because I thought you and Yaz wanted to be alone. Because of the way you were when you were cooking."

"But that was all *her*. And, anyway, at the club – you avoided us. You went off alone."

"For the same reason! You seemed so into each other!"

"*She* was into me, maybe! I was being—"

"Polite. Don't tell me." I've got my arms wrapped tight round my knees, rocking myself. What I really want to do is grab him by the face, demand to know how he feels about me. Instead, I mutter, "Are you saying you *wanted* me to be interested in you?"

"Look, it doesn't matter. It's past. Anyone who could dance with me like you did and then just—"

"You mean – the other week? At that great bar?"

"Yes. We danced so well – you were so sexy, so wonderful. And then – *whoomph*. You just stopped. You started talking about teaching, and idioms, raining cats and dogs. I felt – *squashed*! Like a rat on the road. Under a car. I felt dreadful. So I kissed Yaz again. And now I'm in this mess, and she's angry, and . . . *joder*."

Outside, the rain's stopped. A great spotlight of sun is bouncing off the wet clay tiles; the air's sparkling like magic dust.

"Would you like to know why I stopped dancing?" I croak.

"What?"

"I *said* – would you like to know why I stopped dancing? Well, I'm gonna tell you. I *stopped* 'cos I couldn't take it any more. It was – *overpowering*. Like you. Like you're overpowering. You think you can read people – you can take hints. Well, you've failed with me, mate. Failed atrociously. If you think I don't like you, I mean."

There's a long, long pause. The gecko who lives behind the mirror on the wall pokes his blunt head out, and we both watch him as he skedaddles across the wall and out of the door. "I hope you're saying what I think you're saying, Laura," mutters Juan.

"I think I am," I mutter back.

He gets to his feet, turns to look at me. I can't meet his eye. "Laura, would you come out to lunch with me? Now? I want to ask you . . . *everything*. And here I'm – I'm scared Yaz is going to come back any minute. There's a wonderful place – we can walk to it. It's stopped raining. And then we can talk. And I . . . I need a *drink*!"

"Sure," I say, and I stand up, and my knees are trembling like crazy, but I manage to put one foot in front of the other and walk.

# Chapter 28

We walk in silence to the gap in the cacti and prickly-pear hedge behind the house, go through it, and start to trek across the field. Rainwater is still streaming along the ground, running in gleaming rivulets along the side of the track, forming pools and puddles. The sun feels hot now, and steam is rising to form a soft, lovely mist in the air.

We walk along side by side. It crosses my mind that we could hold hands, but I know we won't, not yet. I'm so aware anyway of him beside me, his easy walk, the way his arms move . . . it would be too much to touch him. "What's the place we're heading for?" I ask.

"*El Fain*," he says. "It's wonderful. It's a big old *finca* – it does lunch a few times in the week, and always at the weekend. They know me – I've worked there, serving at the tables. It gets busy on Saturdays, but they'll find us a place."

"Is it far?"

"Another ten minutes, maybe. Are you OK? It's far quicker to walk this back way than try to drive, the roads'll be flooded again. . ."

"Juan, I'm fine. This is blissful."

It is, too. Everywhere I look there's beauty. The leaves are dropping shining drips of water, and the earth smells good as it soaks it all up. Our shoes are caked with orange-coloured mud. I'm waiting for what he's going to say to me, and I'm starting to feel really, really hungry.

We go through a high white arch into a courtyard with an orange tree in the centre, and purple bougainvillea clambering riotously up the walls. It's exquisite. So is Juan walking across it, up to the vast, conquistador wooden door, lifting the iron ring and dropping it down. After a minute or so, the door's opened by a woman in an apron. I watch her put her arms round him and kiss him on both cheeks. They exchange some very fast Spanish I can't follow. Then he turns and gives me his heart-stopping smile, beckons me over. And we're led through the big hall to a type of glass conservatory at the back, full of busy lunch-time tables.

The woman directs us to a tiny table for two in the corner, half hidden behind a leafy pot plant on a stand. Juan asks for two beers, and she smiles at me and winks at him, and disappears. "She was always on at me about my love life, when I worked here," Juan says, as we take our seats. "Now I bet everyone in the kitchen will come out to look at you. . ."

*Love life*, I think, *he said love life!* "Oh, *great*," I groan, smiling.

"Don't worry. We'll ignore them."

"What about the gossip? You said you couldn't be seen going out with a girl until you'd introduced her to your parents." I go a bit red when I say that, because it's so pushy, like I'm saying I'm Juan's girl-friend, but luckily he's looking confused and hasn't noticed.

Then he bursts out laughing. "Oh, *that*. That was what I said, wasn't it, to make you come to *Las Estrellas* and not leave me on my own with Yaz? I made that up. You didn't think we were that old-fashioned, did you?"

"You *made it up*?"

"Sure I did. I wanted you to come. Why didn't you want to come? You didn't really feel ill, did you?"

A silent waiter appears at our side, with our beers. I seize mine, and drink. "I told you why. You and Yaz were getting on so well . . . cooking that food you'd brought over . . . I felt completely out of it. I was *so sure* you were going to get off with each other. . ."

"And the way you acted, I was so sure you didn't

have any time for me. A Spanish girl – she would've made a sign, I would've known."

"I didn't *want* you to know. Not if you preferred Yaz."

Juan shakes his head, and laughs, and we both take another deep pull of beer. I haven't eaten all day, only drunk that orange juice, and now the alcohol headily infiltrates my brain. Up till now, I've been shy of meeting Juan's eye, but now I lean across the table and look at him straight. I tour fast all over his face – from his eyes to his mouth to his hair falling across his beautiful strong eyebrows – and underneath the table my toes are scrunched up tight with excitement, and I know I'm breathing too fast.

"What you said in the room by the pool," he says, "you know, what you said about dancing with me. . ."

"I meant it. It was fantastic."

"When you stopped, you acted like you couldn't be bothered—"

"Self preservation. Anyway – stop going on about how *I* acted! What about you – drooling over Yaz, making me think you were keen on her. . ."

He looks down at the table. "OK, OK, I was an idiot. And a—"

"*Hijo de puta.*"

"Yes. It was easier to flirt with her, 'cos I didn't care what she thought. You . . . I didn't know how to be with you. I found it hard to even *look* at you. You blew my head up, Laura."

I laugh. "That's bad English."

He laughs back at me, says, "No, it's not. That's what you did."

I have no idea what we're eating, what we're drinking, but it's all wonderful. We talk and talk, and lose all track of time, like you do when what you're talking about is so important that time fails to have any meaning any more. When he's talking fast about real things, his English slips, and I laugh and he pretends to be annoyed and switches to very fast Spanish. He sounds so sexy, speaking Spanish, and his whole mouth moves in this different way, and I get absorbed watching it and can't follow what he's saying at all.

"Translate," I say. "You've got to translate."

"No," he says. "Too flattering."

We go over every hour, practically, since we first met, and how the whole big misunderstanding about liking each other grew, and how glad we are it's cleared up now. We talk about England, we talk about Spain. We tell each other our histories and our hopes, and our philosophy on life, and we agree on so much we keep laughing with sheer pleasure, with delight at finding that we've got more and more in common and what's different is exciting and exotic. Under the table, his foot covers my scrunched-up toes, his leg leans against mine. Then his hand comes over the table top, round my plate, takes hold of mine. We're leaning over the table so close the waiter can barely get the ice cream between us.

"D'you want coffee?" Juan asks.

"No," I say. And we go outside.

There's still a magic landscape out there – the sun's lower in the sky, and everything's charged with rich light. The air's so soft and fragrant from all the rain. Juan takes my hand, and we walk back to the fields, and as soon as we're in the cover of a little copse of trees, we stop, and he kind of wraps me up in his arms, and our breathing's coming out all shaky. Then I pull his head down to mine, and we kiss.

# Chapter 29

I t's dusk. We've stood together in the copse of trees until the sun has sunk right down behind the horizon. We've kissed so much my mouth is beginning to feel numb. Juan's kissing, I decide, is every bit as powerful and wonderful and creative as his dancing. We've talked some more too – we've started to skirt round how we're going to be together, how we're going to work it out, but we daren't say too much about that, not yet.

Then Juan suddenly swears, and pulls back his sleeve to check his watch. "It is Saturday, isn't it?" he says.

"Yeah. Saturday."

"Only . . . it's nearly seven . . . and weren't we going to. . ."

We look at each other, eyes huge, starting to giggle.

"Oh, shit!" I gasp. "Everyone's coming over! For a party! And you said you'd buy the meat for the barbecue!"

"And some beer. Oh, *joder*. And light the fire outside. Come on, we'd better run."

And he grabs my hand, and we race back over the field towards *Pino Alto*. I'd completely forgotten about this party planned for tonight. Probably because it was Yaz who told me all about it, and the way she described it, she and Juan had set it up together and . . . *shit*, Yaz!

"Juan – what about Yaz?"

"What about her?"

"What's she going to say when she sees me and you – you know – *together*?"

"Can't you just – tell her what happened this afternoon?"

"Oh, that'll really go down well, won't it! How's she gonna take it?"

He shrugs, all sullen, mutters, "I don't care how she takes it." Then he grins at me, and I think, *Oh, sod it. If Yaz wasn't so damn sure of herself she wouldn't be in this mess* – and we reach his car and jump in and he roars off, spraying burnt-orange mud. I love it. I love sitting beside him. All we're doing is heading into town to pick up some meat and some beer and it's like the best expedition in the world just because I'm beside him.

We park by the supermarket, fill a wire trolley at

top speed. And have our first lovers' row at the checkout, when Juan tries to bat away the fistful of euros I'm holding out to him. "Look, Juan – I'm earning too. Let me pay for half of this."

"No! I'll get money off the guys – those that don't bring their own drink. . ."

"Well, let me make a contribution, then. Let me pay my share."

"No, Laura, girls don't chip in for *beer*—"

"Spanish girls might not. But I'm not Spanish, or hadn't you noticed?"

At that he goes all googly on me, and he presses his forehead into mine and says, yes, yes he has noticed, and then I stick twenty euros in his shirt pocket, and he groans, says, "We haven't got *time* for this!" and leaves them there.

"What time's everyone supposed to be coming?" I ask.

He checks his watch and groans again. "Now. Now, Laura. Let's go."

We leg it back to the car, accelerate out of Ercos and up the track to *Pino Alto*. And as we park and scramble out, we're practically lasered down by two pairs of very hostile eyes. One Spanish, one English. Both female.

"Where the hell have you been?" demands Yaz. "There's already six people here, and nothing's ready. . ."

"Juan!" interrupts the Spanish girl explosively.

"You promised me a lift – I had to come on Paco's *bike*!"

Juan and I mouth vague apologies, then take shelter by diving into the boot of the car and pulling out boxes of beer cans. "That's Ana," hisses Juan. "She gets possessive."

"Why?" I hiss back.

"She'd like to be serious with me."

"Oh *God*, not another one. So now there's going to be two of them wanting to murder me."

"At least two," smirks Juan, and we laugh and carry the boxes into the kitchen, but I feel this niggle of anxiety, this sudden stab of fear that loads of girls are after him and I'm not good enough for him, how can I be, he's so special and gorgeous and I'm . . . well, I'm *not*.

The feeling disappears the minute we're inside the kitchen, though. Juan shoves the door shut with his foot, puts his beer down next to mine on the counter, and wraps his arms round me. "Let's get out of here," he says. "Let's just get back in the car, and drive off."

"We can't," I laugh. "You were the one who asked everyone. You're the host."

"I don't want to be the host. I want to go away with you and find a dark bar, and sit *really* close to you, and then maybe we can dance again, and this time maybe you'll act like you *like* it. . ."

I laugh. My heart's pounding just with the

thought of this. In fact, I think my heart's forgotten how to beat normally. "I'd love that," I say. "But everyone'll be so pissed off with us if we just clear off, and Yaz will have a *fit*. . ."

The door's suddenly shoved open; we jump apart with the noise. And there's Yaz herself in the doorway, glaring at us suspiciously.

"Hi," begins Juan. "We were just talking about you. . ."

I kick him, hard, out of sight on the side of his shoe. "Yeah," I go, "we were saying – maybe you could make the salad. Because you make *great* salads."

Half an hour later, Juan's digging a shallow pit for the barbecue on a bit of wasteland behind the house and I'm unwrapping the meat in the kitchen. Yaz is washing lettuce and simmering with suspicion, but I'm avoiding her questions. I've made my mind up that there is absolutely no way I'm coming clean about Juan tonight – not with a party going on. I'll tell her – calmly and privately – tomorrow.

"I don't know what kind of night this is going to be," she says, moodily. "These Spanish – they're dead repressed, you know."

"Repressed?" I squeak.

"Yeah – *repressed*. I mean – they're *years* behind our culture. They're still all in awe of what their parents will say, or the priest, or something."

"They don't dance like they're repressed."

"Oh, *that*!" she scoffs. "That's just a substitute."

I don't answer. Her voice is bitter and mean and I know exactly where it's coming from. I grind a last bit of pepper over the steaks, then I say, "Right – these are ready to cook. I'm going to see how the fire's doing." And I make my escape.

I go behind the house, and see wraiths of smoke climbing out of the fire pit. "Hey!" I call out. "Pyromaniac!"

Juan looks up, smiling, and comes towards me. "Pyro *what*?"

"Someone who loves fires."

"I *love* fires," he says, all mock Spanish passion, and gets hold of me.

I push him back. I absolutely don't want to do that, but I do.

"What's the matter?" he asks, stricken.

"Yaz is the matter. I really, *really* don't feel we can just – *present* her with what's happened. I mean, just let her walk in on us together, or . . . or anything."

"Is that why you kicked me so hard in the kitchen?"

"*Aww.* It wasn't that hard, was it?"

"Yes. You nearly broke my foot."

"Sorry. But you saw her face. You know how much she's been after you."

"Oh, *God*. I'll go and talk to her."

"No – I will. I'll – I'll just *tell* her what's happened between us. That's the kindest way. I'll explain."

"Go on then. Go and tell her."

"What – *now*? Just as everyone's arriving? Ever heard of that old song, *It's my party and I'll cry if I want to?*"

Juan shakes his head, laughs. I feel weird, talking about protecting Yaz like this. She's never needed protecting before, not from my success anyway. I've usually had to protect myself from hers. That's not the only reason I'm reluctant to tell her, though. A bit of me is seriously scared of her reaction. Just the way she was looking at me in the kitchen gave me the chills – I mean, if she feels *anything like* as much about Juan as *I* feel about him. . . "No," I go on, "I can't tell her now. I'll tell her tomorrow, when we can talk privately and everything."

"I s'pose you're right. It's just going to be hard, acting all cool and ordinary to you after what happened this afternoon. . ." he trails off, grinning, and I suddenly get an attack of all-out lust for him, standing there so completely fantastic and looking me straight in the eye and – *incredibly* – seeming to want me as much as I want him. It's so fierce and total I get dizzy with it. A little moan escapes my mouth.

"What?" says Juan.

"I said – I feel the same as you. I'll tell her tomorrow. I promise." And I walk unsteadily back to the kitchen.

# Chapter 30

Over the next twenty minutes about two dozen people arrive and suddenly the party's *on*. It's a warm evening, and the sky – having emptied all its rain out in that monsoon downpour earlier – looks clear, so we risk passing the speakers from the stereo out through the windows and standing them on the terrace. Then we turn the music up *loud*, on account of the nearest neighbours being nearly half a mile away. Loads of people bring beer, wine, or extra food. Yaz and I carry plates and salads out and put them on the terrace table, and the Spanish girls take over. They've brought olives and ham and wonderful crusty-looking loaves of bread, and they spread them across the table in a feast.

Gradually, everyone is drawn round the corner to the fire-pit. It's the smell of grilling meat, or the lure of the fire, or maybe the presence of Juan, I'm not sure which. All I know is he's got a whole crowd round him and they're all laughing and swapping words, and I can't get near.

Yaz can't get near either. She's standing on the outskirts of the group, looking all on edge and watching Juan like a hawk. I get this pang for her, I think, *He shouldn't've led her on, he shouldn't've kissed her.* Then I remember the way she cut me out when he first arrived, and I harden my heart again.

The meat's sizzling and spitting deliciously on the grid. Juan calls for plates, starts forking steaks and chicken on to them. Everyone's salivating with the look and the smell of the meat; as soon as they've grabbed a share, they surge back to the terrace and make for the food laid out on the table and the beer stacked up against the house.

I'm on my second beer. I feel like getting pissed, to be honest. I feel like getting out of my skull, 'cos I can't deal with this . . . *intensity* I'm feeling. I can't stop looking at Juan. I'm starting to think – *Did it really happen?* I need to touch him, be held by him.

Juan dishes out the last few steaks, and we all leave the fire and make our way back to the terrace. And Juan and I separate, sit far apart. Yaz picks up a bowl of salad, sails over to Juan and starts scooping some on to his plate; then she sits down next to him and starts talking at him. Her face gets closer and closer to his.

"Want another beer?" asks a boy standing near me.

"Yes please," I sigh, and I finish off my second bottle.

Some of the Spanish girls have gone all domesticated, picking up plates and transferring them to the kitchen. I don't help them out. A few others have started dancing, in that Latino way that's brilliant or showing off, I can't quite decide. I don't join in.

And then Juan stands up and heads over towards me. He puts his empty plate on top of mine, sits down beside me. And it's like I'm back next to the fire again. He puts his hand in his pocket, pulls out a thin wad of euros, takes hold of my hand, puts them into it, and folds my fingers round it. "I got given loads of money for the meat," he says. "Loads of people paid up. Now take your money back, or I'll make a scene."

I laugh. "What sort of scene?"

"Well, put it this way. I'll make it clear to Yaz it's you I'm interested in, not her."

I can feel myself going red. I'm glad it's dark. Then the music from the stereo changes, and something fast and brilliant comes on. Loads more people are standing up and dancing, the boys finally joining the girls. "Come on," says Juan. "Dance with me. Yaz won't notice."

"Yes, she will."

"No. Act indifferent, like you did before. After all, you fooled me."

I laugh. Right now I want to dance with him so much I don't care if she does notice. I stand up, and we weave our way to the edge of the terrace, and start to move.

It would be fake, to keep a big distance between us. All the dancers are close up. It would be fake not to take his hand when he's showing me this flamenco step. And I can't help it when I stumble and he puts his arms round me to hold me up, can I?

He is *so gorgeous*. Now I know he likes me too, I'm not afraid to let the full extent of his sheer gorgeousness infiltrate my brain and my body, and it's so much I almost can't take it.

I make myself look away from him and think – *Blimey, I'm still on planet earth. There are other people here*. Then I look back at him again.

Damn Yaz. *Damn* her. I wish we didn't have to pretend there was nothing going on. I wish we could just *be*. I want another of those amazing interactive kisses, I want to press myself right into his chest and feel him up against me and smell that lovely, wood-smokey, citrusy male scent he has, and. . .

Suddenly, *horribly*, someone's pushing between us. It's Ana. I want to hit her. She launches herself at Juan, squawks, "You owe me at least five dances! As punishment for not picking me up in your car."

Juan's face falls. He wants to tell her to piss off, I know he does. But Yaz is just over there, dancing in a group, watching us, and I panic and before Juan can say a thing, I squeak, "See you later!" and flee the scene.

I spend the next ten minutes wandering about the kitchen, queuing for the bathroom. When I get inside I dreamily redo my make-up, imagining Juan's face in the mirror next to mine, till someone hammers on the door, then I go outside again. The party's spread out; there are still people dancing on the terrace, but now loads are lounging round the table, and a few couples can be seen drifting off into the olive trees. It's a great party – varied, buzzing. And I'd really be enjoying it if I could just be with Juan.

I wander round the corner, towards the fire pit. Amazingly, the heat from the fire and the few hours of afternoon sunshine have dried the earth enough to sit on, and now people are sitting round like it's a campfire, chatting and throwing bits of wood into the flames. I can't see Juan, though. He wasn't on the terrace, either. He must've escaped from Ana. Where is he?

I go back to the house, join a group making a lot of noise around the doorway to the kitchen. Nuria tries her English out on me again, asks me how I like Spanish parties, and I'm saying (in English) that I like them a lot when someone knocks into me, slams me with a shoulder, spilling my beer. Irritated, I look up, and there's Juan's back-view, walking purposefully away, not looking back, along the terrace towards the swimming pool, and without a second's hesitation, I follow him.

# Chapter 31

The door to the old changing-room by the side of the swimming pool is standing ajar. I slide into it, heart thumping, and Juan's there, slipping his arms round my waist, pulling me in close.

I sort of sigh out hello, then I whisper, "I can't see a thing. You could be a mass murderer for all I know."

Which is insane because I know it's him. Every one of my senses tells me it's him.

His mouth lands on mine. I push the door shut behind me, and it gets even darker, but we don't need to see. I reach up and wind my arms round his neck.

"This is all so stupid," he breathes, between kisses. "Acting like – *fugitivos*."

"We are fugitives," I murmur. "It's quite fun. *Romantic*."

"Yes. It's romantic. But I want to be out there *with*

*you.* I wanted to tell Ana – go away. *This* is my girl-friend."

I can't speak, I'm too full of what he's just said. I slide my hands up his neck, into his hair, pull his head down to mine again, and we kiss, we kiss for ages, like we're learning new things about each other all the time.

After a while we just hold each other. "I like it in here," I say. "I like this room."

My eyes have got used to the dark. There's a sliver of moonlight coming in through the shutters over the window on the far wall, and it's falling across our faces and our hands as we hold each other.

"Look," he says, nodding towards the old wooden sunbed in the middle of the floor. "Remember?"

"God," I murmur, "that seems like—"

"– *years* ago. I know."

And yet it was only hours ago that were sitting there side by side, looking out at the rain and begin-ning to mumble out our feelings for each other. Juan sits and pulls me down beside him. His hand traces up from my neck, to my mouth. "You're so lovely," he says. "You're so different."

"*Different?*"

He laughs. "To the girls here. You're tall, and . . . and *elegant*, and you have this wonderful blonde hair. . ."

"It's mousey."

"With the sun, it'll be blonde. And it's not just the way you look. It's you. You're *different*."

He sighs, smiles. And it dawns on me that I, Laura Harvey, with my pale, freckled London face and long, gangly legs, am every bit as exotic and unknown and therefore incredibly desirable as he is exotic and desirable to me. And that kind of fills me full of power, and surety, and I pull him close again, and we kiss again. His hand goes back to my neck, lower; the top button of my shirt comes undone. I can sense rather than see him looking at me, waiting for my response. Very slowly, deliberately, I start to undo the rest of my buttons, one by one.

He's subtle though. He slides his hands round my back, inside my shirt, and this wonderful, voluptuous groan escapes his mouth, and he says, "Your skin is beautiful, it's *soft*. . ."

I push him back, slowly, slowly, on to the sun bed, so we're lying together, side by side. And his hand moves back, and on to my breasts, and we kiss harder, legs entwining, rocking on the hard narrow sunbed, and I don't ever remember feeling as turned on as this before, and. . .

. . .and then my stupid mind starts up. I start wondering what he's feeling, what he's used to, what he expects – and I remember all the stuff I've heard about Spanish boys thinking English girls are easy – and I can't help it, I kind of freeze up.

"Laura – what's wrong?"

"Nothing." I put a hand up to his mouth. "I just—"

"Just what?"

"Oh, God. I just started wondering what you were thinking of me, that's all."

"I've told you – I think you're fantastic. . ."

"No, not that. You know – easy. For letting you . . . for being . . . I thought you might think I was a bit of a slag, that's all."

"Laura, don't – of course I don't." His face is so full of concern that I smile, then he says, "What exactly is a slag, anyway?" and we both laugh.

"*Prostituta*," I mumble, and he shakes me, just once.

"No! How can you say that?"

"Just – you know. Spain. Catholic upbringing and – and everything. I mean – I don't know what the score is here. I don't even know if you can buy condoms!"

"Yes," he laughs. "Yes, you can. Although I don't exactly carry them around with me."

"So are you?"

"Am I what?"

"A Catholic?"

"Well . . . only in so much as everyone is, here. Not practising, despite the best efforts of my mother. She goes crazy 'cos she can't get me to church."

"And your dad. . .?"

"He just bumbles along, going through the motions. Like a lot of men. And he's half American, anyway, so—"

"Oh yes – your American grandad!"

"Did I tell you about him?"

I settle down beside him again, and say, "Yes. The day we first met. I remembered it 'cos I thought it explained why you're so tall. For a Spanish guy."

He laughs. "My grandad's very tall. He was a basketball champ. And in his old age he's become an atheist, to my mother's horror. I love him. I love the way his mind works."

"I'd like to meet him."

"You will." He starts to stroke my hair, back from my face. "Laura?"

"Yes?"

"I'm not lying here next to you thinking, 'My God, aren't English girls slags.' I'm lying here wanting to make love to you. So much."

When he says that, wham, so direct, it's like I'm burning up, like I've got this burning cylinder inside me, right from my throat to my groin, and it hits me I'd sleep with him now, tonight, I would, I would, I want to. After what's happened between us, it's right, it's inevitable.

"Are you upset still?" he asks.

"No," I whisper.

"Good. 'Cos I'm not trying to rush anything, Laura. We don't have to, do we? We've got time."

We stay in the swimming-pool room for a long while after that, kissing, wrapped round each other, going close to the edge but not over. Outside, the party's getting louder and rowdier and nearer. It sounds like people are playing football in the huge empty pool, and it begins to feel like they might burst through the door at any minute and join us. So we stand up, and smooth down our clothes, and then I slip through the door and Juan follows me.

"How long were we in there?" I hiss, as we walk round the corner of the house.

"Dunno. Hours?" He checks his watch. "It's two in the morning!"

"People are looking at us."

"So let them look. And tomorrow – you promise to tell Yaz we're together. And then we can be *out*, can't we?" He grins at me. "I'm going round the back, stamp out the fire. It's time everyone went home. I want tomorrow to come."

I don't know how he does it, but soon after that people start to shift, and leave, and two helpful boys start picking up beer cans and putting them in a bin bag. Juan drives off, waving, with a car crammed full of Spanish girls but I feel so great I don't feel so much as a flicker of jealousy. I do a bit of clearing up in the kitchen, then I head off for bed.

There's no sign of Yaz. She must be sulking, or asleep – one or the other. Too bad. I'll face all that tomorrow.

I'm too restless to sleep though – too restless to

even get into bed. I pace the room and think about what we were on the edge of tonight. It's not like I'm a virgin or anything. Not like it's such a major big step. And the two guys I slept with before – I felt *nothing* for them compared to what I'm feeling for Juan right now. Absolutely *nothing*. Not even with Ryan – the first one who treated me like dirt.

So there's no reason not to sleep with him. None.

I wander to the window, look out. Everything that happened between us today – it's too fantastic. Too fantastic to trust. That's what's getting me, I know it. I feel like – tomorrow, it'll change, it'll dissolve, I'll wake up from this dream I'm in. I want to go right to the end now, I want it all, while I can, before it all dissolves and disappears. . .

I look out at the moon silvering the olive trees. I see Juan's face; hear him saying, "I'm not trying to rush anything, Laura. We don't have to, do we?" And I sigh, and laugh, and get into bed alone.

And it hardly seems I've been asleep for five minutes before I'm woken up again. The door cracks open and Yaz stalks into the room, hissing and mean, saying, "OK, Laura, let's have this out *now*!"

# Chapter 32

"What?" I mumble. "What you talking about?" I'm pretending to be half asleep but I'm *wide* awake. And I'm *scared*. She's always scared me, when she gets like this. Ever since we were ten years old. When prowling round the edge of everything she says is the threat of her not being my friend any more.

"You know *bloody* well what I'm talking about!" she shrieks. "I know where you were tonight – holed up in that *shed* with Juan. *Jesus*, Laura, I do not *believe* you! I thought we were mates! I can't *believe* you'd do this to me – *or* yourself! I mean – *God*. Have you got *no* self-respect or *what*?"

There's a break in the words slashing round me. "Yaz, calm down," I say, breathing shakily. My strongest instinct is to placate her. "What exactly d'you think has been going *on*?"

"Oh, *shit*, Laura, don't pull that snotty, fake-innocent crap with me! I overheard two of the boys talking – they were laughing over you and Juan, the way you'd sloped off together into the shed. . ."

"It isn't a *shed*."

"What fucking difference does that make? It could be the Taj Mahal for all I care. You *bitch*!" She spits that out viciously, like a slap, and I wince, but she doesn't break her stride. "My Spanish might not be that good but I could make out what they were saying all right! From all the *leering* and fist signs! And then I saw you walk round the side of the building together, and him go back to the fire. How d'you feel about yourself, eh, *Laura*? How good did it feel to have a quick shag and then just watch him walk away? Not even a 'Thanks, that was great'?"

I watch her silently. Her face is all screwed up, full of hate. Hateful.

"Maybe it wasn't great, eh? Maybe it was a complete fucking non-event? *Jesus.* It must be awful to be useless in bed *and* a slag. I'd feel sorry for you being *used* like that, if I didn't think you were such a complete bitch going off with him in the first place! You *knew* what he and I had together! You *knew* how much I liked him! And yet you. . . How d'you think I'm going to feel about him *now*, eh? It's so . . . *cheap* and nasty, it's not true! What did you do – manoeuvre it so you went off to get the stuff for tonight and let him know you were up for anything? Were you really that *desperate*? Or was it that he didn't look at you so you had to louse it up for *me*?"

She shudders to a stop, glares at me like Medusa zapping me into stone. And inside, I *am* stone. I'm so stunned and hurt by what she's said, it's like I stop feeling anything. At the edge of my mind a voice is saying, *This can't be put right. Even when you tell her what happened, it won't be put right.* And then I think I'll just kick her out of my room – not bother to explain, she's not worth it. But I don't. Something in me wants to trap her, show her up, expose the way her mind works.

"So it's me you blame, is it?" I say. "Not him."

"You're my friend!" she screeches. "Or *were*. And he's a guy. God knows how easy you made yourself, but he's only a guy, and if someone's on a plate. . ."

"I love your take on relationships between the sexes, Yaz. It's all the girl's fault 'cos the guy can't say no."

"Oh, *don't* give me that sneery, ironic crap, Laura! Not after what you've done! Jesus! I still don't believe it!"

"Good. 'Cos it didn't happen."

"What?"

"I didn't shag him."

"Oh, great. So you just went in the shed for a quick grope, did you? You think *that's* all right?"

I take in a deep breath, then I say, "No. We went into the *shed* because we wanted to be alone. We made love. Not all the way, but that wasn't the point. We made the best love I've ever made in my life."

"Oh, *Laura*, don't be so *pathetic*—"

I take another deep breath and say, "This morning he told me he had a problem. With you. He said you liked him more than he liked you, but you'd kissed a couple of times and he was afraid he'd led you on. And then . . . he said how much he liked me. And since I've been crazy about him from the moment I first saw him, it . . . it kind of went from there."

She's looking at me, ashen. She looks like all the blood has just drained from her face. "You're lying," she croaks.

"I'm not. We went out for lunch, and we talked, and we got the stuff for the party. And the reason we didn't act like we were together – the reason we *sneaked off*, as you saw it – was 'cos I didn't want to hurt *you*. I didn't want you to just see us together. I wanted to be able to tell you, talk to you."

There's a long, long, silence. Then she says, again, "You *bitch*."

"*What?*"

"You *knew* how much I liked him!"

"What are you saying, Yaz? That I should've kept away from him, whatever he thought about me, or about *you*, just 'cos you liked him?"

"If you were a real friend—"

"Oh, *Jesus*, Yaz! What about you being a friend to me? We *both* liked him! Only we didn't talk about it, did we, 'cos we don't actually talk about anything any more—"

"*You knew how much I liked him!*"

"Well you'd've known how much *I* liked him if I'd made it as obvious as you! You honed in on him like a . . . like a heat-seeking missile! I liked him too, but I don't suppose you even noticed that! I didn't get a look in – or a *word* in – with you around, did I?"

"God, Laura, don't blame me 'cos you've got a lousy pulling technique! It's not *my* fault you're so limp!"

There's a silence. Then she realizes the total irony of what she's just said, bursts into tears and runs out of the room.

I wrestle with myself for maybe ten minutes. I think about how evil and vicious she was, the way she yelled at me, the way she thought the worst of me, the way she acted like Juan was a piece of her property, the way she thought the only way I could get Juan to spend time with me was by offering to lay him, straight off. Then I remember how awful I felt when I was sure Juan had chosen her, not me. And the realization floods over me that he *has* chosen me. It's hard not to be kind with that sort of knowledge. I head off for the kitchen.

When I've made two mugs of tea, I knock at her door. "*Fuck off!*" she snarls.

"OK," I say.

And I do.

# Chapter 33

When I wake up on Sunday morning, half of me is dancing with delight because of Juan, half of me is staggering under this horrible hurt weight because of Yaz.

I get up and pad barefoot into the bathroom. I wish Juan was here now. It's wretched being alone in the house with someone I've fallen out with so ferociously. In my head I rerun how Yaz was last night, how absolutely she seemed to blame me and hate me. Maybe she'll have calmed down overnight and be ready to talk, apologize even, but somehow I doubt it.

I clean my teeth, then I look at my face in the mirror. And it's weird because, for once, I really like my reflection. Pale skin, freckles, mousy hair, the lot. My nose and mouth, which usually look too big for the rest of me, just look positive, generous. And my eyes look wonderful. Even without a scrap of make-up, they look deep and wonderful. So it's true, then, I think. Falling for someone is good for your looks. Being liked back helps, too. Or maybe it just changes the way you see yourself. Whatever, it's good.

I wander into the kitchen, put the kettle on. And find myself just staring out of the window at the wrought-iron gates, left half open after the last guest had gone early this morning. I'm longing for Juan to come through them. He didn't say anything last night, about when he'd come back. I just kind of assumed he'd turn up.

Suppose he's had second thoughts? Suppose he regrets it all?

Suppose he's had a car crash on the way here?

*Stop it*, I tell myself. You always do this when things are good – you always imagine them crashing down. Have some toast, then go and get dressed and. . .

A motorbike interrupts my thoughts. It comes careening through the gates, roars to a stop. And somehow I know it's Juan even before the rider pulls his helmet off. I watch his lovely, long, rangy legs swing off the bike and then I rush to the door to meet him. It's only when I'm outside that I remember I'm wearing pale-blue shorty cotton pyjamas.

"Laura!" he says, grinning.

"Hi! Sorry, I was just getting up and. . ."

"What are you apologizing for? You look sensational."

I laugh, pleased, embarrassed. "What's with the bike?"

"It's my cousin's. We swap about."

"So he's got the car today?"

"Yes."

"Right."

And with that, we run out of jerky conversation. And then he steps forward, and I make a kind of rush, and we're colliding, arms wrapping each other up, my mouth slamming into his neck, his mouth coming down. "Oh, God," he breathes, "I thought you might have changed . . . I thought you might have changed your mind. . ."

"I thought so too. Not me, *you* – I thought you might not turn up, I thought you might regret what you said –"

He hugs me so hard I can't speak. We kiss again, and it's just as amazing as the first time in the copse of trees, just as passionate as last night in the swimming pool room. In fact it's better because it's the next day – it's the next day, and I've woken up and it's still *real*.

"Laura?"

"Mmmm?"

"I brought you some breakfast." He starts to walk over to his bike, and as I'm still wedged deliciously under his arm, I go too.

He pulls a striped patisserie bag out of the bike's pannier. "Croissants!" he says proudly. "Almond croissants, and chocolate croissants."

"Oh, *wonderful*."

"Let's make some juice, make some coffee. We can eat out here – the sun's warm already."

"Sure." We go into the kitchen, start gathering plates, mugs. "Keep the noise down," I mutter, as he starts slicing oranges for the juicer. "Don't wake Yaz."

He looks at me. "Have you told her, Laura?"

"Yes," I groan. "I'll tell you when we're outside."

Soon we're sitting at the table on the terrace with the smell of coffee and jasmine and the sun on our faces. The croissants are so fresh, so good, we don't talk for a moment, we just eat, eyes on each other. "*No* English guy would do this," I mumble, mouth full. "Go to the trouble to bring breakfast, I mean. He'd see it as—" I stop. I don't want to offend him.

"As what?"

"Oh, as weak, girly. You know."

"I just wanted to do something nice for you!"

"Oh Juan – it *was* nice! It's lovely!"

"Are you saying English boys are so scared of being thought feminine they don't do nice things?"

"Well. . ."

"They must have a lot of doubt. About being *men*." He gives me this macho, mocking, sexy look, eyebrows all crooked, and he looks so gorgeous I laugh and lean over and kiss him, and he hooks his arm round my neck and kisses me back.

"Oh, Laura," he murmurs. "Have some more coffee, and tell me about Yaz."

"Oh, *God*."

"You told her?"

"I told her, all right. Just after she'd *burst* into my room and woken me up."

"*Joder*."

"Yeah. She'd seen us go off together. She ranted on and *on* – she thinks I've totally betrayed her, and I'm a loser *and* a slag who has to sleep with guys to get them to even notice her."

"Nice," murmurs Juan.

"She was *so livid*. It makes my stomach churn just to think back on it."

Juan turns in his seat, looks nervously over at Yaz's bedroom window like she might suddenly come flying through it and attack us both. "I should've been straight with her," he says. "It's my fault."

"She'd still blame me. Even when I told her everything she still blamed *me*."

Juan shrugs, drains his coffee mug. "D'you want to go out somewhere for the day? That's why I brought the bike."

"I'd love to. But I can't just leave her, can I? Not here all on her own. Not with all this all blown up."

"Don't you think you and I are the last people she'd want to see today?"

"Yes. But—"

"I know what I'll do. I'll phone Nuria – she loves any chance to practise her English, and she gets on

OK with Yaz. And I can explain everything to her. She's a real friend."

"As opposed to jealous prospective girlfriend?"

"Laura! What are you saying?"

"Oh, come on – don't act all innocent. What about Ana last night? What about the girls who drag you off to dance at every club we go into?"

"I dance well, that's all."

"Stop *smirking* like that, Juan – you love it, don't you?"

"OK, so some of the girls here like me. I bet back in England you have boys after you, phoning you up. . ."

"God – *do* I? They queue up at the door, Juan. They lie in wait for me. Last Valentine's Day – I had my own van from the post office, just to cope with all the cards."

Juan laughs, then he suddenly gets hold of my hand across the table, all serious. "Is there someone?"

"What?"

"Is there someone at home? In England? Have you got a boyfriend there?"

"No! And if I had, he would have been ditched as from yesterday. What – you think I'd two-time, or something?"

Juan picks up my hand, presses his mouth into my palm. "No. Just checking."

"Smoothy," I laugh.

"It's great you don't play games," he says. "I love it that you're honest and don't play games."

"You mustn't either."

"I won't. I couldn't, with you. Now – I'm going to phone Nuria. Who is just a *friend*. I'll get her to call round, take Yaz out for some lunch or something. What about that?"

I look at him. I look right into his dark, sloe-shaped eyes and suddenly all I want to do is get on the back of his bike and take off with him.

"OK," I say. "You phone, I'll get some clothes on." And I hurry back to my room.

Within fifteen minutes, it's all sorted and we're on the road and I feel free and fantastic. I've got jeans on and one of my favourite sleeveless tops and I reckon I look careless and sexy, even despite the helmet Juan's made me wear. All I've got in my tiny backpack is a sweatshirt, a brush, a bit of make-up and some money. As we roar along the country roads I press myself into Juan's back, loving the smell of him, loving the way his muscles move as he manoeuvres the bike.

"Where are we going?" I shout above the bike's engine.

He twists back to me; my eyes fix on his mouth. "Jerez," he says.

"Great!"

"It won't exactly be thrilling. . ."

"Yes, it will!" I reply.

# Chapter 34

Juan locks up the bike somewhere in Jerez, and stows the helmets safely in the pannier. "Sunday in Spain is not exciting," he says apologetically, as he takes my hand. "Church . . . sleep . . . long slow meals. . . Sunday lunch is big here. In fact my mother is mad with curiosity over why I won't be at home for lunch."

"Why didn't you just tell her where you were going?"

"We have an agreement. About privacy. And her not interfering." He says this casually, but I catch the sense that Juan has fought long and hard to win that agreement.

We walk the streets towards the centre, past tall, grand buildings painted ochre and pale terracotta. I love the feel of our hands twined up together, the way we fall straight away into a rhythm walking. We stop in front of some seriously fancy iron-lace gates, and stare through at the lush, plant-filled courtyard behind. "Like a cage in a fairy tale," I whisper. "I *love* these courtyards."

The sun moves, bounces off the far wall, casting strong shadows. Juan points up at wide blinds rolled back against the roof. "Look – shade for the summer."

I imagine lying alongside Juan in the shady court-yard, with the sun beating down on the blinds up above. "Oh, I want it to be *hot*!" I sigh. "When will it be?"

"Soon enough," he says. "Then I bet you'll want it to be cool again."

"Never! I love the heat."

"Well, I think the rain's over. The heat's on its way."

We walk on, arms round each other. I gaze at lurid religious plaques nailed to the walls, at yucca plants spiking through the bars of balconies above us. The sheer exoticism of Spain soaks into me, like it did in Seville, only it's indescribably better than Seville because Juan's here next to me. Then a church bell starts to ring, cracked and flat. I laugh, say, "You should hear English bells!"

"Why – are they different?"

"God, yes! They're . . . *musical*. Kind of big and rich and full-throated. It's 'cos we've got a wet climate, it keeps them good. Although thinking about it, I'd go for your crap bells and some sun."

Juan grins down at me. "I really want to go to your country. And not just to hear your bells."

I can't answer – my throat's suddenly seized. I think, *Yes, my country, your country . . . miles and miles apart. Supposing this miracle lasts and we stay together over the summer, what happens when autumn comes and I have to go back home and go to uni?*

*Don't think about it. Don't think about the future, think about the now.*

"Are you hungry?" asks Juan.

"Starting to be."

"There's a square up here, with loads of little restaurants round it – they set tables out in the square. Let's sit down for a while. Have a drink. Order some food."

"Perfect," I sigh.

Jerez is full of people promenading. Some of them look overdressed; some of them look fed up. It makes me want to laugh. How can they be fed up in this beautiful city, with its soft air, its bursts of hot sun? It's bliss, just walking with Juan. It's all I want.

We reach the square; the tables are already filling up, but Juan finds us a good one near two sweet-smelling orange trees. He leans towards me, asks, "Are you bored?"

"Are you kidding?"

He grins. "It's just – the same old Sunday stuff. After church, before lunch. It's . . . *dull*."

"So you're saying *you're* bored?"

He laughs, takes my hand across the table. "No. Of course not. I just think – after London, this must be pretty tame."

"Oh, Juan! It's beautiful here! London – I reckon you'd hate it, after a while. It's so *grey*. The light there – it really is dull and grey most of the time."

"Light?" he shrugs. "As long as there's enough light to see with. . ."

"Yes, but – it's not alive, like it is here. It makes you feel dead."

"All I hear about London is how great it is, how exciting – you have the best clubs, fantastic music. . ."

"It can get nasty, though. At night."

"So there's a bit of risk – so what? You know, what I really like is – you could just get *lost* there. You could be anonymous. You find your own way, find out who you really are – no one breathing down your neck, telling you who to be. In Ercos – everyone knows me. Everyone. It smothers me."

I watch the way his face changes as he talks. I'm burning up with wanting to touch him, to kiss him. "You seem pretty free to me," I say.

"Do I? That's good. I'm not though. Not free enough."

We order our drinks, ask for the menu. Two little kids are running in and out of the tables calling to each other, playing some chase game. No one's tutting, no one's glaring, so it's not a problem, not like it would be in England, any more than the sparrows are, hoping for crumbs. "There is freedom here," I say. "It's just a different sort."

I tell him all about London over lunch, all about my plans for the future. And he talks too. He has no plans, just a burning desire to shake off his folks' wishes that he stay and work in the family businesses of building and olive farming. I love listening to him, I love his energy and determination. We talk and talk; we're the last people to leave the tables on the square.

It's *siesta* time when we wander back to the bike, and on upstairs windows everywhere the shutters have been closed. The shutters look mysterious, sexy – they make you wonder what might be going on behind them.

"Do you have a *siesta*?" I ask.

"Only in the heat," he answers. I know he's looking up at the shutters, thinking the same thoughts as me, wishing it was the two of us up in a room somewhere.

We get back to *Pino Alto* at about five o'clock. The front door is locked, which makes me think with relief that Yaz is still out with Nuria. I go and knock on her bedroom door to make sure; no answer. Juan comes up behind me, puts his arms round my waist. "Which is your room?" he asks.

Without a word, I lead him past the bathroom,

into my square bedroom with its two single beds. "I was sharing this with Yaz," I say, "but when Tom and Ruth left, she moved into their bedroom. . ." I know she was hoping Juan would be joining her in that big double bed. And here he is instead, standing at the foot of my narrow one.

I put my arms round his neck, and we start kissing. We kind of sway, fold down on to the bed together. In my head I'm saying, *I want to make love with you. I want to, now*, but I don't say anything out loud. I pull him down on top of me, loving his weight, loving kissing like that.

After a while he slides off me, props himself on one elbow beside me, starts stroking my neck, shoulders, breasts. He slides his hand under my top, and between us we pull it off and I drop it off the edge of the bed. I unbutton his shirt, slide it off him. He's beautiful. Strong, and brown. "You work out, don't you?" I ask. "You must do."

"No I don't! This is from *real* work."

I start kissing him, all over his chest. He unhooks my bra and I shuck it off. And we stay like that, facing each other, half dressed, stroking and loving each other's skin, each other's faces, until somehow I get lost in it, and it's enough, it's all I want to do, and I remember him saying *we don't have to rush* and I feel so happy as I fall asleep against his shoulder.

# Chapter 35

It's darker in my room when Juan shakes me awake. "I ought to go, Laura. Ought to have a bit of Sunday at home, or they'll get on at me."

I laugh. "'Get on at me' eh? Your English idioms are coming on."

"And *you're* getting more Spanish. You had a wonderful *siesta*."

"Oh, God – did I snore?"

"No. You snuffled a bit. You were lovely."

"Weren't you asleep?"

"I dozed, a bit. I liked just being here, next to you."

"Don't go, Juan."

"I've got to," he sighs. Then he kisses me, swings his legs off the bed, and picks up his shirt. "There's a big building job starting tomorrow. My uncle's coming round tonight to run through it with us."

I can feel my face fall. "Does that mean you won't be coming here to do the pool?"

"Not for a week or so. It's nearly done though. . ."

"Look, I wasn't worried about how much grouting you've got left to do! I just want to see you!"

He laughs, sits back down on the bed and hugs me. "I know. But you work tomorrow morning, don't you?"

"God, yes. Monday. I'd forgotten."

"What time do you get off?"

"Two o'clock."

"Perfect. Will you do something for me?"

"What?"

"Will you come to my niece's birthday party?"

"You've got a *niece*? How old is she?"

"She'll be five. She's my oldest sister's kid. Will you come?"

My stomach kind of dissolves with nerves at the thought. "This is a big family affair, is it?"

"Family, friends . . . but it'll be relaxed, what's the phrase – *low key* – I promise. They've got a clown coming."

"Why d'you want *me* to come, Juan?"

He takes in a breath. "We're going to be spending lots of time together, aren't we? You and me?"

I snuggle deeper into his arms. "Hope so."

"Well, I want my people to meet you, then they can't say they don't know what I'm doing, who I'm with. . ."

"Juan, I'm honoured. I'm also terrified. You mean they've got to vet me?"

"No! It's just – it's like a mark of respect, to introduce you. Then I can say – you've met her. Then they'll get off my back."

I squeeze him hard and gulp, "OK."

"Pick you up here at four? It won't be for long . . . just an hour or so. And after, we can go out. I'll take you out."

"Deal. I'm still scared, though."

"You'll be fine," he says. "They'll love you."

Out on the terrace, kissing goodbye, we both find our eyes straying to Yaz's window. "You didn't hear her come in, did you?" I whisper. "When I was asleep?"

"No. Nothing."

"I suppose there is *just* the possibility that she's been holed up in there all along. . ."

"Laura, you're getting yourself spooked. I'll phone Nuria when I get home – check she's with Yaz. And then I'll phone you here, yes?"

"Oh, *yes*. Please." I'd forgotten there was a phone in the house.

Juan pulls a business card out of his back pocket. It's got *Gutierrez e Hijos* written on it. "That bottom number is my home phone," he says. "If you need me."

I love him doing that. I love the connection I've got with him now.

When he's gone, the house seems very empty, and there's nothing for me to do but wait. Wait for Yaz to come through the gates, dreading what mood she'll be in, and wait for Juan to phone.

Which he finally does around eight o'clock. He tells me Yaz went back to Nuria's house to eat, and she's going out with her again this evening.

"Nuria's a star," I say. "Did she tell you Yaz was OK?"

"She said she was fine. Bit hyper, drank too much – but fine. Didn't talk about you and me at all."

"Good. I miss you."

"I miss you too."

"Come over then."

"Laura, I can't. My mother's cooked the Sunday meal for this evening, just so I can be there to eat it."

"Wow. OK."

"Have you got something to eat?"

"Party leftovers. I'm fine."

"OK, *compi*. I'll be over at four tomorrow."

"I'll be here."

I put the phone down, pace the house happily, restlessly. Then I walk outside into the dark and stand on the edge of the empty swimming pool. I wish it was full of cold, clear water, I wish I could take all my clothes off and swim and swim until my muscles gave up with tiredness.

\* \* \*

I'm nervous, teaching English the next day – I keep losing concentration, tripping over my words. It doesn't seem to matter, though. As soon as I can, I race for the bus, just in time to catch the early one I usually miss. I check my watch as the bus bumps along; I reckon I'll get back to *Pino Alto* at about half-past two. One and a half hours to get ready to meet Juan's family – that has to be long enough, doesn't it?

Yaz came in late last night, after I was in bed – she didn't knock on my door, and even if she had done I think I'd've pretended to be asleep. And naturally, this morning, she was still in bed when I got up and left for Ercos.

I know it can't go on like this. I know we're going to have to make contact and sort it all out sometime. But not *now*. The last thing I want is a big heavy discussion with Yaz when I'm supposed to be getting ready for Juan's family party. I get off the bus and head through the gates of *Pino Alto*, fingers crossed tight that the house will be empty.

And to my huge relief, it is. I scoot into the bathroom and bolt the door, and as I drop my clothes on the floor, and turn on the shower, it goes through my head that I have no idea how Yaz is, or even *where* she is. But I promise myself I'll worry about that later.

Juan drives through the gates on the dot of four, to find me waiting anxiously on the terrace. "You look *fantastic*," he breathes. "Too sexy – but you can't help that. That's not your clothes."

"Blimey, Juan," I say happily, "I'm not sure you should come to England. Girls aren't used to sophisticated flattery like that over there. It'll go to their heads."

He puts his arms round me. "Why would I want to flatter any other girls?"

"I wasn't sure what to wear. This skirt's thin but it's the longest one I've got. D'you think it's respectable enough?"

"Sure. It's great."

"And the top's not too tight?"

"You look fantastic. Come on, let's go."

# Chapter 36

Juan's niece's birthday party is being held in an old hall by a church. The set-up – four lines of trestle tables with little chairs, bunches of balloons in the corners – looks unpretentious, and even reassuringly old-fashioned, like parties I used to go to when I was a kid. But it's *packed*. When we walk through the door it's like about a hundred pairs of eyes swivel round and fix on me.

"Are we late?" I hiss.

Juan shrugs. "Half an hour, maybe."

"Will your grandad be here?"

Juan shakes his head. "He's not too good today."

A tiny mop-haired girl in a sugar-pink dress hurtles up to us and crashes into Juan's legs. He scoops her up and swings her high, rock–and–roll style, says, "Happy Birthday, horror!"

"You're late! You're late!" she squeaks.

"Have I missed the cake?"

"No! No!"

"Then I'm not late, am I?"

Her little coal-black eyes swivel suspiciously round to me. "Who's this?"

"This is Laura. My girlfriend."

"She's not your girlfriend! I am!"

"You're my best girl, Conchita. She's for ordinary."

"Well, *thanks*," I laugh, and the moppet glares at me. "Where's my present?" she demands.

"Don't be so rude, Conchita," says Juan. "Grandma gave you a *huge* present. From all of us."

Conchita glares at me again, and Juan tries to set her on the floor, but she grips on to his hands and mountaineers up his legs with her tiny, patent-leather clad feet. "Ow!" he complains. "Conchita, let me go!"

Conchita ignores him.

"Conchita," says a stern voice behind us. "Behave yourself!"

Instantly, the moppet drops to the floor. "Sorry, Grandma," she says.

Juan turns. And, heart in mouth, I turn too, to meet his mother.

You can see the resemblance immediately. The same large, fine eyes, the same strong bones. But Juan's mother has lines scored deep in her forehead and downturning her mouth, as though life has been one long trial for her.

"Juan," she says, in the same stern voice she used to Conchita, "you're very late." And she turns to look at me as though she knows it must be my fault.

"Mama, this is Laura," says Juan. He sounds formal, detached. "The English girl I told you about."

Juan's mother doesn't kiss me Spanish-style. She extends a dry, chilly hand, which I take and start to shake before it dawns on me that she's holding it completely still. "Hello," I croak, mustering up my best Spanish accent. "I'm pleased to meet you."

She smiles frigidly back at me. "Juan, find some seats. The clown's just arrived."

"*Whew*," I breathe, as Juan takes my hand and we start to make our way to the side of the hall. "I don't think she likes me much."

"Don't take it personally," he mutters. "She never likes anyone I introduce to her."

My next ordeal is to be towed through the ranks of friends and relatives, all of them calling out to Juan, some of them jumping up to kiss him, and all of them staring at me. He's their prince, I can see that – their darling. Some of them smile at me in a friendly enough fashion but what comes over to me loud and clear is that there's no way any girl could be good enough for their golden boy. Least of all a foreign girl and least of all me.

We find two seats and sit there like we're facing a tribunal, and I hold tight on to his hand as though it's all that's stopping me going under and drowning. Then, to my relief, someone outside the hall starts beating a drum: loud, rhythmic, insistent. All the faces look away from us and look towards the noise. And then, drumming furiously, the clown bursts into the room.

The clown's a girl. She's got a white face, smeary red clown mouth, and her hair in lots of little bunches. She's wearing a huge, multi-coloured jumper over bright green tights, big red boots and bands of bells round her ankles. She capers through the crowd up to the group of children sitting at the front of the hall, then she dances a mad dance, jingling and pulling horrible faces. A small boy starts to cry. She ignores him, starts telling a silly story about a pig, punctuating it with blasts on a whistle. The kids begin to laugh, but the adults stare at her, critical and stony-faced.

"*Joder*," whispers Juan. "What an amateur. I bet they got her on the cheap."

"I like her," I murmur back. "I like the way she's not all polished." I also like the way she's drawing the fire from me. And I feel for her, all exposed up there, not being good enough however hard she tries. Her story comes to an end; she bows, and I clap loudly above the lukewarm applause.

Now she produces a silver cardboard crown out of her bag and makes a big fuss out of crowning the birthday girl with it. Conchita giggles and smirks; I can see the audience beginning to thaw. "OK," cries the clown. "Who's your king?"

*Oh, God*, I think, *I know what's coming*. And sure enough, Conchita swings round and points a chubby finger straight at Juan. "There he is!" she squeals. "There he is!"

The clown looks over at Juan, and her face lights up. She was expecting one of the mucky little tykes in the front row, she gets Juan – she must think Christmas has come early. She prances over towards us and grabs him by the hand. He groans, but he has to let her tow him up to the front. He's a good sport; he kneels down and lets her crown him too. Then, at her insistence, he picks Conchita up, puts her on his shoulders, and promenades around with her. His crown has slipped over one ear and he looks goofy and gorgeous. And now the audience has thawed so much it's positively dripping.

At last, the clown lets him go. She's got the audience with her now; she's doing tricks, making balloon animals and floating them down to the children. Juan weaves his way back to me and drops his cardboard crown in my lap.

"Thanks," I say. "But Conchita won't like you abdicating."

He laughs, kisses me on the side of my mouth. I feel really pleased he's kissed me in front of everyone, even if they are all still looking at the clown. "God, how much longer?" he groans. "I'm sorry about this, Laura."

"S'OK. Honestly. You were great, by the way."

"Soon as they've cut the cake – we can leave. I promise. I feel awful, putting you through this."

I squeeze his hand hard, and don't answer. I can't tell him I don't care where we are, it could be any-where, anywhere, as long as I'm with him.

As soon as the clown has finished her act, someone turns off all the lights in the hall and a huge, pink, shell-shaped cake with five fat candles is carried in. Conchita looks like she might pass out with excite-ment as everyone starts singing *Cumpleaños Feliz* to the same tune as *Happy Birthday.*

And Juan leans over towards me, so close his mouth is in my hair. "Eat a bit of cake and we're free to go."

"You sure?"

"Definitely. They'll be playing games after this. There's no way we're staying for that!"

He stays close to me. We're breathing in each other's air. For a crazy minute I think we're going to start kissing, really kissing, right there in the hall with the party going on. But he pulls slowly back, grinning at me. And then someone thrusts a slab of cake on a frilly paper napkin into my hand.

"Eat up," says Juan, as he gets handed one too. "Then we can escape."

We both have a couple of sickly mouthfuls, then we stow the rest on the floor behind our chairs. Juan stands up, holds out his hand for me to take. "Come on," he says. "Let's go back to *Pino Alto*."

I know he's hoping the house will be empty. I am too. We walk towards the door, and I think – all these people, they must know we want to be alone, how turned on we are, how much we want each other. . . The door's right in front of us. And we're nearly through it and free when a voice behind us raps out, "*Juan!* Are you going already?"

"Yes, *Mama*," says Juan, all sullen. "We've been here for most of it."

"But I need you to help me run the games!"

"You don't need me. There are plenty of other people here."

"But you're Conchita's favourite uncle! She chose you as her king!"

"And I played along with that, didn't I?"

"You know she'll cry if you go!"

"Maybe, but too bad – we both know she's spoilt rotten."

Their Spanish is speeding up and I can barely follow it – their voices grow sharp and loud like rifles cracking at each other. Juan's mother gesticulates angrily as she speaks; then suddenly she starts shrieking, really shrieking, and her hand swings out and slaps Juan's face.

There's a kind of gasp in the hall. Juan's looking

murderous. He's got hold of the wrist of the hand that hit him, he's gripping it hard, then he kind of throws it away from him, turns to me, says, "Come on, Laura," and walks out through the door.

# Chapter 37

We drive fast through the twisty backstreets of Ercos, and Juan seethes. "Slow down," I croak. "Juan, *slow down*."

He won't listen. He careens on, face like a mask. "Stop for a minute!" I wail. "You're gonna *crash*!"

At that, he slows, then he pulls up by the kerb and turns off the engine. "Sorry," he mutters.

"Come on," I say. "Let's go for a walk."

I want to take his hand as we walk along, but he looks like he's vibrating with rage and I daren't. After a bit I ask, "What did you row about?"

He shrugs angrily. "Nothing."

"Does she . . . does she often hit you?"

"*No*. It's just all about – *control*."

"What is?"

"Her. Control. Possessiveness. She was punishing

me for wanting something more than – *this*." He flicks at hand at the street, rejecting. "And for taking you along to the party. For making you *important*. Now you've met my family you know why I want to get out of Spain."

We walk on, and I don't ask anything else because I know he won't talk.

"They run bulls along here," he suddenly announces. "Two weeks' time."

"*Run bulls?*"

"*Dia del toro.* They fence off the roads, put up barriers. Then they chase two young bulls down through the streets."

"Oh, that's *horrible*."

"The bulls get their chance. They fight back. I got this, two years ago." He pulls up his sweatshirt, shows me a jagged silvery scar on his back.

"Good!" I snap. "I'm glad it got you. What on earth made you do it?"

He shrugs. "All the young men do. You run out in front of the bulls – you run faster than them. You don't do it, you're a *cobarde*."

"Well, I think it's *horrible*. All those men chasing two terrified animals – why d'you Spanish like that sort of thing?"

He laughs. "Yeah, you *English*. Everything for animals. You put your babies in pens and let your dogs run free."

For a minute, I feel like I don't like him. I turn

and walk on, and he follows. Then he stops by a tiny alleyway. "See this?"

"Yes. So?"

"It was only opened up seven years ago. Before that it had been sealed off, for a hundred years. Orders of the priest."

"*What?* Why?"

"Someone was murdered in it. During a *fiesta*. The priest closed the alleyway off to punish it."

"To punish the *alley*?"

"Yes. For giving the murderer a quiet place."

"And you think the *English* have got their priorities wrong?"

He laughs, gets hold of my arm, and pulls me over into the alley with him. He puts his arms round me and smiles down on me and I stop feeling angry with him. I pull his face down to mine, and we start kissing.

His anger's still there, though. I can feel it. He's kissing me like he's angry, but not with me. He's hotting up, too. One hand's sliding up under my thin skirt, the other's under my top. I'm starting to feel as hot as him. I kiss harder, pressing into him, and he breaks off and breathes, "If the priest saw us now – how long would he shut this alley off for?"

"*Two* hundred years. *Minimum*."

"Let's go, Laura. Let's go back to your house."

Soon we're driving fast along the narrow, bumpy roads back to *Pino Alto*. My heart's thudding, waiting. I know we're going to make love. The car swerves in through the wrought-iron gates.

And there's Yaz sitting at the table on the terrace, deep in conversation with Ruth.

# Chapter 38

"*Joder*," breathes Juan. "*Joder!*"

He turns the engine off, reaches for my hand. There's nothing we can do, though – no way round this. What are Tom and Ruth doing back here – what's gone wrong? And if Yaz has come out of hiding, I need to talk to her. I'd have to be a complete cow, wouldn't I, to just walk by her, towing the guy we fell out over into my bedroom?

I take in a deep breath, squeeze Juan's hand, let it go, and get out of the car. Yaz and Ruth are both staring at me but I can't read much on their faces. I start walking towards them, expecting Ruth to stand up and kiss me hello because I haven't seen her for over two weeks.

She doesn't though. She glances at Yaz, then looks back at me and says, "Hi."

She sounds cold, critical. "Hi," I reply. "Didn't it work out?"

"What?"

"The south."

Ruth laughs, all flat and sarcastic. "Oh, *that* worked out all right. It was me and Tom that didn't."

I feel like she's sandbagged me. "*What?* You're not saying you've split up?"

"I walked out on him," she says.

"*What?* You're here on your own?"

"Yup."

"What *happened*?"

"Well – quite a lot. Like it did here, apparently. Yaz has been telling me." She jerks her head at Juan, who's leaning against the car. "Is he staying? Only I really think the three of us should talk."

She's had Yaz's version of what happened, so she's all set hard against me. But there's something more. This is not the Ruth who left in Tom's car. This is someone strong and determined and altogether different.

I don't reply. I go back over to Juan, reach up and put my arms round his neck. "This is possibly the worst timing in the history of the world," I whisper.

"You want me to go."

"No, Juan – I do not *want you to go*. I really, really want you to stay. All night, if possible."

He smiles down at me, wraps his arms tight round my waist.

"But Ruth is right – the three of us need to talk. We need to sort things out if we're going to be able to co-exist in this house."

"OK," he says.

I love him for just accepting it, for knowing he's got to go. I reach up, kiss him, then I push him away before he can kiss me back, and he laughs.

"Can I phone you?" he says. "Tonight?"

"Better not. Something tells me this is going to be a heavy talking session."

"Then I'll come back tomorrow. First thing. I've got to see you, Laura."

"OK."

"I love you," he says, gets into his car, and drives off.

I let the lump disappear from my throat, then I walk back to the table and sit down. "Ruth," I say, "I'm sure Yaz has told you what a cow I've been, but I hope you know there's another side to it."

"Oh, that's typical, Laura," snaps Yaz. "Jump straight in with *your* problems. Aren't you going to ask Ruth how she is? She's just *hitchhiked* here. And then spent her last euros on a cab."

I turn on Ruth. "You *hitchhiked*? You idiot! You don't even speak Spanish! You—"

"Oh, calm down – it wasn't really hitchhiking," she says, wearily. "They were guys I recognized from the resort – Australians. They gave me a lift right into Jerez, to the taxi rank. They saved my life, actually."

"Saved your *life*? Ruth – what the hell happened?"

"Start at the beginning, Ruth," says Yaz, meaningfully. "Like you did with me."

She sighs. "Well, it was great to start off with. We got down to the Costa del Sol, and got jobs right away in this huge holiday compound. The season was just getting going – the sun was out – the sea was almost warm enough to swim in."

I can see tears glittering in the corners of her eyes. I want to reach out and put my hand over hers, but I daren't in case she chucks it off.

"We were both in the kitchen to start with, doing salads and things, then we got promoted to one of the disco-bars. I was serving drinks to the tables, Tom was on the door. We got given this little chalet, on the beach . . . usually they make the staff sleep in these horrible high-rises, but because it wasn't high season they let us have the chalet. It was sweet, it had its own shower, its own deck. . ." She gulps, stops talking. Yaz reaches down into a carrier bag beside her chair, picks up a bottle of beer, flicks the top off on the table edge, and hands it to Ruth.

"Can I have one of those?" I demand. I'm *parched*. I haven't had anything since some sickly-sweet wine at Conchita's party. Yaz looks at me for a minute, like she'd love to say *no*, then she abruptly hands me an unopened bottle, and opens another for herself.

"The pay was pretty crap," Ruth goes on, "but we got free food, and some free drinks . . . and we got round the guy who timetabled the shifts, we got him to put us on the same ones so we had time off together. He couldn't always, of course. And they started wanting Tom to do extra shifts. And that's when . . . when it happened."

This time I am brave. I take a swig of beer, and take hold of Ruth's hand, and she doesn't shake me off. "*What* happened?" I ask, gently.

Ruth looks over at Yaz, gives her a watery smile. "Sorry. You don't want to hear all this again."

"It's OK," she says. She's looking at my hand on Ruth's; she doesn't like it.

"It's really *sordid*," Ruth goes on, bitterly. "Really *cheap*. He was on late one night. I couldn't sleep. I thought I'd give him a nice surprise – go and meet him at the end of his shift. It was a fabulous night, big, big moon. . . I walked up to the door of the club and saw him talking to these two girls. I stopped. I mean – part of his job was to chat up girls, get them to go in and spend money. Like mine was to chat up the men at the tables, talk them into ordering champagne and stuff. . . we'd talked about it. We'd agreed we weren't jealous."

"OK," I say. "So you didn't want to interrupt. . ."

"Both the girls staggered inside – they looked like they were already drunk. I was just going to go over to Tom when one of the girls came out again. She kept lurching about – she fell against Tom, and put her arms round his neck and . . . and . . . they started snogging. They were *really* going for it."

"Oh, what a *shit*. Ruth, that's—"

"Yeah, well that's nothing, Laura. Not compared to what happened next. Tom was holding on to her and he started looking all around, like he was checking he wasn't being watched. I thought he'd seen me, but he can't've – I was standing in the shadows. I felt . . . *frozen*, to the spot. Then he started pulling her round the side of the building. It was dead dark. I couldn't really see but – there was this shape, this . . . *uuurgh*. Them. Up against the wall."

"Oh, *God*," I say, "you think they might've . . . you think. . ."

"Laura, I don't *think*, I *know*!" Ruth explodes. "I couldn't see but I could *hear* everything! I could hear *Tom*! I do *know* what he sounds like when he's. . ." She breaks off, puts her face in her hands, collapses down on her elbows on the table, and bursts into tears.

"Don't, Ruth," says Yaz. "He's not worth it."

"Let her cry," I murmur. "She needs to. What a *bastard*."

"Yeah, well that's *men* for you," Yaz spits. "Men are all the same when it comes to sex."

*No, they're not*, I think, but I let it pass. "Ruth, I'm *so sorry*," I say. "You must have felt so awful, you must've . . . what did you *do*?"

"The funny thing is, I wasn't angry," mutters Ruth, through her fingers. "It was so gross I think I just . . . shut down. I didn't want to rush over and kill him or anything. I just wanted to *go*. I felt like –

something had died. I felt terribly sad more than anything. I went straight back to the chalet, started to pack. It was like – two in the morning. Then I just sat there, waiting for it to get light. Tom got back about half an hour later."

"What did you do?"

"Nothing. I just sat there. He saw my suitcase and everything, kept asking what was wrong. All I said was, 'I saw you with that girl. I *heard* you.' Then I told him to get out."

"What did he do?"

"Oh, God. He nearly had a *seizure*. It would've been funny if – if just the sight of him hadn't made me want to throw up. He started begging me not to go, he said it was her fault, he said he was drunk, he said they didn't really have sex, not all the way . . . he said anything and everything that came into his sick head. I couldn't stand listening to him. I stood up and walked out, down on to the beach. He followed me. He was pleading with me to forgive him, give him a second chance. He kept saying he didn't know *why* he'd done it, *what* had happened to him, *how* he could hurt me like that . . . how it would break him if I left him. I sat down on the sand, didn't say anything. I think that gave him a bit of hope, then, 'cos he sat down beside me and started explaining about the male sexual drive."

"Oh, *please* – he didn't!" I wail. "What did he come out with?"

"He said it's OK for guys to have casual sex, it doesn't affect anything, it doesn't mean they don't love their girlfriends. He said it's a biological drive going back to the apes, to shag as many women as you can so your genes get spread about. He said ninety-nine guys out of a hundred, if they were offered fast, no-strings sex like he was by that girl, would've said yes and gone for it."

"Hah!" erupts Yaz. "That's for sure. A hundred per cent, probably."

"He started to say if they didn't go for it, it meant they were gay or pathetic or something . . . and *then* he said if only I hadn't seen him, nothing would've changed between us, everything would be as perfect as before. So if I could just forget it, *delete* it, we could go back to how we were. . ."

"*Jesus*," I mutter. "Dream on, Tom. What did you do?"

"Well, it was beginning to get light. I stood up, went back to the chalet, picked up my case. Then I walked out to the road. There's a bus stop there, it brings people into the compound really early to work, and goes back to town. . . Tom came after me. He tried to get hold of my arm. When he touched me I turned round and smacked him in the face so hard he nearly went over backwards."

Both Yaz and I cheer at that, and I put an arm round Ruth's shoulders, and she manages a wavery smile. "He just sort of stood there, and soon after the bus came, and I got on it. I was ready to shove him off, *really* shove him, if he tried to get on after me, but he didn't – I guess he knew what would happen. I didn't have a clue what I was going to do. Then in town I met up with those Australian guys, and they said they were heading for Jerez and they'd take me with them. Which was amazing luck. Then I cabbed it to here."

"I'm so glad you made it back," said Yaz. "You'll be OK, Ruth."

Ruth stares ahead of her. "I'm exhausted. I'm broke. I'm in shock. I'm a *liability*."

"No, you're not," say Yaz and I in unison.

# Chapter 39

The three of us go into the kitchen to fix spaghetti for dinner. Ruth's story is so horrible and dramatic that it kind of dwarfs what's been going on between Yaz and me. But I can sense the hostility from Yaz still. She hasn't forgiven me anything, I can tell. She focuses on Ruth the whole time, being caring and kind, and obviously that's fine because Ruth needs care and kindness, but Yaz manages to do it in a way that makes *me* feel like a piece of rubbish.

We sit down to eat. Ruth is so tired she can barely lift her fork to her mouth. I want to talk to her, I want to tell her my side of what happened with Juan, but it's crazily self-centred to even think of doing that now. After the meal, I tell her she needs to sleep, and while Yaz clears the table I go into my room to make up Yaz's old bed. It's not like Ruth's going to want to go back in the double bed she slept in with Tom. She totters through to my room and collapses into bed and I tuck her up and go back to the main room. Maybe Yaz will talk to me now, I think. We need to sort this out.

But the room's empty. And Yaz's bedroom door is shut tight.

I wish I'd told Juan he could phone. I know I've got his number, safe in my purse, but the thought of his mother answering is too terrifying even to think about.

I walk up and down the long room and the pressure inside me grows, the feeling I used to get when Yaz and I were kids and she'd turn on me, leave me out in the cold for days at a time. And I think, *Wake up, Laura. You're a grown-up now. Why are you waiting for her to come round to you? Why are you feeling guilty? Why are you letting her get away with this?*

I walk up to her bedroom door, bang on it, and walk in without waiting for her to answer. She rears up in bed, hair all over her shoulders. "What the hell do you want?"

"An apology."

"*What?*"

"Yeah, I want an *apology*! You've got *no right* to treat me this way. However jealous you feel. Jesus, it's the first time you haven't got the man you want –

can't you cope with it? You were an absolute *bitch* on Saturday night. You jumped to all the wrong conclusions about me, and when I told you how it really was, you should've apologized! But you didn't, did you? Not only that – you go and repeat the same set of lies to Ruth!"

Yaz has got the coldest kind of look on her face. "I haven't told Ruth any lies," she sneers. "I just told her what happened."

"How *you* saw what happened. You got it wrong, Yaz! He likes me – he always did!"

"Laura – get out of my room."

"I'm sorry you like him so much. I'm sorry you feel so bad. But Jesus – I fell over backwards trying not to hurt you over this, worrying about you and everything! And you – it's like you don't care about me at all!"

She shrugs, looks away, won't answer. I stand there, glaring at her, wanting to smack her one. "You just can't stand it that he wants me and not you," I say, then I turn on my heel, and walk out leaving the door wide open.

As I go along to my room, I realize the pressure inside me has gone. I feel one hell of a lot better. I go to bed to wait for the morning.

Ruth sleeps like she's dead. I lie awake in the blackness thinking over the day, all that's happened in it, thinking about Juan saying he loved me just before he got back in his car, the way he looked at me when he said it. It feels like ages before I can get to sleep.

Then sometime around dawn Ruth wakes me. She's rocking and jerking in her dreams, crying out in this strangled sort of voice. I watch her for a moment, heart thumping. I'm scared, being woken like that, and I'm spooked watching her, but most of all I'm terrified thinking what she's going through, how hurt she is. I get out of bed, crouch on the floor beside her bed and put my arms round her. She fights me off, she's sobbing like she's in pain, and she's trying to talk but I can't understand what she's saying. I'm afraid to wake her; I just stay near her. After a while she quietens down, slips back into deep sleep again. And I get back to bed, but I know I'll stay awake.

It's almost light now; sunlight is beginning to creep through the gap in the shutters, and I can hear birds calling and chattering in the olive grove. I get out of bed, go outside, walk round the side of the house and watch the sun come up like a god over the huge empty swimming pool.

I don't know how long I've been standing there when I hear a motorbike roar up through the gates. I hear footsteps crunching round the house towards me. I smile; something stops me from turning round, something superstitious in me makes me wait until he's right up behind me and he's sliding his arms round my waist.

"You're up early," he says, into my hair.

I turn round into his arms. "So are you. You're even *dressed*."

"Well?" he says, kissing me. "What happened with Ruth and Tom?"

I look towards the house, and suddenly I just want to get away from it all. "Buy me breakfast," I say, "and I'll tell you everything."

Half an hour later we're sitting outside a little café in Ercos, drinking milky coffee and eating rolls and jam. The sun's hot already. It feels fabulous, like it's recharging me. And Juan's so beautiful sitting opposite me, I almost can't be bothered to talk and explain everything, I just want to hold his hand across the table and look at him.

"Come on," he says. "Fill me in."

So I do. I tell him Ruth's story, and I don't leave anything out, and as I talk, Juan's half smiling, half frowning, like it's all too weird for him to get his head round.

"Do *you* think that way?" I demand. "Like Tom? What would you say if someone offered you sex like that?"

"Try me," he grins.

I dig my nails into his hand. "I mean a *stranger*. Someone you'd just met."

"Depends what she looked like. Don't look like that, Laura – I'm only being honest! Anyway, you're missing the main point, aren't you? He had a

270

*girlfriend.* How can he say how much he loves Ruth one minute and then go off like a *perro salido* – you know, like a dog following his . . . his. . ."

"Dick?"

"Yes. Doesn't he think there's a contradiction?"

"Obviously not. That's a perfect description of Tom, though."

"I think – if you have a girlfriend, it changes everything. And she was right to walk out on him, because he was acting like she didn't count."

I rub my foot against Juan's ankle, to show him how very, very much I like his answer, and he asks, "Is Ruth really devastated?"

"I don't know. I mean, she's got over boyfriends before, of course she has. But she's never been as obsessed by anyone as she was by Tom. It was like he'd swallowed her up. Yaz and I used to talk about it, how we hardly recognized her any more."

"Maybe this is good, then."

"Yeah. Maybe she'll get *herself* back. It'll take time though. She's just – she's shattered by it all. She had this awful nightmare, last night."

There's a pause. Juan butters the last bit of roll, hands it to me, and says, "Laura – have you talked to Yaz yet?"

"Yes. Well – talked *at* her. I went into her room last night and let her have it."

"Good for you!"

"She's treating me like shit. She won't even look at

me properly. She's told Ruth all about it, though. Her version."

"Yeah, I could see that yesterday, the way Ruth was acting. You've got to put the record straight with her."

"Not while she's so upset about Tom."

"Are you good friends with Yaz?"

"*What?* Of course I am. We've been friends for years, we've known each other since we were eight or something. . ."

He shrugs. "I don't think she's acted like a good friend, that's all. Right from when I first met you both, I thought she was manipulative – she really cut you out."

I shrug, too. "We both fancied *you*."

"Understandable."

"Bighead."

He laughs. "And now she's trying to turn Ruth against you. Have you finished your coffee? Let's go back to the house."

We pick up some food and white wine because I say I want to make a meal tonight, to cheer up Ruth and be a peace offering for Yaz. Then we drive back to *Pino Alto*. Ruth and Yaz are sitting at the terrace table, drinking tea, and they both turn to look at me as I get out of the car, and then they both look away again. "Oh, crap," I mutter sideways at Juan. "Looks like I'm still in the doghouse. I'll go and try and talk to them. Are you going to work on the pool?"

"In a minute," he says, then he walks over to the table, confident as anything, sits down with them and says: "Yaz – Laura tells me I owe you an apology."

# Chapter 40

I gawp at him. Then I decide it's too late to stop him, so I scoot over the terrace and sit down beside him at the table. I'm not missing *this*.

"Yaz, I know you thought there was something between you and me," Juan says. "That's why you're angry now Laura and I are together. Look – whatever I did to give you the wrong impression, I'm sorry. I really am."

Yaz looks completely stunned. Ruth glances at her, leans forward protectively. "Well, actually, Juan, I don't blame Yaz for getting the wrong impression. *I* thought you liked her, too. You were talking to *her* all the time, not Laura."

"I couldn't talk to Laura," he says simply. "Not in the beginning. I fancied her too much. With Yaz it was easier. I *liked* you, Yaz – I still do. But not in that way, not—"

"Don't give me that!" Yaz glares at him, bright red, offended. "You *kissed* me!"

"Look – you know what happened that night. You know *I* didn't go after *you*."

There's a silence. Ruth is watching Yaz, waiting to see how she'll react.

"Although you're right – I shouldn't have kissed you," Juan goes on. "I'm sorry. You came on to me and I was just – all screwed up over Laura. I thought she didn't like me."

"And I thought *you* liked *me*," spits Yaz.

"It was always Laura. I'm really sorry." He stands up, says, "Look – what matters is that you two don't fall out over this. I'm going to finish the pool." And he walks off.

"*Idiot!*" explodes Yaz. "Give me English men any time – at least they make sense! I'm going to make some more tea." And she stomps into the kitchen.

"Did you tell him to do that?" murmurs Ruth.

"What – apologize? No."

"Not apologize. Come over and confront Yaz with what actually happened."

"What has she *said* actually happened?"

"*Well* – to hear her version, Juan really had the hots for her."

I shake my head. "That's fantasy."

"And then he switched to you because . . . well, put

it this way. Last night she was making all these comparisons between him and Tom. Going for easy sex, I mean."

"Oh, great. So she thought *I* was like that girl Tom had up against the wall? Oh, Ruth, *sorry*—"

"S'OK. And yes, she did."

"Nice," I mutter. "Nice opinion she has of me. You believed it, did you?"

"Laura, last night I wasn't in any state to judge, was I?"

"No. Sorry."

"Plus I was ready to hate *anyone* male. I just took what she said at face value."

"How do you feel now?"

"I dunno. I think – Yaz really fell for him. And that kind of coloured how she . . . interpreted his behaviour. And yours, I s'pose."

"That's one way of putting it. It certainly coloured how she behaved. You know, if she hadn't been so pushy to start off with, so bloody sure of herself, she might've noticed he liked me! *I* might've noticed it!"

"Laura – you've got to get through this. You and Yaz."

"She was really *vicious* to me."

"Yeah, but you've won, haven't you? He's clearly completely crazy about you."

I can feel myself melting. "You think?"

"*Duuuh!* Yes, I do. So you can afford to be generous

to Yaz. And if we're going to carry on this holiday together, you've got to sort it out between you."

"I tried, last night."

"I know."

"I've got food for tonight, I'm going to cook—"

"Laura, that's great. Just the three of us?"

Yaz appears at the doorway. "The bus comes in five minutes, Ruth. Let's go into Ercos. *Big* thrills, I know, but what else is there to do in this God-forsaken hole?"

I watch them go, then I head straight for the swimming pool. Juan is hunkered down working at the far end, and he's taken his shirt off, revealing a scrumptious brown back. I race over to him.

"My hero!" I squawk, grabbing him and planting a kiss right by his mouth. "What made you think of *confronting* Yaz like that?"

He grins. "I just thought we should talk about it when we were all together."

"Well, it worked. Ruth sees my side now, even if she does think it's *me* who ought to make all the running with Yaz, 'cos I've got *you*. Yaz is still being a cow, but maybe she'll come round."

"Would you be really upset if the friendship was over?"

"*What?*"

He shrugs. "Oh, I dunno. I lied when I told her I liked her. What you've said about her – she sounds like a pain to me. I mean, she's fun, yes, but . . . well. People move on." He puts his arms round me. "Don't think about her now."

"I won't. I've had it to here with her. She's out, anyway. She's taken Ruth off to Ercos grumbling about how boring it is."

And suddenly it's very, very still in the empty pool and I can't hear anything but the blood humming in my ears. Juan tightens his arms round me. "So they've gone out?" he asks.

"Yes."

"I don't really have to work on the pool."

"I know you don't."

I climb out of the pool, leading him behind me. I don't take him into my bedroom, I don't want to, not now I'm sharing it with Ruth. I take him into the swimming-pool room. We shut the door behind us, and we stand there kissing for a long time. Then I push him away gently, and he stands and looks at me as I start to take my clothes off. "You too," I say.

I thought I'd be more embarrassed with him – more shy. But I'm not.

I'm glad it's here we're making love for the first time, here where we first found out how much we liked each other. I don't care that the sunbed's hard, digging into my back, or narrow, so we have to be up very close.

He tells me he loves me again. He seems to love me, every inch of me. This isn't just two bodies making love, it's us.

He won't let me hurry it. "We've got time," he murmurs. "Time."

At last, he lets me pull him on top of me. And it's so good, so strong, so completely right, like we were made to be together like this, that I want to cry, but I stop myself.

Somehow, Juan lasts until he's sure I'm too satisfied to move.

"Laura, *my* Laura," he whispers. And then I do cry.

# Chapter 41

"I've got to stop smiling," I say. "If I don't, Ruth and Yaz'll know what's been going on."

"So was it OK?" Juan says, again, putting his arms round me again.

"It was fantastic. Never, ever has it been that good. OK?"

"Me too," he murmurs.

"Juan – come on. We've got to shape up. We've got to get on with this meal."

"Stop being so *English*."

"Stop being so *Spanish*. Get working."

We're standing side by side in the kitchen, vaguely getting a meal together for Yaz and Laura, but it's hard to peel and chop because our hands keep straying to each other.

After we'd made love, we scurried naked,

clutching our clothes, across the terrace and into the bathroom, and drew a huge bath that almost over-flowed once the two of us got into it. We soaped each other and played about until the water was lukewarm, then we got dressed and hugged for a while, then we opened the cold white wine.

"What exactly are we making?" Juan demands, de-seeding a red pepper.

"Well – I was just going to fry the chicken, and stir-fry the veg—"

"Boring. If I was going to be eating this, I'd make it into chicken ragout. . ."

"You still can!"

"Why should I when I'm not invited?"

"Oh, Juan, you know *I'd* love you to stay. . ."

"I know. I'll come back later tonight, yes?"

"Yes! Please!"

"Look, *compi* – maybe I'd better go now. Before they get back."

"No way – not yet! You're not leaving yet!"

I've got him trapped, up against the sink. He laughs, grabs me by the waist, lifts me up on to the kitchen counter. I throw my arms round his neck, hook my leg round the back of his knees, pull him up against me. And then we're kissing, but it's not lazy, post-love-making kissing any more, suddenly we're frantic with wanting each other again, accelerating from 0 to 50 in about two seconds flat. I wrap my other leg round him and his hands slide under my thin skirt, and I'm so turned on I'm breathing all weird, I could hyperventilate, I could faint any minute –

– and he suddenly pulls away and turns his back on me.

And there's Yaz in the doorway, mouth like a steel trap.

"Hello!" says Juan brightly. "We're cooking!"

After that, the meal is not a roaring success, despite the evening being so fine we can eat out on the terrace, despite the food being great (if boring) and despite the icy cold wine. Ruth has slumped back down into despair and hardly eats a thing; Yaz chews sourly, as though I've served her up horse shit. I feel for Ruth but I don't know what to say to her. I even sort of feel for Yaz, but the hostility coming off her is like toxic radiation and it stops me making any kind of move towards her.

And I feel for me, there without Juan.

In despair, I open a big bar of milk chocolate for dessert, then Ruth suddenly seems to come to. "God!" she mutters. "Thank you, Laura . . . that meal was delicious."

"But you hardly touched it!" I blurt out.

"Oh, I'm sorry – I just – what I ate was really nice. I was just – I was miles away."

"S'OK, honestly. You're doing great, Ruth."

"Doing great?"

"Well – you know. You must feel so upset still. . ."

She looks at me, eyes all glittery and naked. "Yeah, I'm upset. But a bit of me's *glad* this has happened. It's like I've . . . woken up or something."

Around the table there's a shift, as Yaz and I realize she wants to talk. "Woken up?" I repeat, softly.

"Yeah. Like I'm seeing things straight at last. You know what's been really *killing* me over the last forty-eight hours? It isn't only that he could betray me like that. It's that he could do it after all the *stuff* he used to come out with."

"What – about how much he loved you?" asks Yaz.

"Yeah. He used to say what we had between us was just about the most amazing thing *ever* – how most people went through life never even getting *close* to feeling what we felt. He'd go on about how we ought to value it."

"I always thought you were a bit over the top," I murmur, "the cards and presents you bought each other. . ."

"I know. But Tom's got a really sentimental side. He used to make a huge big thing over anniversaries and everything. And Valentine's Day he practically bankrupted himself taking me out to that posh place to eat, getting all those roses delivered. . . It was like – we had the perfect relationship, so we had to look out for it. He was always saying how we were meant for each other . . . and if I pissed him off, or wanted to spend time apart, it was like it was this big betrayal, not only of *him*, but of what we had together . . . and you know how he tried to push my friends away. Like everyone else was secondary."

"He's a control freak, Ruth," mutters Yaz.

"Look – I know you loathed him. I know you didn't think he was right for me. But at the start, I thought he was amazing – I thought he was *hot*. And he kept telling me he was crazy about me – it was brilliant to have someone feel for you what you feel for him. I'd never had anything that strong, ever. And his *belief* in what we had, it was magic, I felt so special. . ."

She trails off. I break off a bit of chocolate and hand it to her. She eats it, sighs, says, "When he screwed that girl, it wasn't just him cheating on me – it was, well, if he could do that, then the whole thing was fake, wasn't it?"

"I guess," I say. "Unless—"

"I keep thinking – thank God we didn't go on even longer. How awful would that be – to carry on thinking you had this fantastic relationship with someone, and all the time it was just fake. He hasn't spoilt *any-thing*. He's shown it up for the sham it was. The more I look at it, the more sham it seems. We *pretended* so much. Like I'd have to *pretend* I liked watching him play footie every Saturday – it wasn't enough that I was prepared to go along and support him, I had to go on about how *great* it was. Well – *you* know what I was like. I must've driven you round the bend."

"We did think he'd taken you over," I murmur.

"And he pretended stuff too," Ruth goes on. "Like, when he was fed up he'd make out he wasn't. 'I'm with you, babes,' he'd say. 'Why should I be fed up?' But I knew he was, underneath. It was so dishonest."

"He certainly pretended about being faithful to you," Yaz says.

Ruth's eyes flare. "That's just it. I don't think it was the first time it happened."

"*What?*"

"A few days before, he got out a new packet of condoms. And I was *sure* we hadn't used the old packet up. I asked him where they'd gone, and he just laughed it off, said I ought to lay off the tequila, said what was I doing, asking him about that when he wanted to make love to me . . . d'you know, I actually felt ashamed of myself for asking him. It didn't cross my *mind. . .*"

"Oh, Ruth," I say. "Maybe he just. . ."

"*What?* Just *what?* It's not like he needed to practise putting them on, is it? And you should have *seen* the way he pulled that girl round the corner . . . he looked bloody sure what he was doing! And that shit he came out with about the male sex drive – he believed it. He thought he had the right to have me, totally and absolutely, and as much on the side as he could get away with. For *variety.* He probably still thinks it's all right. *God!* I'm so glad I caught him at it!"

There's a pause, and I'm just racking my brains for something positive to say when Ruth collapses down into her hands and starts to cry. Yaz wraps her arms round her, hugs her tight. "It's OK, Ruth, it's OK," she croons. "Come on, you need to sleep. Come on."

And they get up from the table, and Yaz steers her into the house.

Juan arrives later, on his cousin's bike, soon after Yaz has followed Ruth to bed. We drink coffee out on the terrace under the stars and I tell him the things Ruth was saying.

"You haven't been put off men for life, have you?" he asks. "Listening to that?"

"God, I dunno. It's bad enough having that happen, but when it smashes up what you thought you had in the past. . ."

"From what you've said, she wanted it all smashed up."

"Yeah. Yeah, you're right – or she'd miss it too much. She needs to think their relationship was all fake and rubbish, so she can just throw it all out, so she doesn't hurt too bad. And actually, of course, it *was* a crap relationship. It was like this weird pact they had, to be obsessed with each other and shut everyone else out."

"I thought he was an idiot," agrees Juan mournfully. "But I was jealous of him. . ."

"*You* were jealous of *him*? Come off it."

"I was jealous of the way he was . . . living with Ruth. Of how free he was. I wanted that with you."

I stand up. "And now we've sort of got it."

"Sort of?"

"We can hardly go into my room with Ruth tucked up in there. But there's always –"

"– the swimming-pool room," he says, grinning.

I take his hand and we go there.

# Chapter 42

Over the next few days, things get back to normal, if you can call it normal when you're kind of *humming* with happiness and desire and excitement and passion. Every day, every night, Juan spends as long as he possibly can with me. And when we're not in the swimming-pool room, we go out a lot – into the mountains, into Ercos, into Jerez – because the rift between me and Ruth and Yaz is now a socking great gulf, and it's just too uncomfortable to be at the house. Yaz is still barely speaking to me. Ruth does her best to be friendly but every time she sees me looking all shiny with love she must feel the knife twist again. Basically, I'm happy and they're not. I'm working and they're not. I think *Pino Alto* is paradise and they don't.

No, there's not much common ground right now.

Normally I'd feel devastated at this rift from my friends, but this isn't normal, is it? I'm not worrying about what's going to happen. I'm just living day to day, hour by hour, really living it, absorbed by Juan and loving every minute. I'm accepted now in the group as Juan's girlfriend. I introduce him to Luisa, my teacher friend, and we all have lunch together and she warns me afterwards that he's far too good-looking to be good.

I can't imagine it getting better.

And then it does get better. The heat comes in.

I feel it from the moment I wake up; before I've even pulled back the shutters I can feel it on my face. I go outside and it warms my bare arms. The sun's stepped up a gear; there's no cloud anywhere in the sky, it's all been burnt away.

I put on one of the summer dresses I've had stashed away, waiting for the real summer to start. It's short, bright, brilliant, and it'll look even better when my legs are brown.

Juan phones just as I'm snatching a piece of toast before dashing into town to teach. "Told you," he says. "Told you the hot weather was coming. Grab your swimming things – I'll pick you up at the school when you finish. We can go to the beach."

"You look beautiful extreme today, Laura. For . . . *summer*."

"Extremely beautiful," I correct Manolo, my

second-most-promising pupil. "Although I think that's flattery."

"What is – *flatteree*?"

"When you say something's better than it is."

"No! No flatteree! That colours is good for you."

"You'd say – good *on* me. Or they *suit* me. But thank you!"

He grins at me, pleased. The lesson's nearly over, and it's gone well – we've covered dating, pubs and dining out. I'm building up a real rapport with my students and Concepción's delighted, because she thinks people learn faster when they like their teacher.

"OK," I say, "once more. You're at a restaurant – how do you ask your guest what she'd like to eat?"

"What do you desire?"

"Well, that's a bit formal. Just 'What would you like?' is fine."

"Food, Laura!" someone calls out. "Tell us about food in England. What it is that is most popular."

"Curry," I say, and they all laugh, and then they all pull faces as I describe Full English Breakfast and steak-and-kidney pie. The bright sun's searing through the window, and the ceiling fan's going full pelt. My skin's burning with wanting to get out there, get down to the beach.

"Lau-ra!" coos Concepción, from the doorway. She sounds all sort of coy and teasing, not a bit like her normal efficient self. "Laura, *cariño*, I've got your pay here. And there's someone to see you!"

And Juan appears at the door too, looking astoundingly gorgeous in a white T-shirt. I turn back to the class. "Right, well, I think it's time, don't you? Lesson over – thank you everyone." And I scramble out of my seat, all flustered, with everyone staring past me to scrutinize Juan.

"Hello, *compi*," Juan says, and kisses me straight on the mouth.

"*So*, Laura," Concepción purrs. "*So*. You've been keeping this young man quiet, haven't you? You won't be needing *me* to help you with your Spanish any more!" And she folds my pay packet into my hand and squeezes it shut, all girly and conspiratorial.

"Oh, we speak English together," announces Juan, in English, in his wonderful American-Spanish accent. "We always have. My English has improved so much since I've been with Laura."

The businessmen filing out of the door glance at him sourly.

"I don't suppose you want a job here do you, *hijo*?" squawks Concepción.

Juan laughs, shakes his head and thanks her, then we grab each other's hands and scoot down the stairs. "I'm rich," I gloat, waving my pay packet, "lunch is on me!"

Then we jump in the car, and roar off to the coast with both front windows open.

\* \* \*

We have a fabulous day. We swim; we sunbathe; we eat a slow late lunch of salad and tiny fried fish in a little taverna a stone's throw from the beach. We talk about everything. We analyse Ruth, we analyse Yaz, we despair about Tom. Juan tells me more about his family, how he's feeling more and more stifled by them, especially now he's met me. He tells me how great I look in a bikini and persuades me not to get my hair cut again. "Let it grow," he says. "It'll look lovely longer."

"Maybe," I answer. "If it gets bleached by the sun a bit."

"Yeah," he says, stroking it. "It'll look sensational."

There's one dark bit to this perfect day. I'm watching him walk down to the sea to cool off, admiring every inch of him, and suddenly it's like this cold hand seizes hold of me, this cold voice from the past that says, *Don't feel so much. Or how will you feel when it's over?*

I push it away, refuse to think about what the voice is saying. I tell myself, *Live in the moment*. Juan comes out of the sea dripping wet and throws himself down beside me, and I towel him dry all slowly, and he pulls me down on top of him.

We stay wrapped round each other on the sand and watch the sun drop into the sea before we set off back to *Pino Alto*. As we drive through the gates, it's getting dark. "I wish you had a room of your own," he says.

"Yeah, me too. You'd think, wouldn't you, that Yaz might share with Ruth and let me have the big room?"

"Have you asked her?"

"*No way.* Honestly, Juan, I can't."

"Can I ask her?"

"Only if you want your head bitten off. I thought she'd calm down after a bit – you know, feeling jealous and everything – but she seems to be getting worse. The trouble is, nothing's happening for her."

"I'd really like to stay the night with you."

"Well . . . you could. . ."

"In *comfort* – not falling off a sunbed!"

"I know. It'll happen."

The next day, I'm on a late shift at the school. Juan has to work on one of his uncle's building projects, so I won't get to see him until I knock off at about seven in the evening. I don't get up till eleven, but even so it feels like it's going to be a long day. Yaz and Ruth take off to Ercos on the bus around lunchtime. They don't ask me to go with them, even though I'm clearly not doing anything. I can't blame them though. We've been living so separately, why should they ask me?

I make myself some lunch, then I sit out on the terrace in the sun and read a Spanish novel that Concepción lent me. I'm just getting into it, con-gratulating myself on the way my literary Spanish is improving, when Yaz and Ruth arrive back.

I know something's happened from the minute they walk through the gates. They're loud and laughing, and Yaz shoots me a triumphant look that puts me immediately on my guard. "Hi," she says. "All alone?"

"Not now you're back."

"Laura, we went into that travel bureau," says Ruth, heading over to me with a pile of glossy holiday brochures. "I don't know why we didn't think of doing it before. We just asked the guy in there to suggest places that might be looking for summer workers, and we've practically got the guarantee of jobs!"

"What – here?"

"Hardly," says Yaz, scornfully. She takes the brochures off Ruth, and fans them out on the table in front of me. "*Here*."

"But these places – they're all down south."

"Yeah. That's where all the holiday camps are."

"*Ruth* – that's also where Tom is!"

"No, he's further west," says Yaz. "We won't be anywhere near him."

"This is the one we're heading for," says Ruth excitedly, pointing at an impossibly glamorous picture of a swimming pool opening out on to a beach with palm trees and sunbeds and bright yellow towels. "It's this massive new hotel complex. It's just opened up and they're taking on loads of staff for the summer. We've got a contact name from the travel guy in Ercos – he told us to say he recommended us. It's practically a dead cert."

I feel like I've been hit over the head with something very heavy. "So . . . are you saying this is definite?"

"As definite as it can be," enthuses Ruth. "He went on about how important it was to speak English, and how *personable* we were."

"I reckon he fancied you," adds Yaz, and they laugh together.

"No," I say, "I mean – it's definite that you want to go?"

"It's definite that we're *going*," Yaz corrects me, all aggressive.

"There's nothing for us here, Laura," pleads Ruth.

"And we never meant to stay put in one place for ever," adds Yaz. "We've been here getting on for four weeks already."

*Only that long?* I think, astounded. *It feels like I've taken root here.*

"Anyway, it's up to you," Yaz goes on. "Whether you want to come with us or not."

"But we want you to come," adds Ruth, quickly. "It's going to be *great*."

"But . . . it's great for me here," I mutter.

"Well, I wouldn't want to be here all on my own," says Yaz. "Especially at night."

There's a pause, then Ruth says, "Look, Laura, I

know you've met Juan but, well . . . at the end of the day it's still just a holiday romance, isn't it?"

"And they can go very wrong very quickly," puts in Yaz. "Like other romances. Right, Ruth?"

Ruth laughs, all rueful. "Yeah. I really wish I hadn't left with Tom. I wish I'd stuck with you two."

*Great*, I think. *So now it's my loyalty to my friends that's in question.* "It's not just Juan," I lie. "I've got a job here and. . ."

"Teaching English?" scoffs Yaz. "Well, party *on*! I want something a bit more exciting than that – like the stuff Ruth was doing!"

"It was only waitressing, Yaz, it wasn't great. . ."

"Yeah, but you met loads of guys!"

Ruth turns to me, puts her hand on top of mine and squeezes. "Have a think about it, Laura. You don't want to spend what's left of your gap year stuck in one place, do you? And it'd be great if it was just the three of us again."

I'm silent. I think about the morning Yaz and I walked into the kitchen to find Tom and Ruth's cases packed, and Tom telling us we had a choice. I feel I've got about as much choice now. As Tom would say – I'm outvoted.

# Chapter 43

When Juan turns up that night, I tell him I want to go somewhere quiet. Once we're sitting side by side in a little window seat in a bar in the old part of Ercos, I tell him what Ruth and Yaz just announced.

He looks completely stricken. "You're not going with them?"

"I don't know. I mean – what choice have I got really?"

He doesn't answer for a minute, just stares into his glass. Then he says, "You have a *clear* choice. Go – or stay."

"But that house, on my *own*, Juan. I mean, I know you'd be there as much as you could, but I'd get spooked, being there on my own at night. . ."

"I'd move in with you." He looks at me, straight. "I'd be there every night if you let me."

"*What?*"

"I'm serious. I'd leave home, and move in with you."

"But your *mother*—"

"Hasn't spoken to me for about a week. Things are bad. I'm going to move out anyway."

"But—"

"But what? Bella said you could take care of the house for the whole summer, didn't she?"

"Yes."

"So what's the problem?"

I pick up my glass and drain it, and my heart's thudding with what I want to say, what I want to ask. "Look – it could all go wrong, couldn't it? We could end up falling out, loathing each other. . ."

"I don't think so."

"No, me neither. But actually if we *did*, it wouldn't be such a disaster, would it, I'd just go home. No, the real thing is –" I pause, run my tongue along my dry lips – "if you move in . . . if I *live* with you like that . . . day after day, night after night . . . I might not want to leave Spain again."

"But you have to. You're going to university, in the autumn."

"Exactly. And I can't risk that."

"Of course you can't. It's a great opportunity. You must go."

"Juan, it's not that simple! I'm – I'm half in love with you already! No – I *am* in love!"

"Me too, Laura. *So* much." He takes hold of my hand all solemn, and says, "And that's the first time you've said that to me."

"No, it isn't!"

"It is. I've been waiting. I've told you I love you four times. The last two times – I'm not sure you heard."

I go a bit red then, because he said it at a very crucial time the last time we made love, and I mutter, "Yes, I did – I thought I said it back. Look, will you *concentrate*? I'm trying to *explain*!"

"OK, *compi*. Explain."

"Look – one of the things I wanted from this trip was to have an amazing love affair. Don't smile like that, yes, this is *it*, this is amazing! But at the same time it's gone wrong – no, Juan, *listen*! I want to tell you about what I was *like*!"

He puts his forehead against mine, says, "Sorry. Tell me."

"Ever since I got badly screwed around by a boy when I was sixteen, I've been scared of getting in too deep – getting hurt. It's like I've got a . . . a *reflex* that kicks in when I start to like someone. It slams the lid on when I start to feel things – it's horrible."

"But not any more?" he asks. His eyes look enormous, so close to mine.

"No. Not any more. This trip to Spain, it was like I could let go, here, 'cos I had this guarantee of safety in place – I had to go back home to go to uni. I could ditch this thing I have of always, *always* holding back with a guy. I thought I could have the *real thing*. Just the real thing with a time limit."

He's grinning at me, eyes shining. "Laura, you're incredible! The way you analyse love, like someone in business! 'Guarantee of safety' . . . 'time limit'!"

"Don't laugh at me, *Juan*! I know it's crap. Especially as it absolutely hasn't worked. If you have the real thing, you can't leave it, can you?"

He shakes his head, draws closer to me so we're practically nose to nose. What with the things I've been able to say, and the way I want so badly to kiss him, my throat feels so tight I can only speak in a whisper. "The thing is, Juan, if we carry on like this . . . as fantastic as this . . . only more, because we're living together – how on earth am I going to leave to go to uni?"

"Because I'll come with you."

I spring back from him. "*What?*"

"To England."

There's a wonderful, dramatic pause, and then we both burst out laughing. "I couldn't ask you to do that!" I say.

"Why not? I want to leave, I want to get out of Spain, I've got no plans, I'd love to come to England."

"But—"

"Laura – anything's possible. Anything, if we want it enough. You should let things just . . . *grow*. Not try and control them all the time, direct them all the time. All you need be sure of for the future is you're going to university. Apart from that, we should just focus on what we want *now*. And what I want is to be with you alone in that house. I want that so much I can't think of anything else."

I rest my forehead against his, murmur, "Oh, *God*. This is all so. . ."

". . .*amazing*," he cuts in. "Yes, it is. You should just – *go* with it, Laura. But I know you need to think about it. I'll get you another drink."

I watch him while he's at the bar, and I'm full of the kind of terrifying, exhilarating, wonderful feeling I used to get as a little kid at the top of a helterskelter, when you realize there's only one way to go. He comes back with two drinks, and I smile at him. "I've thought about it," I say. "When can you move in?"

# Chapter 44

"**O**h, *God*, Laura!" explodes Yaz. "I can't believe you're doing this!"

"Are you really sure, Laura?" frets Ruth. "You haven't known him that long. Suppose he changes. . ."

"Yeah, or *you* change. Think of everything you'll be missing out on just to stay here with him."

All in all, my friends' reactions are predictable. Yaz is scornful; Ruth is anxious. But I'm so sure I'm doing the only thing I can do that none of their objections come near me.

"It's so *boring* here," says Yaz. "I mean – beautiful, yes. But working teaching English, and hanging about in those three or so clubs in town?"

"And we're going to be on the *beach*, Laura," adds Ruth. "Right on the beach. You're going to *fry* here –

it's getting hotter all the time. How long does it take you to drive out to the sea? At least half an hour."

"And didn't you want to *travel*? Didn't you want to *see* places?"

I let them wind down to a stop, then I say, "Look, I'm flattered you want me to come so much. But I'm in love, OK? When have you ever heard me say that before?"

"Only when you were too immature to know any better," snaps Yaz.

"Yeah," adds Ruth. "And look where being in love got me."

"Oh, *God*, you two! I'm going to risk it, OK? What's the matter? You begrudge me it or something?"

There's a pause, then Ruth says, "You've really made your mind up, haven't you?"

"Yes."

"And you really are gone on him, aren't you?"

"*Yes*."

"Well, in that case, you're right to stay. Isn't she, Yaz?"

And for the first time in weeks, Yaz gives me the beginnings of a smile. "Yeah. Yeah, she is."

They leave the next morning. They plan to get the bus down into Ercos, then there's a coach that takes them halfway, and another bus after that; they've got it all worked out. They're excited and nervous, and we hold on to each other and hug as we say goodbye. I check they've got *Pino Alto*'s phone number and they promise to ring as soon as they get to the holiday complex. They tell me I can always come out and join them and I say yes, I can, although right now I've got no more thought of doing that than flying to the moon.

I help them carry their bags to the bus stop; I stand there and wave them off as the bus bumps away down the track. Then I walk back on to the terrace, where the midday sun is baking the clay tiles and wilting the vine leaves on the pergola over the table.

I go into the cool of the house, pull the sheets off all three beds, and cram the first load into the washing machine in the kitchen. I sweep out the large bedroom, and dust off the pretty pine chest of drawers. Then I shift my clothes through. Half of them go into the chest, half in the wardrobe, and that still leaves two drawers and one-third of the wardrobe for Juan. It feels weird, so weird I go outside again, all panicky, thinking, *What am I playing at? I can't do this. I can't just start living with him like this.*

I walk to the end of the swimming pool, sit under the shade of the little concrete shelter between the four toga–clad concrete goddesses.

I'm still sitting there when Juan arrives. He's got a sports bag in one hand and a brown paper bag in the other. He looks drained, wasted. "Are you OK?" I call out.

"No," he says simply. "Have Yaz and Ruth gone?"

"Yes. A couple of hours ago. What's up, Juan?"

"My mother. She had a fit when I said I was staying with you tonight. I thought I'd break it to her gently – tell her it was just for the odd night at first. Still, I should look on the bright side. She's so angry I think she'll throw me out for good. I haven't brought all my clothes."

I stand up, put my arms round him. I suddenly feel ashamed of the anxiety I was feeling. He's practically broken with his family to be here with me like this. It's a far greater step than I've taken.

"I've brought you a present," he says, and hands me the brown paper bag.

I look in, and see half a dozen lemons. "Last year's crop," he says. "For your hair. To make it go blonder in the sun, like you wanted."

After that, we drape the wet sheets on the bushes and low branches of the olive trees around the terrace, and then we go inside and make love on the big unmade bed.

# Chapter 45

And after that, incredible as it seems, our life together starts. Juan goes back home and collects the rest of his stuff, and his mother refuses to speak to him the whole time he's there. His father, he says, is keeping his head down, having to seem at least to side with his mother, but his uncle, the builder, is really supportive. He promises Juan lots of work; his wife sends us food parcels. We go round to lunch and are swallowed up in his huge, noisy family of at least seven cousins, and I feel accepted rather than on show.

Juan's American grandad is there too. Juan tells me they don't think he'll live much longer. He's very thin; his height makes him look thinner. His face is all bone. He tells Juan how pretty I am, how he's always loved English girls, and winks. We sit beside him and listen and talk.

I change my shifts at Concepción's school to cope with the heat – no more afternoons. I get the bus at seven o'clock in the morning every day now, and the regulars call out hello. I'm steadily getting browner and browner, and my hair's getting longer and bleached in the sun. Whenever I wash it, I rinse it with lemon juice. Juan says he can get me as many as I like because the new crop will be ripe any day.

He leaves for work early too, and then we're both back home by two. We eat lunch, and then we go into the cool bedroom and make love and *siesta* behind the white shutters. And then the rest of the evening is ours too.

The weekends we have completely free. Juan has taken over the maintenance of *Pino Alto* from his dad – including the fee – so we have to spend a few hours gardening, but I love it. I love the olive trees, and the green lizards slinking about, and the tropical butterflies the size of birds. I love putting on my bikini and watering the plants in the evening, getting as wet as the ground. Juan watches me and laughs – he makes me feel beautiful. I'm keeping an eye on the fig tree – Juan says the figs will be ripe soon, and I love figs.

Juan's still working on the pool, too. Bella wants lights put in now, for night-time swimming, and she wants a new filter system installed. We phoned her once, to check that it was OK with her that we've moved in together, and she was so loudly delighted that Juan had to hold the receiver away from his ear. And she said something amazing. She said, "You know, when I first met Laura, I thought you'd fall for each other." After that Juan makes a joke about her matchmaking and being a witch, or maybe a fairy godmother.

One morning I get a postcard from Yaz and Ruth. It says they've found work and gives the address of the hotel. A line in Ruth's writing says – *You'd hate it here, Laura! The discos are crap and full of piss-heads!* And a line in Yaz's writing says – *PS Sorry.*

Just that, but it's enough somehow, although I know that Yaz and I will never be friends again the way we were in the past. I write back straight away, tell them I'm fine. More than fine.

My Spanish (fed by a supply of intense Spanish novels from Concepción) is now so good I write to the university and ask if I can switch from Italian to Spanish for one of my languages. Juan takes this as a personal compliment and starts speaking more Spanish to me, especially when we're cuddling up together. He says he feels more romantic in Spanish.

It gets hotter, too hot sometimes, but life is sweet. We have more than enough money. We go to the beach, to bars, to a club at the weekend. Sometimes we remember we ought to see other people too and

Juan does something macho with his mates, and I go out with Luisa or Nuria. Or we ask everyone up to the house for a barbecue and it ends up as a party on the terrace. And we *dance*. I love dancing with him. Sometimes I think I like it as much as making love with him. Sometimes I don't think there's all that much difference between the two.

One Saturday I'm woken by the sound of a huge truck rumbling through the entrance at the back of the house.

"Wake up, *compi*," says Juan, shaking me. "I've got you a present."

"Like the lemons?"

"Better. Bigger. Infinitely more expensive. Although I did do a deal over it. You are going to go into *orbit*, Laura."

"Bloody hell, Juan – what is it? A moon-rocket?"

"Yeah, ha ha." He jumps out of bed all gleeful, pulls on his shorts. "Come on, Laura. Get up."

I follow him into the blazing sun, round the back of the house. Alongside the pool is parked a huge, barrel-shaped container-lorry.

"What the hell is it, Juan? What are you having delivered?"

A man jumps down from the driver's seat, unhooks a fat silver hose.

"It's water," says Juan. "In Spain, you can buy water by the lorry-load."

And we stand and watch as the man positions the

hose over the pool edge, secures it to the side of his vehicle and pulls a lever. At the end of the hose there's a white, foaming explosion and then litres and litres of cold, crystalline, shining, sparkling water gushes into the empty swimming pool. I laugh out loud with the sight of it. Within minutes, the pool bottom's covered. Then the water's rising steadily up the sides. I turn to Juan and throw my arms round his neck.

"I did a deal with my uncle," he says, so pleased with my pleasure I hug him even tighter. "And with Bella. She wants us to check the filter system for her."

The water's still flowing, and now the pool's a great lozenge of glittering cold water, reflecting the hot blue sky above. "When can we *swim*?" I breathe.

"As soon as he turns the hose off," Juan replies.

We seem to spend most of that day swimming, moving from the glowing heat of the terrace to the fresh cold of the pool, lying down to rest in the shade on a blanket under the fig tree. Its dry leaves rattle in the heat-laden breeze, and give off the smell of vanilla, and I feel drugged with the lazy pleasure of it. Lizards visit us, and a little olive-brown snake wriggles from behind a stone. Juan laughs at me for being scared and tells me it's harmless. We talk about when we're going to tell our friends in the town about the wonderful water in our swimming pool, and decide that we won't yet, in case we're invaded.

"The house is *perfect* now," I say to Juan. "Like Eden."

"Complete with a snake," he laughs.

I want to say, *Adam and Eve didn't get to stay in Eden*, but I can't bear to. We have a sort of unspoken rule that we don't discuss the future at all. We know it can't last, this idyll, and that makes it all the more precious. It makes us want to live in each moment, just for itself. Then Juan says, "Laura – are you going to let me come back with you in the autumn? Only I think I might have to drown myself if you won't."

"You'll hate England, after this," I say.

"No I won't."

"OK, then," I say. "Of course you can come. And maybe. . ."

"What?"

"Maybe Bella will let us come back here." Then we go off to sleep in each others' arms.

That night, Juan says he has to test the lights in the pool. He turns them on and we both cheer as the six unearthly, greenish lights glow under the water. It's weird, and magical, swimming in the dark. We discover that if you duck under the surface you disappear, disappear completely – something to do with the light reflecting. We play a game for a while, taking it in turns to vanish under the water and then resurface where you're least expected.

"I'm going to make some supper," says Juan. "I'm starving." We kiss, mouths all cold from the water, and he pulls himself out of the pool. I watch him go, and I feel that fear again, fear that it can't last, and I start swimming to the end of the pool.

The concrete goddesses are glimmering in the dark, and the olive tree at the corner of the pool has a face on it in the moonlight, tragic like the moon's face. It's holding out two branches like arms, it's trapped in the earth. It's saying, *Enjoy it. Enjoy it all.*